Acclaim for Ingo Schulze's

s i m p l e   s t o r i e s

INGO SCHULZE

simple stories

Ingo Schulze, born in Dresden in 1962, studied classical philology at the University of Jena. His first book, *33 Moments of Happiness*, won Germany's prestigious Döblin Prize, the Willner Prize for Literature, and the Aspekte Literature Prize for literary debuts. He lives in Berlin.

ABOUT THE TRANSLATOR

John E. Woods is the distinguished translator of many books—most notably Arno Schmidt's *Evening Edged in Gold*, for which he won the American Book Award for translation and the PEN Translation Prize in 1981; Patrick Süskind's *Perfume*, for which he again won the PEN Translation Prize in 1987; and Thomas Mann's *Buddenbrooks*, *The Magic Mountain*, and *Doctor Faustus*. For his translations of *The Magic Mountain* and Arno Schmidt's *Nobodaddy's Children*, he was presented with the first Helen and Kurt Wolff Prize for Translation from the German in 1996.

INTERNATIONAL

ALSO BY INGO SCHULZE

33 Moments of Happiness

simple stories

simple stories

ingo schulze

Translated from the German
by John E. Woods

VINTAGE INTERNATIONAL
Vintage Books
A Division of Random House, Inc.
New York

The Library of Congress has cataloged the Knopf edition as follows:
Schulze, Ingo, [date]
[Simple Storys. English]
Simple stories : a novel from the East German provinces / Ingo Schulze; translated from the German by John E. Woods——1st ed.
p. cm.
ISBN 0-375-40541-0
1. Woods, John E. (John Edwin) II. Title.
PT2680.U453S5513 2000
833'.92—dc21 99-18511
CIP

Vintage ISBN: 978-0-375-70512-0

Book design by Virginia Tan

www.vintagebooks.com

144915995

For Jette

contents

contents

contents

contents

contents

contents

contents

simple stories

z e u s

Renate Meurer tells about a bus trip in February '90—when the wall was already gone, but the two Germanys were not. In celebration of their twentieth wedding anniversary, the Meurers are in the West for the first time, in Italy for the first time. A bus breakdown outside Assisi drives a fellow passenger, Dieter Schubert, to an act of desperation. Shared memories and provisions.

It just came at the wrong time. Five days on a bus: Venice, Florence, Assisi. It all sounded like Honolulu to me. I asked Martin and Pit how they even came up with the idea and where exactly the money was coming from and how did they picture us taking an illegal trip for our twentieth anniversary?

I was depending on Ernst not to go along with it. The last few months had been hell for him. We had anything but Italy on our minds. But he didn't say a word. And in the middle of January, he asked if we shouldn't be making some preparations—we were supposed to leave on February 16, a Friday during school break—and how were we supposed to get over the Italian border, the Austrian border, with our GDR papers? I figured that at the latest, once I'd told him what the kids had told me—how we'd be getting West German IDs from a travel agency in Munich, counterfeit most likely—that'd be that, you could count Ernst Meurer out. But he just asked whether that had been why we'd had the two passport photos taken. "Yes," I said, "the two passport photos, our birth dates, height, and color of eyes—that's all they need."

It was just like always. We packed clothes in our dark green suitcase, put dishes, cutlery, and food in the black-and-red-checked bag: canned sausages and fish, bread, eggs, butter, cheese, salt, pepper, zwieback, apples, oranges, and two thermoses, one for coffee, one for tea. Pit drove us to Bayreuth. At the border they asked where we were going, and Pit said, "Shopping."

The train stopped in every jerkwater town. Except for snow, streetlights, cars, and stations, I didn't see much. We were sitting with men on their way to work. I didn't really think about Italy until Ernst peeled an orange.

At the station in Munich he and Ernst must have recognized each other. I didn't pick up on it. How was I supposed to know what he looked like? I couldn't even have told you his real name.

I remember him from about Venice on. An average-sized man with quick movements and a badly fitting glass eye that never blinked. He was dragging some huge book around with him, one finger stuck in between pages, so that whenever Gabriela, our Italian tour guide, explained something, he could put his two cents in. Your typical know-it-all. He kept pushing back his salt-and-pepper hair, which would promptly fall down over his forehead and eyebrows again.

I recognized the Doges' Palace and the column with the lion from TV. The Venetian women—even those my age—wore short skirts and beautiful, old-fashioned caps. We had all dressed too warmly.

During the day, so that we could be on our own, we took along our bag of supplies with a couple of cans, bread, and apples. We ate in the room in the evening. Ernst and I didn't talk much, but at least more than we had over the last months. "*Una gondola per favore,*" he shouted one morning while washing up. On the whole, I had the impression that Ernst liked Italy. Once he even took my hand and held it tight.

He never said one word about him. Not till the very end. Although in Florence, while we were waiting for everybody to come down from the bell tower, Ernst asked, "Where's our mountaineer?" I didn't pay it much attention or maybe I thought the two of them had talked at some point—Ernst always went down to breakfast before me. Then he mentioned something about doing pull-ups in a doorway. Before that, in Padua, the mountaineer had insisted we stop and visit some chapel or arena that wasn't even on the tour. I turned around—he was sitting way at the back. His glance said that nothing was going to bother him and was directed straight at the windshield, as if we all were there to finally get this gentleman where he was going. Maybe I'm being unfair, maybe I wouldn't even remember if it hadn't been for the brouhaha later on, maybe I've got the sequence of events mixed up, too, but I'm not inventing any of it.

You have to try to imagine it. Suddenly you're in Italy and have a West German passport. My name was Ursula and Ernst was Bodo, we lived in Straubing, Bavaria. I've forgotten our last names. You wake up on the other side of the world and are amazed to find yourself eating and drinking just like at home, putting one foot in front of the other as if this were all perfectly natural. Brushing my teeth and looking into the mirror, I found it even harder to believe that I was in Italy.

Before we left Florence for Assisi on our last day, the bus stopped in a parking lot so we could look back at the city. The sky was overcast. Ernst bought a plate with a picture of Dante and gave it to me—an anniversary present.

Then we drove through rain, and slowly it turned so foggy that I couldn't see anything but guardrails and fell asleep.

When Ernst woke me up, the others were already getting off. We had stopped at a gas station. There was something wrong with the motor or the muffler. Snow was falling on the umbrellas, and cars had their headlights on—great weather for a breakdown. Our driver went looking for a phone. I can still remember his gestures exactly, the way he kept crossing and uncrossing his forearms. Gabriela announced that we'd have to wait for repairs. She suggested we take in the sights of Perugia.

We got our coats out and marched up to the old city in single file, with Gabriela and the mountaineer in the lead. He was upset and insisted he be driven to Assisi, which he claimed could be seen from here in good weather. "So close you can touch it," he kept saying. When we were damn lucky not to be milling around by the autobahn or on some country road.

The snow was sticking to the sidewalks by now. The art museum and the churches were closed—lunch break. Gabriela led us to the Maggiore Fountain, said a few things about the town hall and the cathedral, which loomed up immense, its walls vanishing into the fog. The façade had remained unfinished now for over five hundred years, she said, to which a woman from Plauen remarked that compared to that the GDR didn't come off so bad. She was constantly making cracks. Ernst never reacted. He simply ignored her.

The group scattered into various restaurants on the piazza. Ours was the Victoria.

Up till now we'd spent money only on the Dante plate and a few cups of coffee. Which is why we decided to order something. The waiter in his long white apron snaked his way among the few tables, all suddenly full. Sometimes he would freeze in midmotion and lean his upper body in the direction of a summons. The only place he suddenly went deaf was in front of the TV, waiting for a skier to cross the finish line. At our table were two men from Dresden, a pediatrician and a stage designer, who both could manage a little Italian and explained the menu for us. Ernst tried to signal the waiter while I made sure his finger didn't slip off the line *pizza con funghi*.

Suddenly the pediatrician stood up. And since he was staring out the window, I turned around. People were storming toward us

from the other side of the square, like kids in a snowball fight—
Gabriela wearing mittens, the others right behind her, in a screaming, wedge-shaped swarm.

There was a scraping of chairs all around us, and then a surge
of tramping feet as everyone tried to get past the waiter and to the
door. We followed them to the cathedral, where a little cluster had
gathered on the steps outside the side entrance.

The mountaineer was standing twelve, fifteen feet up, on one of
the little ledges, arms outstretched, shoulders pressed to the wall. It
was strangely silent, as if the fellow up there were a sleepwalker
who might wake up at the slightest sound and fall off. Gabriela
kept blinking up through the snowflakes. Others shielded their
eyes with their hands. His hiking shoes lay on the ground directly
below him.

He thrust his head forward and gazed down at us like a one-
eyed bird. Both socks drooped slightly out over his toes. The climb
looked as if it would be no problem for someone with a little practice. He had probably worked his way up the hewn stones to the
little pulpit beside the portal, got up on its railing, and then used
jutting stones and rusted-out crannies for handholds.

"Don't look down," a man shouted. With that, the mountaineer
let go with his left arm, spun around with one stiff step, and
instantly pressed up against the wall again. His fingers were clutching the next ledge up. His feet groped along the wall. He scaled
higher, his legs moving like a frog's. Then he was able to brace himself on the little roof above the window.

Ernst tugged my elbow. "Let's get out of here!" he whispered.
Herr Sonneberger, a redheaded giant of a man, was the first to start
taking pictures. Gabriela was cursing, "If he dares to jump!" She
wandered about among us, clutching at the turned-up collar of her
coat, and then hurried down the steps toward a policewoman,
whose white helmet reminded me of someone in a carnival
parade. The only part of Gabriela's head visible from behind was

the tall coiled tower of her braid. The policewoman said something into her hand radio.

The woman from Plauen thought that this was getting serious. "Hey, Herbert," she called, "climb down, Herbert! Come on, get down!" Herr Sonneberger interrupted her. We couldn't call him Herbert, he said. Herbert was just the name on his fake passport. With that, everyone fell silent, or just whispered.

I was annoyed with Ernst, at the way he kept tugging at me. I was about to step back away from him when he grabbed me by the arm. "Nothing's going to happen to him," he hissed. "That's Zeus. Come on!"

"Can't be!" It burst out of me. It had been ten, fifteen years since I had last heard that name. "*The* Zeus?"

Gabriela turned around. "Is that his name, Zeus?"

Suddenly everyone was looking at us.

"Is his name Zeus?"

"He's not going to fall," Ernst said.

"Zeus?" someone asked in a loud voice. And now they were all shouting "Zeus, Zeus," as if they had finally found the password that they all had been fervently hoping would break the silence. Cries of apparent liberation: "Zeus, Zeus!"

And they didn't stop until he vanished into swaths of fog. Several people stretched out their arms to point to where they had last seen Zeus. Cameras with telephoto lenses were now turned into binoculars and passed around. One sock fell from the fog into the semicircle we had formed around his shoes. The second followed shortly thereafter. It scared me both times.

Suddenly, like some spook, Zeus appeared again. He bent forward, so far that some people screamed and pushed back. Panic could easily have erupted. It was incredible how he could keep his balance up there. Spit seeped from between his lips, dangled like a spider on its thread, separated, and hit the snow soundlessly. Body in contortions and mouth askew—he reminded me of the gargoyles in Naumburg or Prague—he began to orate.

Of course no one knew who he meant when he talked about "Red Meurer." The Italians didn't understand him in any case. He called Ernst "the big shot in the green anorak" and stretched out one arm to point at us. No one could figure out what he wanted. What amazed me most was how he found the strength to shout, to shout with such rage. It had all happened long ago. And Ernst didn't like doing it at the time, I'm sure of that. At home he'd always just called him by his nickname, "Zeus." His real name was Schubert, Dieter Schubert.

If you didn't look right at him, you just heard stupid shouting. I thought how Zeus could fall at any moment and come crashing down right at our feet. I pictured everyone trying to push forward to get a look at him. And how no one would have the courage to touch him. His body would look unscathed, the way dead animals sometimes look by the side of the road, with only the blood oozing out of them to hint at what has happened. Head lowered, Gabriela was now talking to herself.

It took a long time for Zeus to shut up at last, as if the snow had finally suffocated him. Then he started inching his way toward the gutter on his left. His movements had become much more cautious and hesitant, as if the sleepwalker had in fact awakened.

"It's over now," I said to Ernst, and linked my arm in his. I meant the shouting, of course. Ernst kept his hands in his pockets and stared at Gabriela's towering coiled braid.

Zeus eased his way down the lightning rod. Carabinieri were there to receive him and surround him while he put on his socks and snow-covered shoes. A fire engine pulled up, its blue light flashing. Gabriela crossed herself. She announced the time when we should all be back at the bus, then left with Zeus and the carabinieri. Our group split up again. The waiter in his long apron hurried ahead to the Victoria.

Ernst and I stood there for a while. Only his fingertips were visible from the long sleeves of his new anorak. I felt chilled, and we started walking to the bus.

Suddenly Ernst asked, "Do you smell something?"

"Yes," I said, and thought he meant the exhaust. Everything smelled different here.

"Strawberries!" he cried. "It smells like strawberries." About the only thing we grew in our garden was strawberries, and we kept track of the years according to how many tortes I could make from them. Coffee hour was a very solemn occasion when I announced: This is the last torte. Our last strawberries of the year. I could see our garden before me and the little beer garden, "The Fox Den." And then I said, "The empty beer glasses. Can you smell them, all the empty beer glasses on the side table out in the sun?"

"Yes," Ernst said, "a whole tray full."

I'm certain that we both pictured the same thing for a while, the old scratched tray and the glasses with a red dot at the bottom. And our strawberries.

The driver opened the door. I invited him to eat with us. He had rolled up his sleeves. He wiped his greasy hands on a rag and dug in. Even though all our meals, except for the skimpy hotel breakfasts, had come from our provisions, we still had plenty of everything left, including apples. We were pretty hungry ourselves. We were still eating when the driver eased into his seat to take a little nap before the drive back. The snow had already melted again.

Why am I telling this? Because a person forgets so quickly. Although it's not all that long ago that Ernst and I were still thinking the same thoughts and dragging around canned food in a black-and-red-checked bag.

CHAPTER 2

new money

Connie Schubert tells an old story: A man comes to town on business, gets himself a girl, and disappears. Starry-eyed naïveté and prudence.

Harry Nelson arrived in Altenburg from Frankfurt in May of '90, a week after my nineteenth birthday. He was looking for real estate, and especially for construction sites along the town's access roads. It was all about gas stations. Harry was of average height, had brown hair, and didn't smoke. He stayed on the second floor of the Wenzel, the only hotel in town. Wherever you spotted him, even at breakfast or supper, he had a leather briefcase with him, one with two combination locks.

I started working as a waitress at the Wenzel in September of '89. There wasn't anything better to be had in the area. I would have had to commute to Leipzig or Gera or Karl-Marx-Stadt. My boss, Erika Pannert, I got to know her during training, once said she had been just like me, just as thin and pretty. Of course I know my mouth is a little too small. And when I walk fast my cheeks jiggle a tiny bit with each step.

I liked Harry, especially the way he would come in, nod, sit down, cross his legs, and tug his trousers up at the knee, the way he tasted wine and unfolded his napkin. I liked his cologne and his five o'clock shadow, how he kept confusing the bills of our currency and how he knew our names without having to stare at the name tags we all wore. Most of all, I loved his Adam's apple. I watched it whenever Harry took a drink. I did it automatically despite myself. On the way home I'd try to recall him in as much detail as possible.

The Wenzel was booked full, and anyone who left to spend the weekend at home preferred to pay for the whole week rather than give up his room. Each evening there was a table for six reserved for Harry, because he always had guests. Erika would whisper their names to me, and at the mention of some of them she shook her fingers and blew on them as if she had burned herself. "They never forgot what used to be theirs," she said.

Harry just asked questions. And if he got people to tell their stories, it could run late. Working late didn't bother me. And besides, to this day I still think it's easier to wait tables than leave the house every morning with a briefcase full of contracts to get signed.

There weren't many besides Harry who stayed the weekend. I remember a fat guy named Czisla from Cologne, who owned several stands that sold cassettes and records and moved from town to town on market days, and the Wenzel was where he hired his vendors, young guys from the area who knew something about music. They often stayed to eat and drink here, because Czisla made them wait until the books balanced. Erika took care of Peter Schmuck from Commerzbank, a skinny young guy with big hands and a soundless laugh, who would hang around until she had time to listen to him. There was another guy from Allianz Insurance, we called him Mr. Wella, and a man we nicknamed Shoeshine. They didn't say much to each other during the week. But on Sundays, when you could sit in the breakfast room and watch the line waiting to buy a *Bild* outside the train station across the way—and people bought several copies of the Western tabloid at a time—they would gather at one table and crack jokes about it.

In the middle of June there were photographs in both the *Volkszeitung* and the local weekly showing Harry and the new mayor shaking hands. A gas station was supposed to be built before 1990 was out, a BP station, I think.

Suddenly word was Herr Nelson was leaving. Then I heard he had found an apartment and was moving out. Then they said Harry Nelson would be gone for a week but was coming back. I wanted to put together a package of snacks for him, but I was afraid the others might notice or he might think I was being too forward.

I took a week's vacation and caught up on my sleep. At home my parents talked a lot about the new money that was supposed to be issued that coming Monday. My father, who had joined the German Social Union after his disastrous trip to Assisi, said I was doing exactly the right thing—after all, the Japanese made do with five days of vacation, too. We'd have to put our noses to the grindstone now. Even my mother said this would separate the wheat from the chaff, that we were already in it up to our ears. Sitting in the bathtub one day, I got caught up in the fantasy that I was kissing Harry's Adam's apple.

On Monday, July 2, my shift began at noon. There was nobody in the restaurant. It would be at least three, four weeks, or so Erika thought, before our customers would be prepared to give out Western money for a schnitzel.

Around one o'clock a dark-skinned couple who sold carpets came in—Pakistanis, Erika called them. When they paid I felt like I was starting training all over again, when we used to practice waiting on each other and then paid with play money.

Harry showed up that evening. As he entered with his briefcase he said, "Hel-loo!" and then sat down by the window, at the table that had always been reserved for him. At last I could gaze at it all again: his little ears, his wide fingernails, his Adam's apple. Harry was wearing a short-sleeved shirt, linen trousers, and sandals with no socks. Erika said Harry had quit his job but was staying on here. "A man like him," she whispered, "always needs something new, always keeps on the move."

After the Pakistanis had unloaded all their carpets from a VW bus and carried them up to their room on the third floor, they ordered some soup. Harry thumbed through last week's newspapers while he ate, and I brought him one glass of wine after the other.

Czisla, who had moved out and came by just to pick up a few last things, joined him later. "Well, here's looking at you," he said. "Here's to black ink," Harry said. And Czisla replied, "Here's to us!" I remember that, even though it was totally irrelevant. Since our hotel bar was closed on Monday, the two of them left around ten. I watched them walk past the window and head for the center of town. Czisla had laid one arm around Harry's shoulders, gesturing with the other and looking at the ground. I was left alone with the Pakistanis. The woman was speaking in a low voice to the man, who entered something on his pocket calculator and then turned it for her to see. I said I needed to close the register. They paid and left.

I did breakfast setups at the back of the dining room. That done, I sat down at the table beside the door and folded napkins. The kitchen staff closed up shop. Except for the radio at the front desk, everything was quiet.

About eleven-thirty I heard the protective screen over the front door rattle, and I knew Harry was back. I didn't even have to look up. He stood behind my chair and bent down slowly over my shoulder. I turned my head, brushing his cheek. "Connie," he said, and at the same moment I felt his hands. He touched my name tag and started groping for my breast.

"Don't," I said. Harry pressed me into the chair. He kissed my neck, my cheeks, and, when I pulled my head back, my mouth. Then he stretched out his arm and tried to grab my knees. Turning to one side, I quickly wriggled out from under him and stood up.

He was quite a bit taller than me, his face dark red, his hair all mussed. His eyes wandered down to my white waitress sneakers. I could see his cowlick. There was something reckless about Harry now, something I hadn't noticed before.

"Come on," he said, "let's get some fresh air."

I was afraid I'd do something wrong. I got my sweater, locked up the restaurant, and turned in the key at the front desk. Outside, Harry wrapped an arm around my hips. I would have preferred to be out of sight first, but we stopped and kissed every few steps. We've found each other, I thought, just like that, without a lot of talk.

At the intersection where the main road starts uphill and off to the right is the train car repair shop, he pulled me over to the little patch of lawn.

"Harry," I said, hoping that would suffice. His hands slid from my hips to my butt, moved down my legs, and came back up under my skirt. "Harry," I said. I kissed his forehead, he slipped both hands into my panties and pulled them down. Harry held me tight now and thrust a hand between my legs, then I felt his fingers, first one and then several.

Harry seemed happy. He laughed. "Why not," he said. "Why the hell not?" I looked at his hair, at the nape of his neck. He went on talking. I didn't understand it all, because he was laughing so hard. He and his hand didn't listen to me. Then came a pain that ran from my shoulders all the way down my back. "Raise your arms," someone shouted, "raise your arms!" For a moment I didn't know where I was or what had pushed itself onto me. My blouse was yanked up. And the same syllables again and again: "Raise your arms!"

Harry didn't sound happy now. He braced himself briefly on my wrists, then I didn't see anything. I only heard him and felt him licking and biting. I tried to breathe slow and even. Then I concentrated just on myself. No matter what happened—the important thing was that I keep breathing. That I remember.

Harry was lying on top of me. First I pulled one arm out of my blouse. I tried to turn over and push him off me. The sky was black and the streetlight a big fuzzy dandelion. Harry rolled over on his back, mouth wide open. His shirt was pushed up. His white belly was a triangle, belly button at the top. His penis was dangling to one side, just over the band of his underpants.

"Harry," I said, "you can't just go on lying here." He swallowed hard. I wanted to talk. I kept talking the whole time I looked for my panties. I was acting just like people in the movies do after an accident. I tried to tug my sweater out from under him, but couldn't manage it and just took off.

I kept thinking—just like I'd been doing on my way home from work lately—that I only had to go to sleep, and then I'd see him tomorrow, my future husband, the father of my children, lots of children, who wasn't like anyone else, who would show me the world and understand everything, who would protect me—and avenge me.

What happened after that I only know from letters and phone calls. They didn't hire anybody to replace me, and the Wenzel was closed later in the fall. Erika got a job with an Italian who tried his luck with a pizzeria on Fabrik Strasse. He had to close in April of '91. Erika found other restaurants. But once they had opened and a few months went by, they closed again. That happened to her four times. Before long she had the reputation of bringing bad luck. But not for long, because by then people realized how things were going in general. By that time, Harry Nelson had left town again, taking his briefcase with him. People say he still owns several buildings, but nobody has ever spotted him again.

I found work first in Lübeck, and then, two years later, on an English cruise ship. My parents love to tell people about it. I call them fairly often, or send postcards.

They claim that although I was so starry-eyed and naïve, at least I knew early on—when other people were still caught up in their illusions—clear back then I already knew just how things would turn out here. And in some ways they're right about that, too.

CHAPTER 3

a really good story for once

Danny tells about crocodile eyes. She is writing too little for advertisers and too much about street fights. Her boss, Christian Beyer, is dissatisfied. Peter Bertram's story. At the end, Danny has to come up with something.

February '91. I work for a weekly. People everywhere are waiting for the boom. Supermarkets and gas stations have been built, restaurants opened, and the first buildings renovated. But otherwise it's just people losing their jobs and street fights between Fasci's and Punks, Skins and Redskins, Punks and Skins. Reinforcements are called in on the weekends, from Gera, Halle, or Leipzig-Connewitz, and whoever rallies the most supporters sends the others packing. It's always about revenge. The town aldermen and the district council demand that the police and courts take energetic action.

Early in January, I wrote a whole page about what goes on every Friday at the train station. Patrick took the photographs. A week later, another one of my articles caused a stir. Basing it on eyewitness accounts, I reported how one night unidentified persons broke down the door to an apartment in Altenburg North and almost beat to death Mike P., a fifteen-year-old Punk. He didn't come out of the coma for two days. His younger brother was in the same ward with a concussion. They had stunned the father with pepper spray, the mother had been out taking evening classes.

Beyer, our boss, forbade me to sign the articles. Patrick's name couldn't be used either. That was fine by him, since his girlfriend was planning to move in with him. Beyer seriously considered getting a German shepherd for the editorial offices. "Nobody," he said, "will insure you against vandalism."

I'm more afraid of the old man who lives one floor above our editorial offices. It began with little notes stuck under my windshield wiper—ultimatums for me to give him his money back. Then he punctured the front tires on my old Plymouth. No one is going to insure me for those either. He did it twice. In the evening he waits around for hours on the darkened stairs next to the entrance. I never notice him until he bellows, "I want my money!" I've tried talking to him and have rung his doorbell. Four weeks ago we were on perfectly normal terms. I even carried a scuttle of coal up for him once.

I am working way too hard, and ever since Edgar broke up with me, I've lived as chaste as a nun. I can understand Edgar. I don't even have time to buy a birthday present for my three-year-old nephew.

Besides, I was called into Beyer's office again because I didn't have the article about Nelson Real Estate finished yet. Harry Nelson is one of our advertisers, three columns, four inches, every week, and even with a 20 percent discount, that still comes to DM 336 plus tax, which makes DM 17,472 a year plus tax. "To have and have not," Beyer says. Scholz comes in with cups of coffee and even pours cream for me, which she normally does only for Beyer.

I say a captioned photograph is better than an article and that I can fit four of these entrepreneur portraits on the page, but don't know when I'm supposed to write them, and that we finally have to learn to say no, too. But Beyer starts in again with his DM 17,472, and ends by declaring, "Maybe we're talking about your salary here, Danny."

I stare at the veneer of his old Stasi desk—the furniture from the local state security office was handed over to Helping Hands,

Inc., who sold whatever they couldn't use—all cheap junk. The grain of the desktop reminds me again of Beyer's question in my job interview, about whether I was pregnant or "planning a baby." He claimed he had to go fishing like this, but it sounded to me as if he was trying to justify himself. I stared first at him, then at the desk, and said, "No."

Every time it happens, I promise myself I'm going to talk to the others about this amoeba-like grain in the veneer. We all have to spend our time staring at these lines and squiggles, which at the far left look like a crocodile's eye. But nobody ever says anything, and I keep forgetting it, too, like some bad dream.

I tell Beyer—who when the situation gets unpleasant tucks his forefinger under his middle or ring finger—that it's not good for a newspaper to kowtow to advertisers. Just the opposite. We should be worrying about content, about design and our own organization, and as for the rest, behave as if we *allow* people to be advertisers. He's going at it all backwards!

"Slow down, slow down," he says. "Take it slow, Danny."

Beyer is hardly any older than I am, and it sounds funny for him to address me with formal pronouns, but for him then to call me Danny is just plain rude. He wants to be a pal, wants to be fair, and always lets us talk for a while. But when did he ever listen to us? He doesn't even consider our suggestions. He has no notion of the business, and thinks that if he worries about the money, we'll make a go of it. He says I should supply two photos for the Harry Nelson article—Nelson has had two buildings renovated. Besides which, Beyer asks me to "hold off on the gang wars," as he calls them, for a few editions, and to go after some other leads. Maybe a follow-up on that cesspool of tar in Rositz or the property on the market square that once belonged to Jews, a critical analysis of the proposition: restitution versus compensation.

We agree that we can't turn down anyone who phones or calls on us, and that you have to listen to a lot of people to get a good story, because you never know if there's anything to the information, and if so, just what. He doesn't want any more complaints, or at least not so many, and certainly doesn't want to lose a four-inch, three-column fifty-twoer—meaning Nelson. Beyer shakes my hand good-bye. "See you later," he says, "the auto club meeting is at seven. We can go have a beer together afterward."

I ask myself when I'll be seeing those amoebas and that crocodile eye again and if my life will have changed by then.

But as I pass Scholz, she holds out the mileage book to me, on top of which are the keys to the Renault and a slip of paper: 5:00 p.m. Bertram—address, telephone number, and two exclamation marks.

"He knows you'll be later than that," she says. "He'll wait."

I remember his call. He spoke in a low, rambling sort of way, but it wasn't one of those ragged voices you hear laying into the garage manager or the family on the other side of the bedroom wall. Our paper is the only one he trusts, he says.

Bertram lives in Altenburg North, Schumann Strasse, across from the Russian housing. I find a parking spot right in front of the door. It's a climb to the fifth floor.

He opens the door quickly and offers me his hand. I tell him I have only an hour. He says we can at least get started and pours me coffee from a thermos. On my plate, as on his, is a slice of cream pie and a glazed pastry. Bertram sets a second ashtray on the round coffee table and lights a red candle. "Or would you like tea?" he asks, sitting down in the armchair opposite me. Behind him is a plantless aquarium. I don't see any fish, either.

On the couch are copies of our paper sorted into several little piles. I read a headline: FROM SOUTH AFRICA TO AUSTRALIA TO CANADA: CLAIMS MADE ON PROPERTY IN ALTENBURG, Thursday, October 25, 1990. Before the Skins and the Punks started brawling, our circulation often fell below twelve thousand.

"I envy you your job," he starts in. "Writing makes you look at the world more closely. But you need to be more courageous. . . ." Instead of going on, he picks up the pastry. "Help yourself," he says.

As he bites into it his lips contort and somehow his eyes have a shocked look. The crease between his eyebrows deepens. He chews away at the mouthful with exaggerated thoroughness. Across from the sofa, van Gogh's *Night Café* hangs against a background of patterned silver wallpaper.

I unpack my tape recorder, flip open my spiral notebook, unscrew the cap of my fountain pen, jot down "Bertram," and underline it.

"To be honest," he says, "I haven't told anyone else so far." He chews more quickly and swallows. "And first off, let me ask if you want me to tell you about it. It's pretty gruesome. You're the first, the very first human being to hear this." He brushes the crumbs from his hands onto his plate and leans back.

I ask him if I can turn on the tape recorder. "Sure, no problem," Bertram says. His right arm is dangling over the side of the chair. "It happened two weeks ago, on Thursday. That's the day my wife always goes to see a woman she used to work with. They do each other's hair, and pedicures, too. It doesn't cost a cent and they still have time to talk about all the things women confide only to other women. We men get left out, whether we like it or not. What Daniela wouldn't give to have your hair!"

There's a series of knocks. I don't notice right off that it's Bertram rapping his chair.

"Just like always, Daniela left our apartment about half past seven," he says. "I had told our son Eric—Eric's twelve, but looks older—that he could watch TV or play on the computer till nine. I enjoyed the peace and quiet and was working here in the living room—maybe I can tell you more about that later, but I don't want to waste your time—so far, so good. At nine o'clock I called in to Eric that he should send his friend home and go to bed. And Eric called back: 'Okay, Pops, right away.' I went on working and about ten minutes later heard the front door close. I was glad not to have to remind Eric a second time. I was polishing away at a rather ticklish spot."

"What were you polishing?"

"I write," he says. "And the least disruption, the slightest noise, is too much. And in this building, you know how it is, you can hear a woman sobbing three floors down. So anyway, I waited for Eric to come in and say good night. I heard the toilet flush and him fussing around in the bathroom. When everything got quiet, I figured Eric had simply gone to bed. He does crazy stuff like that recently—puberty, you know. I debated with myself whether he'd even want me to look in and say good night to him. But decided I would after all. And so . . . I crack open the door . . ." Bertram falls silent. I raise my head, and my eyes meet his. Although he seems relaxed, that vertical crease on his forehead remains.

"Just picture it—three kids are sitting there." He gestures with his right hand as if snatching something out of the air. "You have to picture it. Three kids, all about Eric's age, at most thirteen or fourteen, at most. There they sit whispering, not paying the least attention to me. Of course, I have no idea what they're whispering about. All I know is that there are three totally strange kids sitting in my apartment at nine-thirty at night. They stand up, and stick out their hands, one after the other, and mutter some first and last names and—sit back down.

"'Where's Eric?' I ask, and when they don't answer I ask again and then suddenly notice that Eric is lying under the smoothed-out covers, like a corpse—with just a little bit of hair showing. 'Eric,' I call out. 'Eric, what's all this?' And as if to warn me, the three kids put their fingers to their lips. 'Shhh,' they hiss."

Bertram mimics this for me, repeating it, "Shhh, shhh." I start doodling long spirals from left to right across the page. Bertram's head is red with excitement.

"'Don't wake him up,' the tallest one says, 'he needs his sleep.' He pulls down the bedspread until Eric's head is visible, and holds up a razor. 'Nice little ears,' he says, 'cute little nose,' and waves the razor back and forth so that I can get a real good look at it, the way magicians do. 'You don't stand a chance,' another one says. 'So don't do anything stupid, otherwise little Eric'll be missing more than an ear.' 'Who are you?' I ask. 'You're better off not knowing,' they reply. They force me to sit down and tie me to Eric's desk chair. For one brief moment the will to resist rises up in me—you can handle them, you're stronger than these kids, I tell myself while they're tying me up. But they're armed with razors, and by the time I can get to Eric he's maimed or dead. The way they're going about it, this isn't their first job, they've had practice, they're pros."

I keep on doodling snakes around the name "Bertram." He doesn't go on. I take a bite from the pastry and put it back on my plate. Bertram watches me. "A few drops can save your aquarium," says an ad in the paper on top of one pile, and I automatically fig-ure the price: two columns, two inches, plus 50 percent for the back page.

"A quick ring of the doorbell," he says, and clears his throat. "Helpless as I am, I scream, scream for help like a madman, until one of them presses his damp grubby hand over my mouth. Two more kids arrive and have nothing better to do than spit on me. All five of them spit on me, each of them at least three times. Then they gag me with Daniela's washrag and a hand towel. Thank God I almost never get colds. It won't mean squat to them if I suffocate. And then I, too, hear the key in our front door. Suddenly they're all quiet as mice. One of them calls from the hallway: 'Evening, Frau Bertram, your son Eric's not feeling well, come as quick as you can, in here!' I almost go crazy thinking what a shock this is going to be for Daniela, how she'll spend the rest of her life trying to deal with it. But I'm tied up and can't help her. There's nothing more I can do. They close the door behind Daniela and the guy sitting on Eric's bed says, 'Take off your coat, Frau Bertram, it's so nice and warm in here,' and all five of them laugh."

Bertram's voice goes flat. His words come in a rush now, as if time is running out. The boys unzipped their pants, and what was bound to happen happened. Bertram doesn't leave out a thing, although he's long since forgotten the washrag in his mouth.

"This is getting pretty illogical," I say, and turn off the tape recorder. I tell him that I'd rather use our last five minutes telling him a story, too, one that I experienced firsthand and that, unlike his, is true, true down to the last detail.

Just last month I was stupid enough, I say, to visit a man's apartment, the crazy old man who lives above our offices. So there I am standing in his cold apartment because I thought I could talk him out of his wild ideas, and he leads me into his bedroom and starts yelling that I'm a first-class thief, a thief that not even a lock from the West, a brand-new Western dead-bolt lock, could stop. I've stolen two months' rent from him, plus a new pair of pants and his brown sandals. And as if that weren't enough, I've also put candle stubs in with his shaving gear and hidden his ax behind the wardrobe. And to prove it he pulls the ax out from behind the wardrobe and tells me to follow him, says that that's not the half of it. He shuffles past me, turns out the light—total darkness now. There's not a light burning anywhere in his apartment, not even in the hall. I'm standing there rooted to the spot, listening to his footsteps. One blow, and I'm . . . Then a light goes on. It finally gets through to me that I'm in the bedroom of a crazy old codger. With his back to me and the ax between his legs, he unlocks a door, mumbling something about a first-class thief. Thank God the key to the front door is in the lock. I turn it, it sticks . . . I yank the door open, the old man grabs my arm, screams, the ax falls to the floor, the door is wide open, and there on the other side stands Scholz, our hefty Scholz, who shoves him back, uses both hands to shove him back.

"Now that's a really good story for once," I say, and zip my purse up. "Compared to yours, it's downright brilliant!"

Bertram stares straight ahead, looking bored. I tell him I've had it up to here with the kind of crap he's just fed me, and run my hand across my neck as if cutting my own throat. "Up to here!" I

shout, and add that it's beyond me why I still listen to the bab-
blings of total strangers every day. The realization surprises even
me, and I have to laugh.

"You won't get very far thinking like that," says Bertram, who,
still in his chair, begins to clear the dishes. He takes my plate with
the cream pie and the nibbled pastry, my half-empty cup, stacks it
all on his own plate, and blows out the candle.

I tell him he's probably right, and stare at the grain of the wood
that has replaced the plate and saucer in front of me. There it is
again—that crocodile eye under its heavy lid, glowering up at me
from the table, from the wallpaper, cupboards, floorboards, from
everywhere—the world is full of crocodile eyes.

I suggest to Bertram that with stories like that running through
his head, he should buy himself a pistol that fires tear gas or a little
pepper sprayer that fits into any purse, or hire a whore or place a
personal ad in the paper. While I'm saying all this, I stare at the
crease in his forehead, which I'd briefly taken for a scar. I'm making suggestions, but what I'm really thinking about is how many
knotholes, amoebas, and crocodiles there are all around me, and it
dawns on me that this is just the beginning, the start of a whole
chain of things that will follow me until there soon won't be a single thought left that isn't tainted, that doesn't remind me of something crude, that doesn't disgust me.

Bertram closes the door behind me. I grope for the light switch
and hear the click of the relay that turns out the light in Bertram's
hallway.

The Renault's tires are okay. But someone has parked an Opel
so close that I have to get in on the passenger side.

It's still a good while before seven. The stores are already
closed. I don't know what to do till then. I decide to first put the car
in reverse and then make my turn, that way I can slip safely
between the cars parked next to garbage bins on both sides. Which
makes me think of what joy my disappearance will bring—a parking spot still empty, maybe even right in front of the door! I catch

myself in the rearview mirror, laughing. Which makes me think how it's not a good idea to live alone. Not just that it makes everything more difficult, it's unnatural, too. All the same, I'm not going out with Beyer, not even for a beer. I'll tell him that right off. I can always come up with something.

CHAPTER 4

panic

Martin Meurer tells about his career and a trip without a car. His wife rides a bike. His experiences with a tourist and a taxi driver in Halberstadt.

My teaching assistantship wasn't renewed at the University of Leipzig, and from one day to the next I had no income. Andrea, who had already retrained as a bookkeeper, was taking courses in typing and French every morning while Tino was at kindergarten. We put in a request for rent support, resolved to smoke less, and withdrew Andrea's application to a driving school. I gave up my room in Leipzig, applied for stipends and positions on various projects, for jobs as a tour guide, ad rep, and finally as a field rep for VTLT Natural Stone Preservation, Inc., with a guaranteed eighteen hundred take-home.

Before I even took a seat, they told me they were looking for a chemist, geologist, physicist, or the like, definitely not an art historian. I slid into the tubular steel chair until I felt myself touching its back and began talking about medieval architecture, environmental stress, and urban renewal. The whole time I was looking into the owlish eyes of a man named Hartmann. I can stare directly like that only if I don't have to think about what I'm saying.

A week later, two different envelopes arrived, one inviting me to a ten-day training course and the other accepting me for their six months' probation, which wouldn't be in Saxony or

Thuringia, but with the marketing division in Saxony-Anhalt and Brandenburg.

It didn't go bad, it didn't go good. After three months I was just under the quota VTLT required. We managed. Now and then Andrea's parents would send two hundred marks for Tino. My mother gave us things for the boy, and when Ernst, my stepfather, baby-sat for us, he would go shopping with Tino and pay for everything. Plus we had help from Danny, Andrea's sister.

Before the start of the follow-up campaign for UNIL 290, I gave myself a week off in July. We drove our Opel Kadett to Ahlbeck on the Baltic. As I think back on it now, they seem like our last happy days. We collected shells and amber, built sand castles, paddled together on our air mattress clear out to the buoys, and I found a ship-in-a-bottle on sale for Andrea. In the evening, once Tino was asleep, we'd go to the bar in the main hotel, drink prairie oysters, smoke, and dance whenever they played something slow.

At the end of the week, the automatic teller swallowed my Eurocheck card, I was overdrawn. Andrea asked what would happen with our lottery subscription, which got drawn directly from our account. We left the same day.

The following Wednesday, I had just got home for supper when Andrea called me into the bedroom and handed me a folded letter. She smiled, and I thought she might have a date for a job interview.

My driver's license was suspended for a month, and I was to pay a fine of 433.50 D-marks, for doing 146 in an 80-kilometer zone. Plus it counted four points against me. I watched as Andrea, still smiling, began to cry, then threw herself on the bed, pressing a pillow to her face with her left hand. She pulled up one knee, and I stared awhile at the spotless soles of her house slippers. We had our first panic attack that evening.

The worst was over by the next morning. I mailed in my driver's license and worked out a schedule using the train. Somehow the decision to do that even put me in a good mood. At worst we would have to borrow money from Danny or our parents. VTLT would never notice, and I'd keep my job. "You can do it," Andrea said.

She packed for me, putting the catalogs—including the sample from Abenberg Castle, Middle Franconia, strengthened with UNIL sandstone reinforcement and waterproofed with UNIL 290—at the bottom of both my bags, wrapped my test-tube samples (200 ml) in newspaper, and then rolled them up in underwear, socks, and shirts. She had sewn swatches of leather padding to the middle of the shoulder straps.

I spent the day at the Office of Landmark Preservation in Magdeburg and paid calls on both Maculan and Schuster, without ever getting to see the local bosses or their assistants, left our catalogs, and made appointments for half-hour presentations on Thursday afternoon and Friday morning. That evening I took a train to Halberstadt, where I had five meetings scheduled for the next day.

As we pulled in, I looked out the compartment window and there was still just light enough for me to make out the steeples of the cathedral and of both St. Martin's and Our Lady's.

The taxis turned on their headlights. I crossed the station plaza to the two telephone booths on the far side and set my bags down beside the one on the right, which took card calls. With the receiver in one hand, I pushed the door open again with my hip and pulled my bags closer.

When Andrea said hello, the display signal after the decimal went from 45 to 26, and Andrea repeated her "Hello?"

I told her that Dr. Sidelius, the geologist at the Office of Landmark Preservation, had listened to everything, and when I was done had offered me his hand and wished me luck.

One taxi after the other pulled away, and when there were none left I remarked that all the taxis were gone now.

"There's sure to be another soon," she replied, and told me that there'd been an accident just outside the door of our building—we

lived on Brockhaus Strasse in Lerchenberg—but that had not dis-
suaded her from riding her bike up to Tip Co-op on Stein Weg. She
still called it the co-op. She said that riding a bike was no longer a
problem and that she'd be doing it from now on. She even wondered why she hadn't done it before. Besides, that was the best way
to get in shape for next week. She wanted to go on a little bike hike
with Tino and Danny, who had arranged for her to use a bike with
a child's seat. They had only decided to do it that noon.

The 2.88 became 2.69 and then 2.50. A taxi pulled up and
stopped, the headlights went out. Tip Co-op even had a big bike
stand, Andrea said, with an ad attached. I was supposed to guess
which ad. But she blurted it out. "Prince Denmark, my brand."

"You wouldn't have risked it a week ago," I said.

"You're right! And now if they build some bike paths . . ."
Andrea said, and followed up with a couple of French words I
didn't understand. I laughed. She had to wish me luck, I said,
unloading some of this stuff tomorrow.

"Don't call it stuff, Martin. It's so important!" she cried. "What
good is the whole of art history if all those beautiful buildings
crumble away. And they're all crumbling, Martin, what with all the
filth in the air." Another taxi pulled up, and this time I told her
about it.

"Hang up, quick!"

"It's okay," I replied, and then, suddenly frightened, turned to
one side. My bags were still there. "I love you," I said, and then
added that I wasn't just saying that because I was all alone here
without a car. "That's nice to hear," Andrea replied.

At first I thought we'd cut it off at 1.17, but then it went down
to 0.98 and then 0.79, and after she said "Bye" it jumped to 60
pfennigs, and I called out "Darling," but she had already hung up.
So I did too and removed my phone card. There were three taxis
now. The driver of the first was leaning against his open door, his
arms crossed. In front of him stood a woman in a red short-sleeve
jumpsuit. He shook his head while she held up a slip of paper

and turned around toward me: a Japanese woman with large eyes, white face, and permed hair. She turned back to the driver, but I asked in English, "What do you want?" She handed me the slip of paper: "To Magdeburg." And then, while I was putting one bag down on my foot and handing the other to the driver: "To Frankfurt."

"Not in the trunk!" I shouted, and lifted the second bag onto the backseat myself. I kept only my briefcase and walked back through the blue swinging door into the station with the Japanese woman. She was rather tall for an Asian.

There were no more trains to Magdeburg and none to Frankfurt, either, but there was one to Göttingen in ten minutes. I said that best I knew it wasn't that far from Göttingen to Frankfurt. She nodded, but her eyes continued to look worried. The little creases in her brow didn't disappear, either. I also couldn't think of the English word "platform." And since she stopped nodding her head when I said "From number three," I walked her down into the underpass and showed her the second set of stairs. "Number three," I repeated. But on one sign there were only a "4" and a "5," and on the other "1" and "2." So I escorted her up to the platform, where a diesel engine with two cars was just pulling in. There was a schedule here, but it showed no connection to Göttingen, or even to Magdeburg. Gazing at me in desperation and clutching her handbag, the Japanese woman asked what she should do now.

I ran after the conductor who had got off the train that just pulled in. She laid a black notebook on a bench and thumbed through it. I could hear the Japanese woman's high heels, then I felt her hand on my arm. I looked down from the buttons of her jump-suit to the fine print of the schedule, while the conductor paged back and forth, shaking her head. The Japanese woman's small breasts rose and fell, and you could even make out her belly under the fabric. If the taxi driver had left his clock running, I was the fool in all this.

"She can ride with me," the conductor said, "on the ten-seventeen to Oschersleben, then take a taxi from there for sixty marks and be in Magdeburg at half past eleven." I translated. "And to Frankfurt?" The conductor shut her eyes for a moment, closed her black book, ran back to one of the two cars, and set a foot on the lowest step.

"Well?" Her trousers were stretched tight over her short thighs. I asked the Japanese woman if she wanted to go with her. She could probably find a hotel room here for sixty marks. She nodded. I thanked the conductor, who grabbed the pole beside the door, let her left leg follow, and climbed up, body bent forward. Her rear end seemed to expand in those uniform trousers.

Descending the underpass stairs, I asked the Japanese woman where she was from.

"From Korea."

"Goslar," I burst out as we passed the schedule hanging in the station waiting room. "This isn't the timetable for Halberstadt. It's for Goslar!"

"Thank you very much," she said.

Trying to make conversation, I said it was wonderful that she had set out all by herself. She nodded. I told her I was an art historian and that I was writing my dissertation on the unusual figures of Adam and Eve in the Halberstadt cathedral, and asked if she had ever heard about Dresden.

"Of course, Dresden." Her lips, bright with lipstick, were still slightly open. She looked at me and nodded, and I held the swinging door open for her.

When I asked the taxi driver, "Do you want to drive the lady to a hotel or me to Pension Schneider?" he turned up his nose and slipped in behind the wheel. Pension Schneider was at the other end of town and somewhat out-of-the-way, but the hotels were only a few hundred yards ahead in the center of town. I walked the Japanese woman to the next taxi. Like the one before, this driver—a fairly young guy, tanned, wearing shorts—stood with arms crossed behind the open door and replied that there weren't many hotel rooms, most of them not very good, and nothing for under a hundred marks. You could go a long way on a hundred marks, to Magdeburg for instance. I translated. My taxi driver yelled that his time didn't come free. The Japanese woman said, "To Magdeburg." Then the driver vanished into his taxi and pushed the passenger door open from inside. The Japanese woman turned around once again, called out, "Thank you very much," and got in.

"To Magdeburg!" my driver yelled. He had jumped out of his car. "To Magdeburg!" He was spraying spit like an actor. "I gotta be dreamin'!" Another burst of spray in the rays of the streetlight.

I yanked open the rear door of the taxi, just grazing the driver's belly, squeezed in beside my two huge bags, put my briefcase on my lap. Both doors slammed shut at the same time. "Two days' worth!" His roar struck the windshield and set the car reverberating. He turned the key and grabbed the fleecy steering wheel. "He gets a hundred, I get fifteen!"

I wanted to apologize, but before I could open my mouth, the radio started booming. The little ventilator on the armrest shook. And in the next moment I realized: This wasn't the way to Pension Schneider. I knew my way around here pretty well.

We picked up speed, the tires thump-thumping over cobblestones. Then the car made a sharp right, my head banged against the window. There were no more streetlights. I slipped deeper into my seat, thighs splayed, knees against the back of the front seat. The car suddenly took a hard bump and then another, a dirt road.

It came to me that I should have sent the Japanese woman to Braunschweig or Goslar, it would have been cheaper than to Magdeburg, and the connections were better. Or I could have called the pension and asked if they didn't have an inexpensive room for a Japanese lady. All in all: I was an idiot. My driver had lost two days' income because of me, I hadn't even contested the speeding ticket, and I'd given up my driver's license. I was lugging our vacation bags around and selling snake oil, while my wife was practicing riding a bike to go to the grocery and borrowing out-of-date French textbooks from the library. We were using money her parents had intended for Tino to pay for our lottery subscription. And at the drop of a hat, I would have cheated on Andrea with a Japanese woman. Who knows what damage I could do in the next few hours, days, or years.

I had a good idea what the driver was up to. But I wasn't going to defend myself. He was right! He had every right to toss me and my test tubes into the nearest ditch.

Suddenly we stopped. I could see the sign in the headlights: PENSION SCHNEIDER. The music died, a little light went on above my head.

"Twelve-twenty," he said.

"Make it thirteen," I said.

He held his long waiter's wallet with its neat, unwrinkled bills up to the light and took my hundred-mark bill with his right hand.

"Are the streetlights out?" I asked. It was pitch-black out here. He thrust a bundle of bills back at me and counted out seven one-mark coins into my open hand.

"Thanks," I said, cramming it all into my breast pocket. He looked at me in the rearview mirror. I pointed to the color snap-shot dangling in front of the ventilator. "Is that your wife in the bikini there?" The scrollwork frame had been cut with a jigsaw.

"Hey," he said, "you paid up. Now get out."

I dragged out both bags. I closed the door with my knee, moved to the front of the car, and trudged to the pension. Stepping to one side—I couldn't make out the doorbell in my own shadow—I carefully set my bags down. The beam of the headlights slid down across the door, hesitated at the threshold, turned aside, and now shone straight ahead down the street. I heard the radio again for a moment.

Groping for the doorbell, I managed to trip over my bags. It sounded awful. But I didn't fall. I kept my head high and my body almost stiff, bent forward only slightly. There were little flurries of rustling off to one side. A mouse probably, or a bird. Pension Schneider had melted into the darkness. You couldn't even see it outlined against the sky. If I moved, the UNIL 290 samples clinked against one another. All I had to do was wiggle a toe or lift my heel just a little, yes, that was enough, or shift my weight from one leg to the other, just bend my knee slightly—and there was that clink again.

CHAPTER 5

migratory birds

Lydia tells about Dr. Barbara Holitzschek, who claims that she's run over a badger. A long conversation about animals. The scene of the accident. A puzzling ending with no badger.

Today is Monday, and actually we're closed. But at ten-thirty I'm supposed to give a seventh-grade class a tour of the museum. School classes are the worst. I'm tired. Hanni, my boss, steps in, holds the door open. "Dr. Holitzschek has run over a badger," she says. A short woman in her early thirties with long hair, a navy blue skirt, and a gray shawl-collar sweater now appears, stands there in the doorway, tapping the jamb with one finger.

"Holitzschek," she says without looking at me. "I ran over a badger."

"Lydia Schumacher," Hanni says, pointing at me, "our taxidermist."

"Hello," I say, and stand up. Her hand is cold. "Do you have it with you?"

Dr. Holitzschek shakes her head, tugs a tissue out of its pack, and turns to one side to blow her nose. "I don't have it with me," she says.

"An adult?"

"Yes," she says with a nod. "It gave off a strong, gamy smell. And its front paws went like this." She presses the backs of her hands to her cheeks and wiggles her fingers as if shoveling something aside.

"That's supposed to be a badger?" I ask. Hanni, who is half sitting on my desk now and stroking the head of my whitethroat warbler with a bent forefinger, rolls her eyes.

"It was still twitching," Dr. Holitzschek says.

"We need a badger, don't we?" Hanni exclaims.

"Sure," I reply. "We could use a badger."

"And there's one on the road near Borna. Dr. Holitzschek is in a hurry. Maybe you can go have a look at it and bring it back if it's in good condition?"

"And the tour?"

"There isn't much choice," Hanni says, giving me her meaningful glance and continuing to stroke the whitethroat. Dr. Holitzschek blows her nose again and tries to smile. She says, "Then it won't all be for nothing," and tosses her hair back over her shoulder.

When I get in her car, a dark blue Golf hatchback, my knees are pressed against the glove compartment. She leans across and brushes my ankle as she searches for the lever under the seat. "Push," she orders. A red tree-shaped deodorizer dangles from the rearview mirror. She turns the key with some effort.

"Hanni told me about the last badger. How could anyone pull the plug on a deep freezer! Who'd do such a thing? Nobody can be that stupid!"

"They probably needed the wall plug for the vacuum cleaner," I say.

"What did the badger look like? How did you even get it out again?"

"I turned the deep freezer back on," I say, "aired it, and then opened it up again a week later. Expected worse."

"That would've done it for me!"

We pull out onto the road and make small talk about people who work for cleaning firms and security agencies.

Her car looks new. Spotless, no dust anywhere. I ask what kind of doctor she is.

"I work at Dösen. I was on my way there—when it . . ."

Dösen doesn't mean anything to me.

"Psychiatry," she says. "Actually, I'm a neurologist. Aren't you from around here?"

I tell her I've been living in Altenburg for only two years now. When Dr. Görne died, there was an opening for a taxidermist, and I wanted a permanent job, no matter where.

"There are big-city people and country people, and then there are small-town people, too," she says.

"Maybe I'm a big-city person," I say, "or a country bumpkin."

Dr. Holitzschek stalls the car waiting for the stoplight at the entrance to the playing-card factory. But then we race up Leipziger Strasse hill.

"Have you always been a taxidermist? I wanted to work with animals once myself."

"But?" I ask.

"My parents had a Skoda with tan fur seat covers, synthetic of course. And the first-aid kit had fallen onto the backseat, with the sun beating in through the windows. The kit's plastic melted, and when we got into the car, my mother ripped it off the backseat. All it takes to make me shudder even now is to think of that gray mis-shapen blob with patches of fur. I was fourteen and just couldn't get over it. My mother thought I was putting it all on so I could sit up front with my father. Told me she didn't want to hear about my wanting to work with animals ever again." While she talked she kept looking at me instead of the road.

"I don't get it," I said.

"Anybody whose stomach gets turned that easily . . . Besides, I'm afraid of dogs. I like birds though, crimson rosellas or kook-aburras or emu wrens. Do you know those?"

"All Australian," I say.

She nods. "Have any pets?"

"No," I say, and tell how my mother is a patsy for people want-ing to get rid of cats, that die within two years at the latest. "Either rat poison or kidney problems or they get run over. Then she calls me every day for a week and promises me that she's going to be really tough from now on and not take any more in. But as soon as she starts in about how kittens aren't asked to be born either, I know it's pointless even talking to her."

"A neighbor found a seagull with a broken wing and took it to the vet," Dr. Holitzschek says. "He amputated it without even asking. What good's a bird with just one wing? Our little Island Zoo isn't going to accept maimed animals. And now the gull hops around in his front yard, which he digs up for it, and it eats anything—like a pig. When it spreads its wings, and there's nothing on one side—I expect it to fall over every time. It'll eat anything! Komodo dragons don't just eat everything, they can even digest the hooves. All that's left behind is chalk, pure chalk. Crazy, isn't it? You don't have Komodo dragons, do you?"

"No," I say.

"Animals shouldn't be caged," she says. "When even the dolphins start biting . . . all because of stress. They're like people, animals are, I mean they need to be treated like people. You can disappoint them the same way. And they're just the same with each other, too, egoistic and ruthless. Did you read about those temple baboons? What goes on with them? The females miscarry because the lead male will bite their babies to death if they're not his. He wants to propagate his genes. That's all. Pure egoism," Dr. Holitzschek says.

"Does that surprise you?" I ask.

"At any rate, it was in *Der Spiegel,*" she says. Her hand on the gearshift knob is trembling. We wait at a construction stoplight this side of Treben. It's windy. The sky has the light of late afternoon. Dr. Holitzschek sneezes. "Sorry," she says, and sneezes again. A few tiny droplets stick to the windshield. Or it's something on the outside, pebbles or insects. She feels for her purse on the backseat. The car in front of us starts to move. She needs a tissue.

"What was that, the little bird on your desk?"

"A whitethroat warbler," I say, and look at the clock. The school class will be trudging into the museum about now.

"A whitethroat warbler?" Dr. Holitzschek has accelerated too fast and has to brake. "Is that the bird that burns up its own intestines as it flies? That's its secret, miraculous way of staying in shape. It eats about eighty percent of its body weight, and then loses it again. Whitethroat—I think that's the one." We are now the first in a whole long line moving behind an empty cattle truck. "What I don't get is: 'integrated orientation systems.' How do they find the same bush from last time? Sea swallows fly twenty-five thousand miles a year. And the golden plover takes forty-eight hours to get from Alaska to Hawaii, just a weekend!"

After this, Dr. Holitzschek talks about global warming, the rising sea level, how the wetlands where birds rest are drying up, their food disappearing, and how the seasons are out of whack.

"These mild autumns have reset birds' inner clocks. They take off for their winter grounds ten to fourteen days later. Which means that by the time they get to their resting places everything has already been eaten. With some species at least," she says, and reaches for her purse again, "it takes only a few generations for them to store data in their genes about new nesting grounds and flight patterns. Some of them are already wintering in southern England instead of Portugal or Spain. With most blackbirds, for example, the urge to migrate has been totally erased."

Dr. Holitzschek is the only driver who could possibly pass the LONG VEHICLE ahead of us.

"The worst part," she says, "is that when nightingales or orioles arrive at their breeding grounds, the best spots have been taken by run-of-the-mill birds. They're more aggressive and well-rested than the true migratory birds."

The truck ahead of us comes to a stop on the other side of Serbitz. Dr. Holitzschek starts in on attempts to crossbreed sedentary and migratory birds. I open the window. One after the other the cars behind us turn off their motors. Traffic flows past us from the other direction. The sun is blinding when it appears between clouds.

We start moving again, but a vehicle with a flashing blue light is stopped in our lane. The police wave us on by. "Another bad accident," I say. As we drive past, however, all we see is an ambulance, no tow trucks. Dr. Holitzschek says: "And meanwhile about seventy percent of our indigenous birds are on the endangered list."

Without using a turn signal or even braking, she turns left onto a country lane and stops. And now she's going on about swarms of moths that can be seen only once a generation. I interrupt her and ask about the badger. Dr. Holitzschek blows her nose, undoes her seat belt, extracts the car key, gets out, and runs off. Sticking the folded blue plastic bag in my jacket pocket, I follow her in the direction of the police car. As I walk I start pulling on my rubber gloves.

With every gust of wind Dr. Holitzschek turns to one side and lowers her head, as if someone were pulling her hair. Sprinting between two passing cars, she crosses the road and runs on along the other side. I've hesitated too long and try to at least stay even with her.

A policeman comes toward her. He spreads his arms wide. Just before they collide, they both come to a stop. Or, rather, Dr. Holitzschek tries to get around him. They're both speaking at once.

A semi rolls slowly past. I puzzle out the blue letters against a white background: PLUS and under that: POSH LIVING ULTRA SAVINGS. I'm standing in the middle of exhaust fumes.

Dr. Holitzschek crosses her arms. The policeman stares at her breasts. They talk and suddenly look across to me.

Another semi passes, this one with a double trailer.

The policeman is standing there alone now, chewing his lower lip. He watches me pull on the gloves. Then, without turning around, he saunters back to his car.

Dr. Holitzschek is ahead of me again, the wind at her back now. She is clasping her elbows. I call out. She doesn't react and vanishes behind a bus.

When she crosses back, she's limping. Her right knee is banged up. She stops in front of me, puts her hands over her eyes and forehead, then pushes back strands of hair.

"He claims there's nothing here. I told him to let me through. He says they've searched the whole ditch and embankment, and if there'd been a badger there, they would've found it. It was dead, don't you see, it twitched, but then it was dead."

I ask about her knee.

"It was dead," she says. "They won't let anybody through, no one. But if they find something they'll call the museum. I'm sure they'll call. If they don't we'll have to come by here again this evening or afternoon, when they've——cleaned up here."

"Cleaned up what?" I ask.

"They won't say. Won't tell you a thing."

"Let me drive back," I say, crooking my left arm so that she can take hold of it. There are two honks. We don't even look that way.

"Want to bet they've called by the time we get to the museum?" Her yellow key ring looks like a traffic sign: KOALAS NEXT 10 MILES. I open the passenger door for her. "They'll call in the next few minutes, I'll bet you anything, and Hanni will wonder what we're doing and think we've stopped someplace to live it up instead of looking for that badger. You'll see, you're going to get into hot water with her. But I'll explain things. I can't believe how they just brush a person off. It's always the same old bunch." Dr. Holitzschek sneezes and rubs her hand back and forth under her nose. "Just because he was so pigheaded, you may end up in hot water. They love it when they can catch you at something, when you give them something to latch onto."

I rotate the dial that moves the seat a little farther back and turn on the engine. Dr. Holitzschek reaches for the lever under her seat and freezes in that position. Her knee is bleeding.

"My bracelet," she says. "I'm caught. Would you mind helping?"

She doesn't move. She sits there bent far forward, one hand under her seat. My fingers touch the ball of her hand. I can feel her pulse, and the back of my hand bumps her calf. I have no idea how I'm supposed to budge her hand, her forearm, to get her unhooked. I grope for the catch. She is completely dependent on me. I turn her arm. She can go ahead and throw those panty hose away. I bend down lower, my head is close to her thigh. All the while I'm looking up over the dashboard and out through the windshield. The traffic has disappeared beneath my horizon. I can only see the roofs of the trucks, and above them the cloudy sky.

Suddenly her hand comes free. I sit back up. An ambulance drives past slowly, with no lights flashing.

During the drive back I'm careful to keep my distance from both the center and the shoulder stripes. My hands hold the wheel the way they teach you in driving school: "ten till two," that is, right and left both a little above the middle.

I halt at the first stoplight intersection because she hasn't answered me. I don't know where I'm supposed to go. Finally she haltingly provides me with the name of a street and a number.

"Is that on the canal?" I ask.

I can park right at the entrance. "We're here," I say, and turn off the engine. I busy myself a little, slide the seat forward, readjust the rearview mirror, take out the key.

I ask if she's sick to her stomach. In the rearview mirror I can see two boys with schoolbags and can hear their footsteps on the asphalt. One passes the car on the right, the other on the left. When they're walking side by side again, they turn around, but without stopping, and look at us. I sit there awhile longer. Then I say that I'll be going. I get out, wait a moment, and finally slam the door.

The seventh-grade class is raising a ruckus outside the museum. The teacher and Hanni are talking at the ticket window. "Do you know each other?" Hanni asks, and looks from him to me and back again. "Bertram's my name," he says. We shake hands briefly. The kids have dragged autumn leaves with them into the exhibition rooms. There's a half-eaten apple lying in front of the glass case with "the Rat King." Still on the stairs, I can hear the telephone in my office. Once it stops ringing I unplug it and sit down to the whitethroat on my lab desk.

Hanni comes in and stands there behind my back. She is the only person who never knocks. She pulls my jacket away from my shoulders and begins to massage the back of my neck. She expects me to thank her for taking over another tour.

"Still have that headache?" Hanni asks. Her thumbs slip farther down my spinal column, wander back up, and move to the tips of my shoulders. I spot the inflamed cuticle on her right forefinger.

"Can't you afford a manicure?" I ask. It's funny that a woman like Hanni always has such banged-up fingernails. She sighs deeply to demonstrate the torment I cause her and how difficult it will be for her when she has to let me go—this year or next, or in two years' time. She's not just my boss, she's also been here for a good while and has a child, a daughter.

"Where's the badger?" she asks. I hear her heels click on the tiles.

"I didn't know you knew each other," I say.

"I thought I was doing you a favor. Did she make a pass at you?" Her hand stirs in the pocket of her smock. The knuckles she sometimes counts on to check how many days there are in the month can be seen clearly under the fabric. The cries of the schoolkids are more distant now. "Everybody knows everybody here. That's just how it is. Your Patrick keeps calling, by the way." She moves a few steps toward the door. "You didn't sleep all weekend?"

"Do you sometimes long for the old days, too?" I ask.

"What's that supposed to mean? You didn't have anything to do with all that," she says rather calmly. "My God, Lydia," she cries angrily when I try to respond. "All you're expected to do is to stuff a few animals. The worst that can happen is that you have to give a school class a tour or the power fails or somebody pulls the plug on the deep freezer. You don't even have a child to worry about, not even that!" Her back to me now, Hanni lights a cigarette and blows the smoke toward the ceiling. "What's with the badger?"

I can feel the car key still in my jacket pocket. "I forgot it," I say, and hold up the key by its yellow koala ring as if I could prove something by it.

Hanni doesn't look at me, she doesn't even turn back around. She walks out and starts down the stairs. With each step her hand raps the wooden banister. Hanni is cursing. I can't understand what she's saying even though she left the door open. I pull my jacket back up on my shoulders, lay the car key on the desk next to the whitethroat, pull my chair closer, and go back to work.

CHAPTER 6

so many hours in a night

*Patrick tells about the problem of finding an address in the
dark. A birthday celebration in the country. Return (with hot
pursuit) and a party at a gas station.*

It's Tuesday, April 7. Tom is celebrating his thirty-fifth birthday.
Two years ago he inherited some money, and soon afterward Billi,
his wife, inherited even more. They're living near Leisnig now, in a
old farmstead built around a courtyard. Billi takes care of the twins
and the garden and gives flute lessons. Tom is still turning out
wooden sculptures—gigantic heads with gigantic noses—that he
doesn't have to sell anymore. Lydia knows them both from Berlin,
when they were still students, education majors.

I run into Tom and Billi regularly, whenever I'm photograph-
ing gallery openings in Leipzig or Chemnitz. And every time Billi
says: "You must drop by sometime." And Tom says: "You two really
have to see the place."

When I call at a little before eight to ask about the quickest way
there, Billi answers. She says that they had expected us earlier,
much earlier, and that as a passenger she never pays attention to
the road. It sounds as if she's greeting other guests at the same time
or gesturing as to who is to sit where at the table. "Tom's setting up
a new Ping-Pong table in his studio," Billi says in closing.

Lydia has had her hair color touched up. She's wearing the silver necklace I gave her for her birthday for the first time. In her lap she's holding the 1990 Automobile Club atlas, using the spine that's fallen off as a bookmark. Lydia and I talk about what we would do with an inheritance—a million, say. Except for a trip around the world we can't think of anything, and even that's not such a good idea, since we'd have no jobs waiting for us afterward. So we'd need considerably more money.

Lydia asks if I know anyone who's in the same boat we are, who's not going to inherit anything. "Sure," I say, but then feel less certain. At some point it always turns out that the in-laws have a bungalow on a lake or Grandma owned those five acres that just happen to lie between Berlin and Potsdam. Lydia knows of an unmarried woman who apparently got two million for a piece of potato field needed for the new autobahn ramp near Schmölln. Neither of us can understand why lottery millionaires should be unhappy. Lydia says that maybe they were unhappy before. I hold out my hand to her, and she gives it a quick squeeze. I take the wrong road out of Rochlitz and have to turn around after a few miles. Once back at the intersection, I'm still not sure. Lydia thinks we ought to follow the sign that reads ALL OTHER DIRECTIONS. It seems to me as if I'm doubling back in a large circle.

We've been driving for an hour already when Lydia says it's embarrassing to arrive so late. She wants me to turn around, there was a sign we missed. And my driving so fast isn't going to help now, either.

"Well finally!" I say as we reach the fork in the road where we're supposed to keep right. Lydia closes the atlas and combs her hair. I drive slowly now, my brights on. After an eternity we arrive in the next village. "Keep right at the fork" is all I know. Ten minutes later we're back at the fork, smack next to the road sign. I turn around. "That has to be it," I say, and flash my lights. "Straight ahead."

"What *are* you doing?" Lydia says. I turn off the headlights. And in fact I think I can see a light off in the distance on her side. Although the farm should be on our left. Anyhow, we look for a road leading to it.

We bump along a deeply rutted path. Clumps of grass brush the undercarriage.

"Billi and Tom have a Jeep, don't they?" she asks.

I nod.

"Only way it can be done," she says.

We soon make out the silhouette of the shed, a transformer station or the like, lit by a single bulb and surrounded by a chain-link fence. The sign reads DANGER! HIGH VOLTAGE!

"In the middle of a field," Lydia says.

I kill the engine. I can't put it in reverse because of the muffler. Lydia says not a word. She should get out and direct, but of course in those shoes that would be absurd.

By some miracle I manage to turn around. For a moment I'm as happy as if we'd actually arrived.

"Maybe you can stop somewhere and ask," she says.

"And where would that be?" I ask. "All the farmers are asleep by now anyway."

I now take the other fork.

"This is pointless," Lydia says.

I avoid the splayed body of a dead cat. A little farther on, a crow is pasted to the asphalt of the left lane. One wing's vertical, moving in the wind.

"Has your headache come back?" I ask.

"I thought you had them explain the way to you."

"Turn right at the fork," I say. "I'll ask. If I see a light anywhere, I'll stop and ask."

"Tom drew a little map at some point," she says. "Would you please turn around!"

She rummages in the glove compartment. We pass the crow again and the cat. Lydia stops in mid-rummage and leans back. For the first time I notice the little lamp in the glove compartment. Last Christmas it was left open and she ripped her panty hose on it. I say there's no help for it now and that we need a telephone, and ask if she can remember where she last saw one. Lydia doesn't even bother to shake her head.

A couple of miles ahead we stop for a construction stoplight, a white Ford in front of us. I turn off the motor and read the bumper sticker: GOD IS CLOSER TO YOU THAN YOU ARE TO MY BUMPER.

"What idiocy!" I say. "The things people come up with."

"We always do things wrong," Lydia says after a while. "We do everything wrong." She stares straight ahead. One hand rests along the edge of her seat, turned upward, fist half closed. You could lay something in it.

"It's green," Lydia shouts, "green!" and with a slap of her hand shuts the glove compartment.

The courtyard is packed with cars I don't recognize, including two with Wiesbaden license plates. Billi and Lydia hug for a long time, rocking back and forth. I'm holding the presents: for the twins, two little expensively wrapped Lego sets that have been lying in our entryway for days; for Tom, an art book, *Sculpture of the Renaissance: Donatello and His World.*

Billi says that Tom really chewed her out. Lydia and Billi hug again. "Oh my," Billi says. And while still in the entryway she explains that Enrico is here, Enrico Friedrich from the theater. "He came on the bus, drank himself silly, and now he's asleep in my bed, all curled up like a fetus." I say that we can take him back with us.

"But you only just got here!" Billi exclaims, grabbing Lydia by the wrist and leading us into the kitchen.

There are only women sitting there—no one we might know. We circle the table and shake everyone's hand. That done, two plates are set out for us: potato salad, little warm meatballs, and steamed cucumbers. Billi keeps saying that we should take our time eating. All the others sit leaning back in their chairs, watching us.

Then the men appear. We stand up and congratulate Tom, who's wearing his usual carpenter's trousers and vest today too. He says he tried to call but we'd already left and that we both have to play a game of Ping-Pong now. A few couples take their leave.

From the studio we can hear cars pulling away. I first have to get used to the aluminum table and lose almost every point. Tom asks if Lydia and I aren't getting married soon, what we think about children, and when there's going to be an exhibition of my work. Now and then he praises one of my serves. He'd pay for sparring partners who were his equal, he says.

I ask about Enrico.

Tom grimaces. "He's telling everybody he's got stomach cancer and will be leaving for Brazil on a development project in two weeks—his working motto is, This is our last time together. Don't believe a word of it! Besides, he wasn't even invited."

Billi comes up the stairs. Tom is supposed to say good-bye to somebody. Surrounded by gigantic heads, I wait awhile in the studio. Then I go back to the kitchen. Lydia is talking in a loud peppy voice to the people from Wiesbaden.

They're staying the night. Enrico is asleep. Everyone else has left. We should stay, Billi says, and give our presents to the twins in person. Lydia looks very elegant, almost unreal here in the kitchen.

One of the men from Wiesbaden is a wine wholesaler. He nods toward the two women, while Billi pours them a refill, and says that they're sisters. He's been a fan of Tom's work for a long time. He didn't like them painted at first, but couldn't imagine them any other way now. Then we all talk about Tom's development. Billi says that color is becoming increasingly important for Tom. There's a pause. The wine wholesaler repeats his remark from before and then adds that he's already said that. We all nod to each other. Lydia asks if we shouldn't wake Enrico.

"I'm no baby-sitter," Tom says, and makes a grab for the plate of potato salad. We all sit down at the table. Lydia goes on about the old days, which of late she's taken to calling her "Berlin life." Chewing and swallowing, Tom tells the story of an opening back then, when first the lights went out and then you could hear conversations echoing off the ceiling. Billi and Lydia snort with laughter. Tom explains it was a malfunctioning bug that had reversed itself and was working like a sort of loudspeaker. The Wiesbaden couples are now laughing too.

Billi sits down next to me and, putting her mouth to my ear, asks if Danny—we both work for the same newspaper—has taken in her nephew just temporarily or for good. "The kid's mother, Danny's sister, was killed in a bicycle accident, wasn't she?"

"I didn't know you even knew Danny," I reply.

Billi recalls other hit-and-runs and the shock that must come with causing such an accident, and says a driver really ought to be allowed to plead extenuating circumstances. I'm against that, because otherwise every bastard could worm his way out. "True," Billi says, "but you do have to take shock into consideration. Each is an individual case."

"What are you two talking about?" Tom calls over. He invites Lydia and me to come for a whole weekend, in May or June or when Billi puts on a recital with her students. "You know the way now," Billi says. Our present is lying still unwrapped on a stool.

As we say our good-byes, she hugs me, too. It's a good while before Lydia finally gets into the car. We wave from behind the windows and smile, although no one can see us.

"Half past one," Lydia says. She opens her purse and riffles through the cards. "We've been invited to the North Sea, to Zittau, and to Wiesbaden." She stretches her legs and crosses them at the ankles. I suggest she let her seat back and sleep.

"Did I talk too much?" she asks.

"No," I say, "not at all."

When I stop for the construction stoplight, Lydia has already fallen asleep. The newly resurfaced lane is a straight, well-lit line through the deserted town. I don't pay any attention to the red light. Suddenly there's a car behind us flashing its lights. Once through the construction site, I slow down. We turn left at the next intersection. They follow. The flashing continues. I check my lights, parking brake, temperature, gas, turn signals. If our taillights were out, Tom would have yelled after us as we drove away.

I flip the rearview mirror up, glance to my right. But they're not trying to pass us, either. Their front bumper is about even with our back axle.

The streetlights end at the last house, open fields on both sides, a sickle of moon overhead. I floor it, turn on my brights, and steer the car to the middle of the road, the stripe between my wheels. We race at eighty toward a patch of woods. They're in hot pursuit—Romanians, Russians, Poles, who knows. . . . What if a tree's fallen across the road? I ask myself why we didn't bring Enrico along.

I have to stay calm, do more than just react. We've got a quarter tank of gas. That makes the car lighter. We're in a densely populated country, not in Siberia. My knees are pins and needles, but my feet feel okay. In the next straightaway I lean across and try to press down the button on Lydia's door, but can't reach it. I grope for my own button.

If he bumps us, it'll send us flying off the road. We don't have disc brakes, or air bags, not even on my side. We do have our seat belts on. I wonder about side-collision reinforcement—that we might have.

More fields, no buildings, a construction zone, the road narrows. In my side mirror I can see their headlights growing dimmer.

The warning signal is flashing at the railroad crossing this side of Geithain, the barriers are already lowered. I lean across Lydia and lock the door. The brights behind us are switched on high again.

"Geithain," I tell Lydia, who opens her eyes.

"Your hands are ice-cold," she says.

"There are some crazies behind us," I say.

"Who are they?" she asks, turning around.

They've pulled up so close now that their lights no longer blind us. I can make out a broad childlike face.

"Some crazy," I say. He's sitting bent forward, as if driving a backhoe, his chin over the steering wheel. He stretches his neck. His forehead touches the windshield. He gives us a bump.

"What does he want?" Lydia flips her visor down.

"He gave our bumper"—I swallow hard—"gave our bumper a nudge."

"What does he . . . ?"

The train is coming. The tracks give beneath the cars of grain. I extend my right knee out full, and my foot slips on the brake pedal to the middle of my shoe sole.

The next bump sets our car rocking. I clutch the wheel tight. All we can hear is the train. I concentrate on the distance between my radiator and the bottom edge of the barrier. The road is dry. The train just won't end.

Then I wait till the barrier is completely raised and the warning signals have stopped flashing.

"The car's not responding right somehow," I say, and bang the steering wheel.

Lydia wriggles up a little higher, her head against the backrest. I get the middle stripe between my wheels again. He's right behind us, even as we pull out of curves.

"He can't follow us forever," I say.

Suddenly Lydia says, "A UFO." She doesn't sound the least bit upset. There's a glow behind a hill in the middle of a field.

"Miami," I say. The road bends toward the light, which now turns blue, a radiant blue. An Aral station. I signal a turn.

"Slow down!" she cries, "slow down!" The crazy shoots past us. I brake, pulling into the middle lane of the gas station.

"There's a party going on," Lydia says. I get out and unlock the gas tank. A couple of women and men inside raise bottles to us in a toast. They're leaning against two round snack tables shoved together in front of the coolers. A man with a buzz cut grabs the arm of the woman next to him and waves for us to come in. He points to me and to Lydia, who gets out and stands beside me.

"Surprise, surprise!" they shout as we enter. A red-haired woman cries: "Herrrman, Herrrman!" "Surprise, surprise!" the others answer in unison. All of them are older than we are.

The attendant rips open a six-pack of Becks, nods to me, and opens the bottles. Three in each hand, he carries them to the table. "Herrrman, Herrrman!" they shout again. One after the other they greet Lydia.

"They're waiting for their taxi," the attendant says when I pay. "I can't just make them stand outside. You want something, too?"

I take two ginger ales for Lydia and me. My hands are still cold. Which is why I don't want to shake anyone's hand. Lydia says that we're looking at six bookkeepers, all of whom want to become tax consultants. They nod earnestly. Then the man beside me shouts "Surprise, surprise!" and laughs so hard he chokes. A large bottle of Jim Beam is passed around.

Someone whispers into the ear of the woman across from me. "No way!" she cries, and gives me a once-over. "No way!" she cries a second time, and accepts a hug. Lydia puts the bottle to her lips and drinks. Someone claps me on the back.

"Besides, old pal . . . do you see a taxi?" I don't know what he means. They roar with laughter, and Lydia wipes her mouth. The attendant passes his price gun across containers of yogurt. I chug the second ginger ale and stand there with both bottles in my hands.

"Herrrman, Herrrman, refills!"

Lydia points to an inflatable cow above the cash register, a cow lifesaver. "That's mine," she says, and is greeted with applause because it's the only one left and has to be unhooked from the ceiling. Plus she demands a card good for five car washes.

"Not until after six a.m.," the attendant says. Lydia insists.

"It's really great here," she says, "and I want to make sure we come back." She starts shopping. Goes about it in a very ladylike fashion, the handle of a blue plastic basket in the crook of her elbow. She studies each package. Two cartons of milk, a six-pack of country eggs, mozzarella, sliced multigrain bread. On top lie Varta long-life alkaline batteries. "The only thing they don't have is muesli," she says.

While I'm maneuvering the cow into the backseat, Lydia says good-bye to the others. They get into their taxi two by two. Lydia collects more calling cards, including some from the women.

When they wave to me, I just lift one finger from the steering wheel. I'm sure they long ago decided I'm a wet blanket and party pooper. I imagine Lydia leaving with them. The attendant comes out. "She forgot this," he says, handing me the red rectangle for the car washes and some cleaning rags sealed in plastic. He raises his hand and waves to the departing taxi. Lydia holds the Jim Beam above her head like a trophy.

"You didn't pay any attention to me when he was trying to bump us," Lydia says. She has left her door open, as if she's about to get out again, and holds the bottle clasped tight in her lap. "You could at least have given me your hand or said that I shouldn't be afraid, that you'd protect me, or something."

"I didn't want to make a big deal out of it," I finally say. "It was some dumb kid."

"You don't understand," she says. "We were each of us on our own. You sat there, and I sat here, that's awful!"

"That's not true," I say.

"Of course it's true." She screws the cap off the Jim Beam. "You just don't want it to be true, you always twist things around your way." She drinks, one hand around the neck of the bottle.

I feel sick to my stomach. I want Lydia to stop drinking, to buckle up and close her door.

I get out and walk over to the vacuum cleaner setup. Just beyond it I take a piss. The cold air does me good. My urine steams. I stand there awhile with my fly open. Then I give the air pump a kick. The nozzle jiggles back and forth and hisses.

The attendant has rolled a display case with cigarette lighters, stuffed animals, and chocolate bars back inside the entrance.

Lydia is fixing her makeup. I take in the pleasant smell inside the car, it's familiar, as if it's always been part of my life. Although we only bought the Fiesta last fall.

"We don't even have a screwdriver handy to defend ourselves with," she says. In her right hand she holds a lipstick, in her left its cap. "What's amazing," she says, "is that people aren't constantly attacking each other."

Her door is closed. I start the engine and pull out to the road. I adjust the rearview mirror.

"If I take out a life insurance policy, should I put down your name as the beneficiary?" Lydia asks. Suddenly she leans over, throws her arms around me, and begins to kiss my right ear. She brushes my other ear with the lipstick. Her mouth wanders down my neck. I can feel the car-wash card in my breast pocket and her elbow pressing against it, while over my left shoulder she sets the cap back on her lipstick.

I put my arm around Lydia. I can see the Jim Beam between her feet and the inflated cow in the rearview mirror. Lydia's dress has slipped up over her knees. Then I look in the side mirror, and when it remains dark, I drive off.

s u m m e r   a i r

*How Renate and Ernst Meurer fix up a deserted weekend
cottage. A broken windowpane. Ernst stays behind alone and
goes for a walk. In the night he hears singing.*

"Nobody's saying it's not a piece of luck! It's just that a place like
this one here is a lot of work." Ernst Meurer wiped his lips with his
handkerchief, set his plate on the cutting board, put both on the
tray, and, picking up the glasses and empty bottles of malt drink,
followed his wife. "And he didn't tell you anything about the broken windowpane, either."

She spun around. "Stop griping all the time. How's he supposed to know about that? Who's going to tell him?"

Meurer stopped in his tracks. From the kitchen came the rumble of the fridge going off. And the jingle of the bottles on top.

"And when it comes to gift horses . . ." she said into the silence.

"It's not so much that. . . ." Meurer snorted, but said nothing
more.

"He offered it to *you*, not *me*. Sure, there's things to be done.
Do you suppose otherwise he would've . . . You know Neugebauer!" She held the tray higher as if trying to hand it to him. "And
you're a man, after all," she said, and turned away.

In the kitchen Meurer put the glasses and bottles on the edge of
the sink. He shook open the dish towel, grabbed the bread knife,
and stabbed at the air with it. "For when the Romanians come," he
said.

"The filthy scum!" she said. She scrubbed the fork tines on both sides with a wooden brush.

Meurer pulled the drawer open and laid the knife to one side of the silverware tray. "At least they didn't do anything worse to their victims," he said, accepting a glass from her.

"Wasn't that nice of them! I'd like to see what you'd do if they—see how you'd like it." She pulled the stopper and scrubbed the sink. She filled the skillet halfway with water, set it on the stove, and moved to the bedroom.

"The papers always exaggerate," Meurer shouted. "We'd better go." He hung the dish towel over the bar and rolled down his sleeves. He left the kitchen window open. For two days now they'd put up with the draft, but there was still the odor of mildew and the unpainted wood they had dusted with a damp cloth. When she came out with her suitcase, he noticed she'd buttoned her blouse with wet hands. "We'd better," she said.

They walked the road in this direction for the first time. Meurer tried to imagine how it would look once he was used to it all: the pavement, the wooden fences in front of the narrow yards, the spring water dripping from the iron pipe with the algae-covered screen below, the stone archways into the farms. In the crack under one courtyard door a dog's black-and-white muzzle appeared, laid itself on its side, and barked away. Maybe someday he would even greet people.

Meurer carried the bag with the curtains his wife was taking back to wash. He would be coming this way again on Friday at the latest, to meet her bus. That evening, then, he would hold the ladder and hand the curtains piece by piece up to Renate. He would tell her that if the house had still been bugged, about the only thing they would have heard out of him for the last five days and nights was snoring.

Her calves were almost transparently white. Under the straps of her sandals was the soft reddish sheen at the top of her heels. In bed he had tried to shove his feet between hers, and felt where she had filed off her calluses again. Because the mattresses were longer than the sheets, they had spread towels over the foam rubber at the foot.

Later he had woken up. He decided to close the window, but when he sat up he realized that the noise wasn't coming from outside, but from his wife.

From the moment she had tapped on the bus window and said "The second one on the left," Neugebauer's cottage had disgusted him. The whitewash was flaked and faded. Underneath it was a dark gray stucco, which closer to the ground was almost black from the damp. "Bad as the damn Russians," Meurer had cursed. A path of crushed roof tiles led from the garden gate to the front door. And finally, there had been the windowpane somebody had broken. He had found the stone under the table, picked it up with a handkerchief, put it on the dresser between Neugebauer's wedding picture and the barometer, and then folded up his handkerchief again. Otherwise he had just followed his wife around, looking over her shoulder into the bath, toilet, and kitchen and watching as she put her weight to the jammed back door. The pump in the overgrown backyard worked. There was a hammock dangling between two fruit trees. The roof looked solid—but there were no keys for the two rooms upstairs.

Meurer had turned soil in a plot beside the house, not even bothering to remind his wife about lunch. She had been crawling around hyperenergetically on her knees, humming Papageno's aria, but bursting into song whenever she got to the line "so merry, hi ho, nonny no." She wasn't shy about touching anything, but scrubbed the toilet and shower, wiped cobwebs from corners with her bare hands, tore up an old pillowcase, and thumbtacked it to the window frame to cover the broken pane. It was all Meurer could do to press down on a door handle, and later that afternoon he even resisted letting her put a Band-Aid from the first-aid kit on his blistered palm. Only after she had agreed to first wash the dishes twice had he held out his cup for coffee, and even licked his spoon after stirring with it.

They were walking now along the shoulder, between stripe and ditch. Cans and bottles seemed to grow in the long matted grass. Meurer had often thought of gathering up all this litter. If you got other people to join . . . in a well-organized, countrywide campaign for cleaning up roads and railroad beds—now that would be a great job for him.

A man his age was waiting at the bus stop, looking at the schedule. Meurer nodded to him, and when his greeting wasn't reciprocated, he said "'Fternoon" and turned away.

It was still very warm, but the draft from passing cars didn't cool things much. She put her hands to her thighs each time to keep her skirt from flying up. His summer trousers flapped.

"Takes some gall," Meurer said softly, without looking at his wife and pointing at the white stripes in the road that were fading at the edges, "to call this a bus stop."

A year ago she had had him explain the various makes of cars to her. If he ever did buy one, it would be a German car, or at least one with a German firm behind it. He was thinking of Seat and Skoda. But not even counting those two, the Germans had six different makes, the Italians four, if you included Ferrari, and the French only three, despite Renault. "Germany's number one import!" they wrote across every hood. Whereas the Golf was number one in Europe. The Japanese had five different makes. And nobody could really tell with the Americans. And boats like that weren't meant for our roads.

When the bus arrived, Meurer attempted to kiss his wife on the mouth.

"Give me a call tomorrow," she said. "But not before eight, you hear?"

Meurer passed the bag up, supporting it from below while she paid. "And remember to get a glazier," she said, lifting her baggage in front of her knees with both hands and moving down the narrow aisle toward the rear. He kept even with her outside and waved. Just as the bus pulled away, she sat down. He held his breath. He thought of Subaru and Isuzu, and somehow that spoiled his mood.

When Meurer took in air again, he could still smell exhaust. He crossed the street. On the other side was a narrow concrete slab road. NEW HOMES, he read on a bent sign. The ground floor of the two-story unit behind it looked unoccupied.

He wanted to get quickly past the development on his left, too, with those high peaked roofs just like Neugebauer's. A Saint Bernard in a kennel gave deep, throaty barks. Meurer couldn't recall the last time he had been alone in a strange town. The sun was shining on his back, and he thought he could smell the stale warmth under his shirt. He liked the idea of walking and not knowing where or when he would have to turn back. He didn't want to meet anyone, either, and definitely didn't want anyone asking who he was and what he was doing here, even if the villagers figured he was a friend or relative of Neugebauer, who was already risking showing his face again, offering tax tips in the "Useful Hints" column of the *Volkszeitung*. But people here probably didn't know about that. Maybe for the villagers he had always just been someone who drove a Wartburg sedan, worked in his garden, spoke with a Saxon accent, and for some reason or other had now vanished and was letting his place fall into disrepair.

Meurer wondered if he should take off his shirt. But it wasn't like him to run around half naked. There were tall barriers of nettles on both sides of the path.

After ten minutes Meurer came to a brick barn whose gutters and downspouts were cobbled together out of plastic segments of various colors and had come loose at several points. A rusted farm implement—and he had no idea what it had once been used for—lay overgrown with weeds just outside the gate.

Fields of grain stretched over the gently rolling terrain as far as a hill where the road's slabs of concrete were no more than a dark stripe. A car was coming from that direction.

Meurer heard the distant rumble of an airplane. If they wanted, they could afford a real vacation and make a down payment on a Golf, and still have money left over. After all, the currency exchange had left them with 12,000 D-marks. It was three months now since they'd thrown mud at him—that's how his wife put it— in the local paper.

Meurer stepped off to one side so that the car could stay on the slabs. The white Fiesta slowed down, and the driver, who was younger than he but already balding, waved.

The Meurers paid the rent with his unemployment check and saved what little was left. Her salary as a secretary in Neugebauer's accounting and tax-consulting firm covered their other expenses. They'd bought a stereo color TV, a CD player, a juicer, and a new hair dryer. In February of '90, they'd taken a bus trip to Venice, Florence, and almost to Assisi. They wanted to spend a week this fall in the Burgenland of Austria.

Before climbing the hill, the road led through a reedy low spot. It was cooler here. Meurer bent down and watched a large shiny black beetle scramble around the cracks in the concrete. A man could, given the right conditions, learn something about nature here. "Dung beetle," he said. He could also identify ladybugs, potato bugs, and June beetles. Then again, maybe it wasn't a dung beetle.

Of course Meurer was not the only person who knew a lot about Neugebauer. But so far everyone had kept their mouths shut, even the newspapers. But with the offer of this "cottage" for the summer, it had become clear to Meurer that Neugebauer was still afraid. Or that he needed a free house-sitter. Or was simply sending him, Meurer, on ahead just in case people here had gotten wind of his, Neugebauer's, old position.

A small tractor approached, and bouncing behind it was a trailer with four or five men inside. Meurer again stepped to the small earthen shoulder beside the concrete. They had spotted him before he had seen them. He gave his first wave when they were still a good ten yards away. As they drove past he nodded to them several times. The tractor veered off the slabs in a whirl of dust. One of the men shouted something at Meurer, something about "passing" or "panic," and through the dust cloud he saw the man upright in the trailer, one arm raised. The others were propping him up. Meurer held his breath again.

Fifteen minutes later he reached a crossing. A country lane led off to the right toward some woods, disappearing into them as if into a cave. Meurer turned left.

The air was growing warmer. He thought of his favorite vacation, the honorary trip to central Asia in September of '86, when they had wandered the narrow streets of Bukhara after dark and his wife had said that it felt like an oven.

The fields on both sides had already been mowed. There was something round, silvery, a foot or maybe a foot and a half in diameter, lying in the stubble. Meurer walked in that direction. He guessed it might be a motor, a little electric motor, or a land mine, or a tiny UFO. While still a few steps away, he turned around and gathered some pebbles. Back on the path, he fired away at the rippled, dull silver hubcap with the Opel logo in the middle. Each time he hit it, there was a brief "puck," like the dull chink of champagne glasses filled to the brim. Meurer used up the rest of his stones and wandered on. Without that Opel logo he would have had to get even closer to have recognized it as a hubcap. He didn't believe in UFOs, although those Americans on Channel 7 hadn't sounded like liars. He wasn't going to exclude the possibility of UFOs, but until they made the evening news he wasn't going to take them seriously either. Without intending to, he had been heading for the highest point in the whole area. That sort of thing just happens. Maybe it was a natural urge, something in the genes, that made people want to conquer high peaks. That could be an advantage in the Darwinian struggle of the fittest.

Meurer looked out over the plain stretching far to the north. Two power plants towered on the horizon. Below him, on the slope, was a village with a fieldstone steeple. Meurer tried to judge its distance from him, and then how far it was from there to the power plants. He had had a different picture in his mind of Neugebauer's cottage, and the foothills of the Harz in general, had expected them to be tidier, friendlier. The scene he had imagined rose up clearly before him again for a moment, as if that's where he would return from his walk. He listened, chin jutted up. But all he heard were larks.

At home, in their ground-floor apartment in Altenburg North, he was constantly getting headaches, which could come on in a matter of minutes. Old man Schmidt, who was so proud of being officially certified as a victim of the Nazis, swept the sidewalk every day. Worked over each section three or four times. The awful part was when his broom batted against the wall. And then there was the way he cleared his throat. As soon as Meurer heard him in the stairwell, he would retreat to the bedroom or go shopping. Meurer admired efficiency, liked killing two birds with one stone, even if he was just sitting around. People with time on their hands could chew the fat with old man Schmidt about this, that, and the other. At noon all the kids came home, and banged their soccer ball against the house till evening. Once they had broken the Meurers' cellar window. Ever since, he expected each kick to be followed by the shattering of a pane of glass. Of course he was oversensitive, but that awareness didn't change anything.

Whenever he took out the garbage, he expected to hear his name screamed from one of the windows, to be followed by a volley of curses until he took to his heels. A week ago his wife had been going through the closet, and he was supposed to take what she wanted to discard to National Solidarity. Meurer had got the address mixed up and stood there puzzling over the buzzer box of the old folks' home, until a woman's voice above him had asked what he was up to there. When several more heads appeared, he ended up returning home with the plastic bag still stuffed full.

Last Thursday, he had been on his way to the supermarket when he ran into a handyman in the entry. As if he somehow had to legitimize his own presence, Meurer had taken the newspaper from the mailbox, wedged it under his arm, and then forgotten about it. He didn't notice the moist warmth in his armpit until he was at the checkout. He laid the paper among his items on the conveyor and paid for it.

Meurer had kept to the same path, which led down to the village on the far side of the hill and ended at a barracks, behind which some concrete columns towered. He didn't know if something was being built or torn down until he saw the NO DUMPING sign.

Meurer had to hurry on the way back, and as he moved briskly alongside a field of grain the evening sun was in his eyes. He thought about the open pits of the mines that had been closed down and how he'd read that if they were left alone, if man didn't intervene, life could originate again in them just as it had millions of years ago. And maybe he was doing the right thing himself by doing next to nothing. Meurer flinched. He stared at the grain.

Something was moving beside him. It had to be good-sized—a wild boar maybe. And not twenty feet ahead a doe leapt up, and right behind her a fawn and then the doe again. Both rose up like targets once more, but then stayed under cover, traceable only by the sound of their plunging through the grain. It was almost dark when he crossed the "Avenue of Workers," passed the fire-department pond, and turned onto the main road through town. In front of the church were two linden trees, and between them a stone memorial to the dead of the First World War. The area around it had been weeded and raked in a zigzag pattern. Set in the wooden fence around the memorial—the planks looked bright and new—there was a little gate with a bolt you had to slide to one side if you wanted to get closer by way of a white gravel path.

Meurer decided to visit the stone tomorrow, to count the names and take note of some of them. He was certain that in marching off to war most of these men had been leaving this area for the first time. Maybe any kind of travel was unnatural, or at least superfluous, in the age of television.

Only Neugebauer's place didn't have a satellite dish. An adhesive label had been stuck above the old name plate on the gate. "R. Neugebauer/E. Meurer," it read in his wife's handwriting. He unlocked the door and called her name.

In the bedroom the pillowcase was now dangling from the windowsill. Two thumbtacks were still in the wood. The outline of the hole in the pane looked like a head wearing a beret tilted upward to one side. "You pansy," Meurer said. That's what the man in the trailer had yelled. At last he understood. "You pansy," he clearly heard the fellow shouting.

Meurer didn't turn on a light, but went out the back door into the garden, held his head under the pump, and dried himself with his handkerchief. He rolled up his trousers, jiggled his feet, first one, then the other, under the stream of water, shuffled back toward the house, and tried to slip in through the jammed back door without touching it. He undressed down to his underwear, stood beside the bed for a moment, groped for his pajama top, and pressed it to his nose—the smell of fabric softener and an iron reminded Meurer of home. In the kitchen he gazed for a long time at the skillet on the stove, still half filled with water. He gave it a squirt of dishwashing liquid. Then he took the bread knife from the silverware drawer.

Once under the blanket, he slipped off his underpants and stuffed them under his pillow. He could smell his sandals, their inner soles still greasy from his walk. He grabbed first one, then the other, by the heel strap and dragged it under the bed as far as his arm could reach. A fly or something even bigger kept banging against the wall and ceiling. There were other noises, too: cars out on the street, the fridge, the water heater, the dripping tap. He listened so raptly that he held his breath, and then had to struggle for air.

Meurer had no idea how long he had slept. He was sitting up in bed—legs drawn up, pajama top pulled down over his knuckles, his back against the iron rods of the bedstead—and staring at the outline of the man with the beret, while the pillowcase flapped against the wall below. He again heard the crash of shattering glass that had awakened him. He heard it over and over, a noise that swelled until it swallowed every other sound, became the culmination of every rattle, knock, tinkle, and crunch, racing through the air like a bird or a cloud until it crashed into a window. Inevitable. Without taking his eyes off the windowpane, he touched his nose to his knee. Only then did Meurer realize that his wife had been singing Papageno's aria the whole time.

CHAPTER 8

breath on my neck

Dr. Barbara Holitzschek tells about a late-night telephone call. Playing a game, Hanni makes a confession and asks about what life is like with a famous man. A daughter, a cat, and a turtle.

"Yes, sure, an eternity," I say, crooking the receiver at my neck, getting a good hold on the phone, and tugging the spiral cord apart with my other hand.

"Did I wake you?" Hanni asks.

"What time is it?"

"Oh, shit," Hanni cries. "I did wake you! I'm sorry, Babs. But I thought you two were night owls. Otherwise I never would've called."

The leather of the tubular chair is cold. I try to fish for Frank's shirt. For a moment I have to take the receiver from my ear. ". . . read the article," Hanni says, "where they wanted to know when he does his best work, and he said, at night, when there's peace and quiet, inside and outside. I hardly recognized him from the picture." While she talks, I slip on Frank's shirt. "What's it like living with a famous man?"

"Oh, Hanni," I say. "What time is it?"

"Almost midnight," she says, and then says something to someone else. "Babs?"

"Yes," I say. "Where are you?"

"At a birthday party."

The people behind her are all talking at once, and a man bursts into laughter. "Is something wrong?" I ask.

"No, why do you ask? Everything's fine, Babs," Hanni says. "We're playing a game, and part of it is that you say it. And now they're standing here waiting for me to say it, you know? It's a game. So I'll say it now."

"What kind of game?"

"If you lose you have to call up someone that you loved once, but never admitted it," she says in a rush. "Just a game. Are you mad at me?"

"Do you want to talk to Frank?"

"But Babs, it's you, of course. Are you mad at me?"

"You loved *me*?" I ask.

"Well, yes, I did. Do you hear that, the applause? It's for us, Babs!" she cries. "When I read the article in Saturday's paper about you and Frank—I felt really nostalgic. I got out my old diaries. I wanted to talk with you again. And then I lost the game. You probably think it's ridiculous, don't you?"

"No," I say.

"Men always make fun of women who admit such things. They can't deal with it. I've always admired you. Just your being nice to me made me happy. But you were nice to everyone. I wanted you to be my friend, just mine."

I wait for her to go on, and then I tell her that I'm basically shy.

"I don't believe it," Hanni says. "Understatement—that's why you say things like that. But there's a reason you've got the best man here. Shows how special you are."

"How's your family?" I ask.

"My daughter?"

"Yes," I say, "Rebecca."

"You mean Sarah. Otherwise there's only Peggy and Fridolin." Hanni's smoking from the sound of it. "Fridolin's just a turtle, sad to say. When I'm as old as he is, retired and all that—if I ever make it that far—Fridolin will still be alive, and I'll have to find someone to pass him on to. Crazy, isn't it?"

"Yes," I say. "Hard to imagine."

"Such a faithful man. . . . The move discombobulated Peggy. She's totally off-track."

"Peggy?"

"Our cat. I should open a pet psychology clinic. Pets are just like us, totally loony."

"I read your articles," I say.

"'Articles' is good, Babs, helpful hints corner in a local adver-tiser. But I don't have time for anything else. People like Frank, our representatives, are constantly asking us to write proposals. And so I'm always writing proposals and arguing with the construction crew. And if it's not that, then I'm batting my eyes at bankers or giving lectures at the Rotary Club, because they've promised us a new slide projector. You still working?"

"Why wouldn't I be?" I ask.

"Well, if Frank's people win, seems to me you'll be a cabinet minister's wife, at the very least. I voted for the Greens once, but I can't go biting the hand that . . . there'd be even less money for museums then. . . . Do you realize we've known each other eigh-teen years?"

"Since ninth grade," I say.

"Always makes me feel queasy, a number like that."

"Which number?"

"You see, I knew it wouldn't affect you the same way. You've made something of yourself. But for me it's a crisis, I really panic. Thirty-five, that's two-thirds of the way already."

"Hanni," I say, "half at most."

"No," she says sharply. "Not for us. Men have a different half-life. Not us. I have no illusions left. You're married, Babs. . . ." Hanni takes a drag on her cigarette.

A light goes on in the hall.

"And the worst part is that everything that once was is gone, all those people, gone."

Frank is standing in the doorway, leaning against it, head tilted forward, as if trying to listen in. "Hanni," I whisper to him. He grimaces. There's a greenish-blue bruise on his hip.

". . . and I know why, too," Hanni says, "because I can't be alone. I mean, I can manage being alone all right. But somehow I think that a person ought to be with other people and be in love. Anyway, married couples never let me even get close anymore. They're all scared."

"You think so?" I ask. Frank is suddenly kneeling between my legs.

"Do I think what's so?"

"I'm wondering if you mean it the way you said it?" Frank pulls the shirt to one side and kisses my breasts.

"Of course," Hanni says. "What else should I mean? I see it all around me. People with any brains make themselves scarce, and those left behind play these little games. Today's my birthday, Babs, my birthday!" I have to raise the receiver because Frank is pressed up against me. He's really warm.

Hanni goes on talking. ". . . day before yesterday, Sunday, I'm still asleep. Suddenly there's one helluva racket somewhere in the building. Doorbells and slammed doors, and people running around. But I'm only half awake. And then my doorbell rings. But by the time I get to the door, there's total silence. And I think if they want something, they'll try again. That's how it works, right?"

Frank bites into my shoulder.

"If they want something, they'll be back. I get back into bed, it's only half past five, still pitch-dark. And then I hear these women again. No sooner am I in bed than I hear them again. Do you know what they're up to? They're making a date for breakfast. I stand at my apartment door, and I can hear it all. They're making a breakfast date because they can't go back to sleep. Me neither. Once I'm awake, I'm awake, I get it from my mother. But I can't just open the door now, either. Not now. And I think . . . ah, forget it. A water pipe broke somewhere. And yesterday morning on the bus, there was this woman, thin as a rail, sitting across from me and eating one muffin after the other. She peeled the paper off with her fingernails, and then crammed the muffin in her mouth. Crumbs everywhere. And her shopping bag, with the bag of muffins in it, kept slipping from between her knees. She ate and ate, and every once in a while her bag would fall on the floor."

"You didn't have to watch," I say. Frank has stood up and heads for the bathroom.

"They're all a little off the wall here. I don't know what else I'm supposed to do. It's just like back then. Everybody's leaving. Sarah wants to move in with her father now that she's sixteen. I don't see her at all anymore anyway, or as good as never. Let her move in with him, too, then I won't have the worry. And won't he look dandy once he's got her, he can play Papa and show off his daughter. But when I had to go to emergency every night, because of her asthma attacks, there was no Papa anywhere. And he only pays what he has to. Quiet as a mouse then. And so now I get a call from the little man. Sarah's been crying buckets for a week, and all of a sudden she wants to move in with him, and she smokes like a chimney. I figured you didn't want to have anything to do with me anymore, either."

"Because I'm married?"

"I just put all my eggs in one basket and called. You were so strange the last time. And then I never heard from you again. And if I don't call people—nobody calls me. That's just how it is."

"I really wasn't doing very well," I say.

"On account of that badger?"

"Yes," I say, "on account of the badger."

Then Hanni doesn't say anything. For the first time there's a long pause, a nightmare of a pause. I can hear Hanni breathing.

"Do you have a badger by now?" I ask. My voice sounds perfectly normal.

"No," Hanni says. "I'm just sorry that the two of us didn't go that day. But Lydia, our taxidermist—if she has to lead a tour, just one little tour, she gets behind in everything. She's total chaos. She'd be a case for you, really."

"No problem," I say. Frank comes out of the bathroom. He leaves the hall light on.

"I'd love to see you again, Babs, just see you, and then we could spend a nice evening together, the three of us, or just us two, that's all, and talk and gossip. Do you think that's silly?"

"No," I say, "not at all."

"Just to see someone, from back then. Does that make sense?"

"Sure," I say, and promise to call her and not wait forever to do it.

"Babs," Hanni says in closing, "I really love you, that's all. Do you believe me?"

When I hang up, the spiral cord twirls and catches on itself in a couple of places like a zipper. I lift the phone with both hands and lay the receiver on the floor. The cord gets longer. I hold the phone higher, until the receiver starts turning pirouettes just above the carpet. It takes at least a minute of spinning back and forth for it to untangle. I set the phone on the table and hang up the receiver.

"Is something wrong?" Frank asks.

"No," I say, taking off the shirt and tossing it toward where I think the back of the chair is. "She was pretty drunk," I say, bumping my shin on the bed. "She thinks you're famous and give big parties every night, and that I'm playing First Lady."

Frank puts his head on my shoulder and angles his right leg over my knee. Slowly I begin to recognize the outlines of the wardrobe and clothes tree plus hangers, the picture frames, the two lamps, and the mirror with my necklace dangling from it, and the chair.

I can feel Frank's breath on my neck, warm and even. We're both totally exhausted every night. I know I won't be able to fall asleep now. The feeling's only too familiar. It's six long hours until six-thirty.

Smartest thing would be to get up and get some things done. I need to write my mother and ask about her plans for Christmas. We want to go to Tenerife, till the second week of January. My mother never used to be a problem. But ever since our last visit—I bent down to tie my shoe in the entry and there was a huge dust ball with hair clinging to my shoelace. I thought the glob would fall off on its own. But it was caught in the knot. I had to untie the knot, carry the mess to the garbage can, and wash my hands. My mother watched, but didn't seem to care. At least she didn't say anything. She'll be sixty-eight in February. Until now I've only been amazed at how lackadaisical she is about shopping, just prepackaged lunch meat and cheese from the cooler, hardly ever anything fresh, and nothing but Nescafé, even though she claims it tastes better, Nescafé Gold. Those pretty blue-and-white goblets have been standing unused behind the roaster for years now. At her place we drink from Czech mustard glasses that used to have a gold rim. She just uses dishes right out of the dishwasher, then puts them back again. I never even realized my mother has become an old woman and that maybe I'll soon have to start worrying about her.

Frank's leg jerks. His breath is hot and keeps blowing on the same spot on my neck. I tuck my legs up a little. I can feel my toenails against the covers.

I didn't even wish Hanni happy birthday. I don't know what I ought to wish for her. "Frank," I say. The spot where he bit my shoulder still hurts. Light is coming through a bent slat in the blind. I can see the uneven places in the wallpaper. I try to make myself sleepy by picturing the telephone receiver doing pirouettes.

His breath is unbearably hot. "Frank," I say softly. His forearm presses against my ribs, his fingers brush my spine. "Frank," I whisper, "I killed someone." I turn over toward him, on my side. We are rocked by my heartbeat, it sets the whole bed swaying.

Sometimes a nap toward morning helps me forget a night like this. Then the hours I've lain awake melt into a single moment and evaporate like a dream, as if it were nothing.

I should get up and do something useful. But I don't know where to start. I calculate my life in cat-years. You multiply by seven to get cat-years. You have to divide for turtles. But there's no such thing as turtle-years.

CHAPTER 9

dispatcher

Why Raffael, who runs a taxi business, can't create a job out of thin air and why Orlando is unsuitable as a driver. Intentional and unintentional confusion. Too warm for this time of year.

Raffael is sitting in the office. His forefingers wander over the keyboard. His eyes shift regularly from the screen to a book and back. On the edge of the desk lies an empty box of Toffifee. He keeps wiping off the palm of his hand on his thigh.

Raffael hears footsteps in the stairwell. He looks toward the door and flinches at the sound of the bell.

"Raffael?" The door handle moves. The bell rings a second time. "Raffael, what's up? It's me, me!" A shoe tip bumps the steel door, which springs open after a short buzz.

"You'll wake the whole building." As he stands up, Raffael buttons the top button on his pants. "First shut the door right."

Orlando sets down his suitcase, presses his knee against the door, and jiggles the handle. "Shut," he says.

Raffael comes toward him. "Well, how you doing? Have you grown?" He raises his hands. "Careful—I'm infectious. You trying to found a folk costume club?"

"It's called a janker," Orlando says, unbuttoning his jacket and unwinding a scarf from around his neck. "I can start work."

"When did you get out? You've got new shoes."

"Today."

"And headed right here, kit and caboodle?"

Orlando nods.

"Not put on disability?"

"I can drive, no problem, really."

Raffael has returned to his chair and plops into it. "You've put on weight, Orlando."

"They fed me right."

"Ever since I stopped smoking . . ." Raffael pats the inside of his thigh. "Fat for the winter. I always notice it here first."

"Give me a car, please."

Raffael raises his hands again, and lets them drop on the arms of his chair.

"I was a good driver."

"I know, Orlando." Raffael slides forward in his chair and thumbs his pocket calendar.

"I really was a good driver! You said so yourself."

"For five weeks, Orlando, five weeks." Raffael flips page by page. "Four weeks and five days, to be precise."

"Six days a week, seven days, twelve, thirteen hours."

"Do you know how long *I've* been holed up here? You ever thought about that? I don't even have time to go get some aspirin. I should be in bed, I've got a fever. Want to feel?" Raffael puts the flat of his hand to his forehead.

"I'm a taxi driver."

"Everybody's a taxi driver nowadays, Orlando. Everybody thinks he can drive a cab. Every asshole thinks he's a taxi driver. Don't make this so hard for me."

"I'll do anything you want."

"It was a trial run, Orlando. Please, I gave it a try, and it didn't work out. Like it really, really didn't work out."

"He was drunk."

Raffael expels a sound almost as soundless as a sudden sigh. "You don't say!" He closes his calendar and stands up. "Last home game today."

"He was drunk, and now he's doing time in jail, Raffael."

"Which team're you for? Take a load off. Can I make you some tea? Drink a cup with me?" Raffael goes to the mini-fridge, on top of which stand a coffee machine, some dishes, bread crisps, and two jelly jars. "Last year shitty weather saved us, us and the fuel dealers. And if it doesn't start in again soon, then . . . silly V. That's life. We always used to hope winter would come late and be over fast. All the same, I always volunteered to drive, to be on call for the first snow, that's if I wasn't already on duty. And at the first real snow, I'd be out with the plow, usually at night, when there weren't even any tracks in the road, and you're all alone, and there's nothing up ahead but virgin snow—it's incredible!"

"He's doing time, Raffael. It's not gonna happen again."

"'Not gonna happen again.' You can go to Berlin maybe, to Hamburg or to Leipzig for all I care. But you're not staying here! Don't you get it? 'Not gonna happen again.' Next time, maybe, the knife won't be in your back. . . ." Raffael empties the coffee grounds into the wastebasket, rinses the glass pot, and pours water into the machine. "Okay, Orlando. Even if I am exaggerating, I still don't have a car available."

"But you said—"

"I said that I'd help you. That's what I said. But I didn't say that I can create a job out of thin air." He wipes his hands on his trousers. "Leave your fingernails alone. You don't even notice it anymore. Go pay a visit to Holitzschek, our Landtag representative. I read in the paper how he wants to help you. Why don't you go see him tomorrow, thank him for his visit and the flowers, and ask him just what he meant by lending a hand to people of color." Raffael turns on the coffee machine. "That made you sit up and take notice! Can you tell me why we have health insurance if the firm has to shell out for six weeks? I'm paying five times as much for car insurance, but gas isn't getting any cheaper. And meanwhile the town council has eliminated the taxi stand by the pond, and to the cops one car's the same as any other. And to cap it all, my dear sir"—Raffael suddenly grows very calm—"to cap it all, you're a mechanical engineer, with a diploma from Havana and another one from Dresden Tech, and that's not even counting the retraining you did. Besides which, you know ten times more about computers than the whole bunch of idiots that installed this thing here for me. But you're not a taxi driver, *dottore*. And aren't you getting full unemployment again?"

"No." Orlando wrinkles his nose. He turns away. Raffael grabs him by the shoulder.

"Makes no difference," Raffael says. "Look at me. You're not a taxi driver, *dottore*, not a cabby, got it? I can't make it snow and I can't make palm trees grow by magic. Everybody wants help. Everybody's got problems, everybody!" Raffael raises an extended forefinger to his temple. "That's how it is! And bang"—his thumb retracts—"bang! I can't save the whole world. What I can save is four and a half jobs. That takes concentration, Orlando. I don't want any more excitement, no more confusion, understand? And stop chewing your nails, damn it!" Returning to the fridge, Raffael opens it. "Do you know when the last time was that Petra and I . . . the last time I even touched her? Easter! I see David on weekends, sometimes. At the end of the month I just break even, with shit left for me. Payments on the vehicles, rent for this place, telephone, salaries, insurance . . . I just cover that. What's the time?"

"Nine o'clock."

"Second half. Did you ever ask me why I'm a Dortmund fan?"

"Because of Sammer?"

"No."

"Because of Andy . . . Möller maybe?"

"Want to know why? If Borussia Dortmund makes it this year, then I will too. I know it. And if they don't, we go belly-up. I'll throw in the towel. You can have all my cars then. What's with the grin? It has to end at some point, one way or the other. Petra pays for everything, the apartment, food, stuff for David, Christmas presents. And I wanted to be the first guy to get his family out of

Altenburg North!" Raffael gives the coffee machine a slap. "Needs to be decalcified. What kind of tea you want? Maté, green, peppermint, Earl Grey, wild cherry, English breakfast? I got Christmas tea, too."

"There's always somebody who's had enough or leaves town. You said that yourself, Raffael."

Raffael polishes the tea glasses, hangs a tea bag in each, and tosses two cork coasters on the desk. "I can put you on between Christmas and New Year's. And now will you sit down!" He grabs a handful of sugar cubes from the box.

"No," Orlando says.

"You won't sit down?"

"Not as a sub, Raffael."

"I'm out of lemons." He sets the milk carton between the glasses, sits down, and picks up two telephone receivers at once. "I keep thinking somebody must be sabotaging me. Can you tell me why nobody calls? There are forty-eight thousand fat butts in this town! Or say forty-seven or forty-five—once there were fifty thousand, Orlando, fifty thousand butts. Why doesn't one of them want to sit in a taxi? Why isn't the phone ringing off the hook? You can have my job. I'll gladly switch, love to. Unemployed, and with no debts. You're free! You can do whatever you want." He bangs the receivers down.

"Vacation weather," Orlando says, "not taxi weather." He puts a cigarette between his lips and lays the pack on the desk.

"If people's pockets are empty, it can rain cow pies! That's a fact! Get that through your head. And don't smoke in here, Orlando." Raffael probes at the opening of the milk carton. "Why don't you leave? What's keeping you in this backwater, huh?" Raffael licks milk off his thumb. "I saw a guy this morning I knew back in school. So I walk right up to him. He just gapes at me and doesn't say a word." Raffael stretches his head out and holds both hands like binoculars up to his eyes. "About like this. I didn't ask if he's working. Even if he does have a job, I can guarantee you he thinks he's not making enough. Everybody here thinks I'm a big cheese, you, too, probably. And so I ask about his family, his kids, and so on. And that did it!" Raffael buries his face in his hands, as if everything's been said, and rubs his forehead. "You'll never guess. He blows his stack! If anybody knows how they are I should, he says—after all, I'd learned about it before he did. I have no idea what's stuck in his craw, why he's so pissed at me. His baby double chin is wobbling like a turkey's. 'You're way out of line!' he roars at me right there on the street. And do you know why? Because he claims I knew before he did that his wife had given birth to a daughter. I can't remember anything about it, not even now. I don't even know his wife. And so how did I know that, I ask. Who's supposed to have told me about it? He just yells that I'm way out of line. And the whole thing's supposed to have happened six years ago, Orlando, think about it, six years ago! He probably has me confused with somebody else. But even if I were the guy he thinks I am . . . do you understand it?"

"No," Orlando says softly. The coffee machine hisses. Steam rises. The water in the glass pot is just below the first line.

"For somebody to carry that much anger around in his gut for six years, Orlando . . . do you know what that means? It means that I'm getting off easy with just scratched paint and slashed tires. Best thing would be for me to never leave this office. The telephone's all I need. All the rest just ends up a hassle and confusion."

"I can start right away, really I can. It doesn't hurt anymore. Want to see?" Orlando takes off his janker and sweater. He unbuttons his shirt down to his belt and slips out of the left sleeve. With his back to Raffael, he leans out over the desk and pushes his undershirt off his left shoulder.

"No bandage?" Raffael stands up and leans across the desk.

"It's supposed to get air. Heals better that way, they said."

"Just like you imagine it." Raffael reaches out an arm and traces the scar with his fingertips. "And the stitches? They hurt?"

Orlando shakes his head. "Just tickle," he says.

Raffael pats him on the shoulder. His hand glides down Orlando's arm. He helps him pull the undershirt strap up. At the next touch, Orlando shoves away from the desk.

"So it does hurt," Raffael says, and sits back down.

Once he has closed the door behind Orlando, Raffael pulls out the doorbell wires. He goes to the window and tips open the transom. He watches Orlando lift his suitcase onto the backseat of the taxi and get in on the passenger side. Then the taxi drives off.

Raffael looks across to his old office. Both windows of the bus station are dark.

"Dispatcher," Raffael says. "Dispatcher, dispatcher," he repeats, "dispatcher, dispatcher." He says it faster and faster, until the syllables are disconnected and sound as strange and meaningless to him as they do to most people when he answers "dispatcher" to the question of what he used to do. "Dispatcher for local public transit in the districts of Altenburg, Borna, Geithain, and Schmölln. Dispatcherdispatcherdispatcher . . ." The longer he speaks, the more unexpected sounds there are. Raffael enjoys his self-made confusion. It doesn't always work. The word often remains clear and unambiguous, no matter what he does with it.

He had once believed "dispatcher" was one of the few job designations used worldwide. At least West Germans ought to understand it. The word was English, after all. "Dispatcherdispatcher."

Raffael is at the telephone at once and grabs for the receiver. He hesitates a moment. Then he picks it up and says calmly, "Günther Taxi, good evening."

"It's me."

"Already?"

"What do you mean, already?"

"Did he carry your suitcase up for you?"

"I'm fine, Raffael."

"If you say so."

"Have forty-seven thousand Altenburgers been calling?"

"Who?"

"Had any more calls?"

"Oh, sure. Christmas parties, couple of times."

"What about Dortmund?"

"What?"

"They win?"

"Did they?"

"I'm asking you. . . ."

"Let's hope, I hope so, sure."

"Just heard the weather report. It's going to stay above freezing. They don't know yet what next week will be like."

"But always pretend they do. That's what really pisses me off."

"Right."

"It can all turn around by next week."

"Sure it can."

"Orlando?"

"Yes?"

"I'm sorry . . . I've got this fever. I didn't mean . . . will you take a look at my computer tomorrow?"

"You got it."

"Nothing's working right anymore."

"I'll have a look, sure."

"That'd be great, really great."

"You staying till eleven?"

"Till eleven, right."

"Got enough chocolate?"

"Chocolate?"

"Instead of Raffael, your name should be Raffaelo, Raffaelo Ferrero, like the chocolate."

"Has to do with the painter. But nobody knows that now-adays."

"Raffael?"

"Yeah."

"What's the connection?"

"There isn't any. I'll tell you sometime."

"Do *you* paint?"

"I'll tell you sometime, not now."

"I wanted to suggest something, Raffael—you listening?"

"Yes."

"I could drive until it's all made good. It came to me when I got back here. You tell me how much it cost, the sick pay and the repairs and—"

"What?"

"I could drive until it's all made up for, sick pay, repairs to the car—"

"You're talking bullshit, Orlando."

"I'll be by tomorrow. You know where you can find me other-wise."

"Hmm."

"Well then, Raffael."

"Hmm."

"It's your move."

"What?"

"Whoever gets called hangs up first."

"So it's up to me."

"You can count to three if you want."

"I'm going to have to cut this short."

"It's your move."

"Right," Raffael replies, and hangs up.

"Dispatcher," he says aloud, and looks up at the two wires above the doorframe. Their shiny points look like feelers. His shirt is stuck to his armpits and back. Raffael rolls up his sleeves. He walks to the windows, opens both casements, bends under the crossbar and leans out. "Dispatcher," he says, "dispatcher, dispatcher." He keeps repeating it, loud and fast. Raffael thinks he can see the smoky wisps of his breath and for just a moment the bus station even looks snowed in. But he's not cold. Not so much as a chill or a shiver. It's really still way too warm.

s m i l e s

Martin Meurer tells about seeing his real father again after twenty-four years. An unexpected confession. Believers don't get sick so often and they live longer. Potholders and the act of an apostle.

It's hard for me to talk about meeting my father, about how it felt at the time, I mean, to give an account of the impression he and his story made on me. Not because my memory's poor—it was barely a year ago—but because I know more now. I might even say I've become a different person.

One morning in March '69, our mother came into Pit's and my room and said, "Your father's gone west for good." She pulled back the curtains, opened the window, and left again. I was seven, Pit was five. "No matter what they ask you at school, you have nothing to hide, absolutely nothing," she cautioned me before she left to take my brother to kindergarten. And for a long time, that's all she said about it.

After Tino was born on February 13, 1988, I sent my father a snapshot of the three of us. He slipped a hundred West German marks in his congratulations card. My wife, Andrea, was killed in an accident in October '91. I wrote him about that, too. There was another hundred marks in his sympathy card. Later I also got a greeting card from a day trip to Murnau.

Shortly after his fifth birthday, Tino, our son, moved in with Danny, my sister-in-law. She simply got along better with the boy.

A few weeks after that, Thomas Steuber, who used to be our neighbor, phoned and asked if I could pick up a year-old demo for him, a BMW 500, in Gröbenzell near Munich. He offered me 250 marks, plus the train ticket and expenses. He must have heard I was unemployed. I said yes on the spot.

I suppose that at the time I didn't even know myself why I called information to get my father's number. Maybe it was just simple curiosity or because I hoped to get a little money from him. After all, he'd been a staff physician.

He seemed tentative on the phone and called me "my boy." I jotted down the name and address of a café where he could be found on weekdays after four. The next evening my father called me back. I did know about the state of his health, didn't I? He didn't want me to be surprised. We hadn't seen each other for twenty-four years.

I didn't have to wait long at the dealership in Gröbenzell. All I could think of was how long it had been since I had sat at the wheel of a car. It was an hour's drive from there to the English Garden, and I even found a space where I could park without putting it in reverse. I walked the last little bit.

Round tables were set outside the café on the wide sidewalk, two chairs per table. As soon as anyone paid, passersby would stop, wait, then push their way to the seats while the waiter was still wiping up. I sat down at a table where a woman was sunning herself, her tinted glasses shoved up into her hair. The coffee came with the bill and a little cookie in the saucer.

I looked to one side, then the other, like a man at a tennis match. I even watched for any slow-driving taxis. Meanwhile I dunked the cookie in hot coffee, poured condensed milk into my cup till it was brimful, and lit a cigarette. Whenever I thought of my father, I pictured the wedding photo we boys had hid in our room. I was just imagining how in the next moment I would toss my cigarette aside and forge a path between the chairs when here came a short, slight man walking toward me. His long coat seemed to get caught between his knees at each step. Just before he got to me, he stopped, cut a wide semicircle toward our table, stretched his right hand from its sleeve, and said not a word as his long dirty fingers filched sugar cubes from the bowl. Suddenly in shade, the woman opened her eyes. The next moment, we saw coattails fluttering at his ankles, and he was gone.

Four o'clock, and I was standing at the curb across from the entrance. A couple of times I thought I saw his face.

Then I recognized him at once. He was making very slow progress, dragging his leg but without using a cane. I moved directly into his path.

"Hello, Father," I said. I had never called him "Father."

"Afternoon, my boy." His head turned a little to one side. "I can see only out of my left eye."

My father linked his arm in mine, and we entered the café together in step. He was shorter than I.

"Your father's pretty much of a wreck," he said. "At least physically. Wouldn't you say?"

"No," I said, "why should I?"

The waitresses wore tan uniforms and white aprons with crocheted trim. One of them pressed her back to the display case filled with tortes, cakes, and pastry, to let us pass side by side. "Dr. Reinhardt, good afternoon," she said. My father stopped, turned his head, and gave her his left hand. "My boy," he said. She raised her eyebrows. "Hello. Pleased to meet you, Herr Reinhardt. Nice to have you with us." We shook hands as well. Then I felt my father's arm in mine again. A couple of guests were watching us and smiling. There were loud greetings from waitresses coming toward us and passing from behind.

"Do you still go by 'Meurer'?" he asked.

"Yes," I said, and helped him out of his coat. Without actually touching, we took a few steps to the round table he had pointed to in the corner. There was a good crowd in the café, a lot of women sixty and over, mostly in twos and threes, but only a few couples.

A very young waitress jotted something on her pad before she came up to us. "Afternoon," she said, removing the RESERVED sign and sticking it in her apron pocket. We ordered two cups of coffee.

"You'll have to come in summer when the beer gardens are open. You really have to come then." He laughed just like in the wedding picture, except that it didn't give him little chubby cheeks. He looked at me closely now.

"I used to think that you'd end up fat someday. You could eat for three, polish off all the leftovers, incredible—fourteen dumplings plus stewed fruit. We kept asking ourselves who you got that from. Most big eaters end up fat and die young." Using his left hand, he raised his right arm from the table. "As you see," he said, "I've got a lame paw." I searched his face for traces of paralysis, but saw none. He looked good, still had a nice head of hair, an attractive man in his mid-sixties. His fingertips checked his tie.

He told how he had got up one morning to go to the toilet, and when he came back to the bedroom, he saw a chair tipped over. He set it upright. And a vase fell off the table.

"That's how it started," he said. "I was knocking things over without even noticing. And then—a lightning bolt. It wasn't *like* a lightning bolt, it *was* one, absolutely, and not a stroke like they all thought. I felt no pain. Just a lightning bolt, and you're left paralyzed."

My father turned to the waitress who brought us our coffee, and he kept smiling till she left.

"I've had to start over, start all over again. And it was so long before I could even start! I thought it would just go away, like when your leg falls asleep and then wakes up."

I watched him put his cup to his lips. He drank quickly. Set it back down without trembling.

"Is sugar a problem?" he asked.

I reached for the sugar bowl.

"Ah, my boy, I meant do you have *diabetes*? I do." He took another sip and gazed at a spot beside his crumpled hand. "I had to start over, begin again from scratch," he said. "Because back then, when I first came here—that was starting over, too."

"Keep starting over myself," I said, "but don't ever seem to keep it up."

"There's a purpose behind it all, Martin, a purpose behind everything," he said, reaching for his right hand and pushing it away from the saucer a little. "Even if *we* can't see the purpose, or at least not right off."

Although I said nothing, he grew more animated. "I know what you're thinking. But all the same, it's what the years have taught me." He pulled out a folded handkerchief and wiped his lips.

I wondered what I should say in reply, and in the shared silence drank my coffee. I was sure he had planned each sentence, had prepared himself for our meeting as if for a lecture. And that his silence was presumably part of the rhetoric, too.

I told him about the man who had filched sugar cubes from the bowl. "And poof!" I said, "he was gone."

"And?" my father asked. We fell silent.

"Anything new with you?"

"No," I said.

"No girlfriend?"

"Oh that," I said. "No."

"How long has it been now since your wife's accident? A year?"

"A year and a half."

"And the driver? Did they ever . . . ?"

"There wasn't any driver," I said. "At least they haven't found any traces of one. Maybe somebody passed her too close, or something else frightened her. She just had a stupid accident . . . on the other side of Serbitz."

I said that I felt I was to blame for Andrea's death, because after my driver's license was suspended, I insisted we didn't need a car. "That's why Andrea was trying to ride a bike. She was terribly unsteady on it."

I had often talked about her death like this. Suddenly, however, I said: "I wanted Andrea to die, and then it happened."

I stared into my cup and was dumbfounded to think I could have said such a thing, and to him of all people, who had deserted us and thought he could find just the right card for every occasion.

"You probably never really loved her, or at least not long enough. You never know beforehand." My father set his cup on the table and shoved the saucer and cookie toward me. "You want it?" I put it in my mouth, got it down somehow, and asked whether it would bother him if I smoked. He preferred I didn't.

"And what about you?" he asked after a while.

"Who needs art historians," I said, "especially one without a Ph.D."

"I could have told you that."

I started to talk about Bohemian wood-painting, about school, the demonstrations. "None of us finished," I said. "We did everything conceivable, except work on our dissertations. And then, all of a sudden, bang, new prof, new assistants, bang."

He never took his eyes off me. "They tossed you out?" he asked.

"Yes," I said, comparing his left eye with his right again, but without detecting any difference.

"Were you in the Party?"

"What makes you ask that?"

"I'm sorry," he said, "but I know Meurer. Red Meurer! That's what they all called him." My father squinted. "The hardest part was forgiving him. I hated that man. But I've forgiven him."

"What have you forgiven him?"

"Ah, my boy! When your own children suddenly end up in the hands of a man like that . . . I didn't want you all rotting away there. I tried so hard to persuade your mother that we should all go together. But she was stubborn, plain stubborn, stubborn to the core."

"We didn't want to leave either."

"You were children, Martin. You can see what it got you."

"I've just had bad luck, that's all," I said. "All I need now is to start drinking and lose my apartment." I wanted to go on, but couldn't. I thought of Andrea. My throat was dry and sore. I felt tears welling up and was on the verge of slipping into warm self-pity.

But my father refused to pay me any attention and simply started talking again. Mother had once called in the police when he had been very late getting home from a walk. "She was asleep, and you two were huddled in front of the TV. You never wanted to get out in the fresh air. First she alerted the forest ranger. She thought I was lying somewhere, gored by a wild boar." He laughed until his eyes squinted tight. His forehead was shiny. "I always think about that," he said, and looked at his watch.

"My boy," he began, sitting up straight, "once I got here and divorced Renate and married Nora . . ." He stroked his temple. "Nora and I were married for almost twenty years. I'd open my eyes every morning, there she was beside me, and I could still feel her hand when I fell asleep. Even after two years of taking care of a cripple. . . . Of course, I thought: Nora is the dearest thing to me in the whole world, without Nora . . . And then——I want to tell you about it——then I tempted fate. It hunted me down and wiped out all the illusions I never knew were illusions, because I was too pig-headed, too wrapped up in my happy little world." He gave his hand another push. "There was this Bible-thumper, that's what I called him then, who was forever ringing our doorbell. I didn't have much use for people like that, but at some point Nora let him in. We had hardly anybody to talk to, hardly any visitors. I couldn't walk and had no hope I ever would. So this Bible-thumper sat himself down, and we listened to him and made fun of him. He sat there patiently, didn't try to defend himself, and——suddenly started praying. I can still picture him very clearly, his knees squeezed tight, hands folded over them, head down, a deep furrow between his eyebrows as if he were in pain."

My father brushed the handkerchief across his lips again. It's his story to tell, I thought, I don't have to say a thing.

"Don't you want a bite to eat?" he asked, putting the handkerchief away. "Nora and I sat beside our praying evangelist and waited till he was done. He said good-bye as if nothing had happened, but there he was two days later—this time with flowers. He visited us three, four times a week. I kept thinking, If only he weren't so nuts—" my father said gruffly. "Ah—I'll make it short. When he and Nora took off together, I realized who I'd been living with. Do you know what kept her with me all those years? First my savings account, second my insurance, third the pension I'd get someday—money, money, money. When Nora told me she'd be flying to Portugal the next day with Boris, the preacher, she also said, 'Now you don't have to hide your money from anybody.' My Nora, my life! I mean, we'd always had everything we ever needed, and then some."

My father paused. It looked to me as if he first had to get control of himself again. But when he started speaking, his voice was firm.

"So that's the end, I thought at the time. But I had farther to fall. It even felt like some kind of relief. So that's what they're like, I thought. That's what's behind all the sanctimony. The world's that simple. I was an enthusiastic masochist. But," my father said, squinting again as if laughing ahead of time at some joke, "do you know what, my boy? My life was only beginning. All alone? Anything but! Jesus Christ was never so close to me as in that moment! Who are we to be offended by those who bring us the message?"

What my father said came like a bolt out of the blue. I had never even been baptized. I just figured that believers live longer and don't get sick so often. I had read that a couple of days before, in an issue of *Psychology Today* at our local library. The tone, the cadence of my father's voice had suddenly changed.

"Brothers and sisters visited me every day. They helped me,

stood by me, read God's Word with me, let me pray with them," he proclaimed, never taking his eyes off me. "You can see how I can take care of myself now. I'm walking into retirement, head held high." He tried to reach for my hand. "If you're lonely and in despair," he said, "Jesus Christ is right there beside you. All you have to do is say yes, Martin. Just say yes."

"I'm not lonely," I replied.

"Of course not!" His fingertips touched my finger. "You're not alone, Martin." He got a firm grip on his right arm and leaned back.

I no longer recall what else we talked about. At any rate, it wasn't long before I said I had to go if I wanted to drive partway before dark.

My father plucked a ten-mark bill from his pocket, laid it on the table, reached into his pocket again, and handed me a little dark green package that felt soft to the touch. "Look inside if you want."

I tried to peel the Scotch tape back carefully to keep from tearing the wrapping paper. "I designed the pattern myself," he said as I held up the two potholders—both bright blue with a white eight-pointed star in the middle. A little tag was attached to the loop of each: Dr. Hans Reinhardt, Building C, Room 209. "It's something everybody needs," he said. "You can always use some-thing practical."

I thanked him, and he paid the bill.

Then I helped him into his coat. He asked if his scarf was tucked in right. I pulled it more to the center. He linked his arm under mine, and we started off. One waiter lowered his head in a brief bow. As I looked up, I saw a lot of eyes trained on us. Women were even calling one another's attention to us and smil-ing. I tried to keep my head held high. The waitress who had first greeted us opened the inside door. Two women entering through the pair of outside doors held one panel open and waited. They were smiling, too.

His taxi was waiting at the curb. When I nodded, the driver got out.

"Good luck, Martin," my father said. I felt his chin against my right cheek.

Clutching the passenger door with his left hand, he let himself fall backward into the seat. The driver lifted his feet in for him. I put out an arm to wave in case my father turned around. The car was already moving when he turned his head, but not far enough to see me.

I walked fast in the direction I had come from and did not look up until I could be sure there would be no one smiling at me. I found a telephone booth, dialed Steuber's number, and told him everything had gone fine and that I'd probably be back sometime between ten and eleven.

"Fabulous!" Steuber shouted. "We'll be waiting. The whole family's waiting for you."

"Well then," I said.

"Have a good trip!" his wife shouted into the receiver.

"Have a good trip," Steuber said.

"Thanks," I said, pressing my ear to the phone, listening for voices in the background.

"Bye," Steuber said, and hung up.

I dialed Danny's number. I wanted to talk to Tino. I just wanted to say hello, but then I hung up again before I heard the first ring. I could just as easily call him tomorrow, and it'd be a local call. I walked to the car and pulled out of the parking space without having to shift into reverse.

I know now that what my father told me is a real Saul–Paul story. You can read about it in the Acts of the Apostles in the New Testament, how a persecutor of the Christians became their most important missionary, the proclaimer of Good News.

The two potholders—and my father was right about that, too—are hanging next to my stove so that I just have to put out an arm whenever I need them.

two women, a kid, terry, the monster, and an elephant

How Edgar, Danny, and Tino move together into a modern apartment with balcony. The smell of bratwurst. Big and small catastrophes. Spots on a chair and a kilim.

"Eddie, good God! Not the monster!" he heard Danny say. Edgar straightened up. He held the gray wing chair like a giant helmet over his head, his forehead lost down to his eyebrows in upholstery. It was merely a question of balance. He audibly let out air. The chair back pressed against his shoulder blades. Tino went "Wow!"

"Eddie, why in the world . . . it doesn't have to go today. . . ."

Danny's feet were wiggling on the burgundy carpet in front of his shoes. Edgar guessed she was touching the chair. He pictured her slipping in under its arms to join him, grabbing his hips with both hands. They would kiss without Tino being able to see—and then dance slowly back and forth.

"What a big strong man Eddie is," Danny said, and patted the front of the chair. In reply Edgar first made an effort at two little hops, and then followed her, ducking where he guessed the lamp was. Without bumping into anything, he made it to the doorway in the entrance hall. "Scratch me there." The tip of his right foot pointed to his left calf.

"Don't think so," Danny whispered, and opened the apartment door for him.

"Scratch me there!" he said, not budging.

"There's a draft, Eddie, quick, please, Eddie . . ."

He ducked again and took a long stride to miss the doormat, where black letters formed a semicircle that read WELCOME.

He heard footsteps on the stairs, a woman in a knee-length dress. Edgar tried to guess her age from her shoes and calves. His greeting went unanswered. At the last step she pushed past him and held the front door open. He said "Thanks," but heard nothing more.

With his right hand Edgar groped his shirt and pants pockets for the car keys. He crouched low, bending shoulders and head forward till the chair legs touched the asphalt. He slipped out from under the back, stood up quickly, but missed as he made a grab for the chair, stumbling forward with it and banging against the Ford Econoline's left taillight.

The woman was gone. He gave the chair back a shake, and yawned. It was muggy.

"And where was this?" Tino was asking as Edgar stepped into the living room.

"In Ahlbeck, on the Baltic," Danny said. "Well, Eddie? We're impressed. Any room left?"

Edgar nodded. "The keys?"

"What about this?"

"About what, Poops? You mean who's that on the donkey there?"

"No, this!" Tino held the photo album up. "This here."

"Wait a sec, Eddie, the keys—I don't know, Poops, really—in the kitchen maybe?"

Edgar stepped in a puddle in front of the fridge. He spread a rag over it and watched as the water formed islands and the rag stuck to the floor in the form of Sicily. He kicked at the edges of the rag and carried the wet blob to the sink. He repeated the procedure a couple of times. Then he opened the cracked fridge door wide. The black key pouch was dangling from the freezer.

In the living room Edgar tried not to look in Tino's direction. "Should I take anything else?"

"Take this!" Danny pointed to the box beside her. "And two cans of food for Terry."

"That was really a great idea, really great," Edgar said.

"It's *his* dog, Eddie. *He* has to decide what's good for his dog and what isn't. Terry will get used to his new surroundings, and we'll have some peace here. I think it's a good idea." Danny knelt down beside the wall unit, shook an old newspaper, tore off a double page, stuffed one crumpled half into a beer glass, and wrapped the other half around it. Edgar pulled a page toward him with his shoe toe. "Lust ends in the ditch. Masturbation behind the wheel" read the caption above a picture of a jackknifed semi. He held the short article out to her and laughed out loud when he thought she'd finished reading.

"Good God," Danny said, "how do they know that he was . . . doing that while he was driving."

"Doing what, Moms?"

Edgar turned the page over.

"Doing what?"

Danny stared straight ahead.

"An accident," Edgar said. Patches of red were rising on Danny's neck.

"An accident at the zoo. Leo the Elephant leaned against the wall, and his keeper got stuck in between."

"Is that true, Moms?"

"Why don't you believe Eddie?"

Edgar tore out the zoo article and folded it into an airplane. He raised his arm and aimed at Tino. The plane dived to the carpet in a tailspin. On the second try it landed next to the photo album.

"Did they shoot the elephant?"

"Oh, Poops. He didn't do it on purpose."

"And then?"

"They took the keeper to the hospital to make him well again, and his family and other keepers will come and visit," Danny said, packing a champagne glass. "And when he goes back to work, Leo the Elephant will be there to greet him with a bouquet of flowers in his trunk."

Putting chin to shoulder, Edgar made trumpeting sounds and swung his right arm.

"March nineteenth!" Danny interrupted. "It's from Friday, Friday the nineteenth. So it happened on Thursday, right?" She looked back and forth between Edgar and Tino. "Well, my two good men, Thursday, March eighteenth, well? What happened that day? I know you know. Poops, Eddie?"

"Aha!" Edgar said.

"Come on, Poops, don't you remember—Southeast, Southeast, hooray, hooray—our new apartment's ours today!"

"While we were counting the trees, the elephant squashed its keeper."

"Eddie, cut it out."

"Moms?"

"Oh, Poops," Danny said, shaking her head, "he didn't squash him." She pushed the flaps of the box down. Edgar stared down the top of her blouse.

"Enough for today," Danny said, then stood up and ran ahead again to open the door.

. . .

Edgar braked. The car rolled into the pull-off where the city bus line came to an end and stopped beside a log-cabin kiosk. A blond woman in a wine red anorak was busy folding up the stands for copies of *Bild* and *Focus*. She waved.

"Calling it a day?" Edgar shouted as he rolled down his window.

"Called it long ago. You got Betsy with you?"

"Terry, his name is Terry," Edgar said, and got out. "We took him to the new apartment in Southeast this morning, so he could get used to it. Any cake left?"

"Wasn't any. In weather like this, the grannies stay home. I've got something for . . ." She pointed her head toward the lamppost, against which was leaning a canvas bag topped by a little package wrapped in aluminum foil.

"Terry, just Terry. . . ."

"Terry-Eddie-Betsy, whatever."

"Terry, because he's a fox terrier." The kiosk shutter rattled as she rolled it down.

"Hi, Ute," Edgar said as she got in. "Tino hid the car keys in the freezer today."

"I would think he'd be happy when you leave?" She laid the aluminum foil package next to the hand brake and grasped the knob of the gearshift with her left hand. Edgar started the car and put in the clutch. She put it into gear. And they drove off.

He caressed her neck with his right hand, inserting his thumb under the collar of her sweater. She smelled of French fries and the Sabatini perfume he had given her last week.

"We'll need the van tomorrow from seven till noon. It's yours for the rest of the day."

"Fine by me," Edgar said, leaning over and whispering, "Ute mine."

"And what about Tinko?"

"His name is Tino . . . no *k*."

"I call him Tinko."

"A terror, the whole day. Yesterday evening I petted his dog . . . you should've seen Tino carry on. Jealousy pure and simple, outright hate. And since she still feels guilty somehow, she keeps telling him she loved him while he was still in his mommy's tummy."

"What does he call you? Uncle Eddie?"

"He doesn't talk to me."

"What does he call her?"

"Moms."

"Mom?"

"Moms, not Mom. She's his Moms."

"And why does Moms want you all to move in together? One last try?"

"Well, now that she's lost her job—it's better if there's only one rent to pay," Edgar said. "Besides, it's almost out in the country."

"In the country! Here you volunteer to move to Southeast, and give up a really nice apartment. You feeling guilty, too? Or do you really love her, hm? All that curly hair? You feel guilty because she got fired on your account."

"Beyer accused her of 'spying.' What sort of big secrets were there supposed to be? Danny was an editor, she didn't have anything to do with ads."

"You don't get involved with the competition. That's logical enough. Next thing you know, your rag will can you."

"Nope," Edgar said. "Not me. Beyer had the hots for Danny. That's all. And when he realized that we'd patched things up again . . . he's suddenly the big Zampano."

"What?"

"The big wheel, he throws his weight around."

"And Tinko's dad?"

"What do I know. Pit, his brother, says that he's not all that good with kids. Doesn't know what to do with them. At least not when they're small."

"What a holy mess you all've got yourselves into." She took her hand from the gearshift and pulled a pack of cigarettes from the bag between her legs. "When a kid is put through something like that, all you can do is take cover." She lit her cigarette and blew the smoke into his lap.

On the far side of the town woods, at the dump for broken asphalt, Edgar turned right onto a dirt road and stopped.

"Need some air," he said, sliding open the side door. "Now for a surprise."

"What sort of surprise, that monster there?" She moved up beside Edgar.

"Exotic," he said. "Or romantic, whichever you like."

"What about the prayer rug?"

"The kilim?"

"Your flying carpet."

"Too hard," Edgar said. When she got in, he could smell French fries and perfume again. He slid the door closed after her, then climbed in through the right door at the rear and pulled it to behind him.

"Do you know, sometimes I picture him as a little girl, or even a nice boy. I like kids. I don't ask for anything more than fairness, a little bit of equality. We only do what he wants, and if we don't, we can forget it."

"Tell me how to get over this." The back of the seat came up to her shoulders. She pulled the red terry-cloth band from her hair and bent over. The boxes behind her were labeled in blue letters: THIRST.

Edgar pushed the chair right against a plastic box and patted the left arm. "Okay, jump!" With a cigarette between her lips and already without shoes or slacks, she came scrambling over, a towel in her right hand.

"There are always problems," she said, unzipping her white and red anorak.

"What's that for?" Edgar asked.

"What?"

"That rag there."

"To protect the monster. Think about the carpet yesterday, how we—"

"They don't show me any consideration either," he said, tossing the towel behind the chair and pulling both his trousers and underpants down at once.

"And now?" she asked.

Edgar sank to one knee, spread his arms, and squeezed her ass with both hands.

"Cold," he said with a smile. "Pretty cold, Ute mine." She put out the cigarette on the van's roof, pressing her thumb against the butt for a while. Then she let herself fall back into the chair.

It was drizzling when Edgar collected his three blue plastic buckets from the parking space closest to the entrance to the building. He slowly backed the Ford up until its wheels touched the curb. He opened the rear doors, reached for the arms, and lifted the chair out. Still standing there with its front edge braced against his stomach, his arms crooked and quivering from exertion, he heard the barking. When he reached the sidewalk he let the chair slip down to his thighs.

"No, Terry, no!" The dog was standing with its front paws in the empty flower box. One story down, curtains moved. "No, Terry!" Edgar patted his pockets, went back to the Ford, grabbed the aluminum foil package, and ran into the building. He already knew each floor by its boxes of greenery and the calendars for shared chores. On the third floor, between Baron and Hanisch, there was nothing in the way. But one floor up there was a rickety bamboo affair with two sansevierias and a brimful watering pot of hammered brass. He had banged a box of records against the long spout yesterday. Water had dripped down the stairwell, all the way to the cellar.

Terry jumped up on him and yowled. Edgar broke off little pieces of bratwurst and tossed them over the dog's head into the hallway. At the threshold to the living room, Edgar stopped in his tracks.

"The bastard," he said softly, "the little bastard." The only thing in the room was the kilim rolled up against the wall. The cardboard and plastic boxes with Edgar's dishes, his slide trays, his records and books were stacked up out on the balcony. Gusts of wind drove the rain against the windowpanes.

Bracing himself on the railing, Edgar bent forward. The empty flower box squeaked in its hinges when he gave it a slap. The gray armchair was blocking the sidewalk below.

The dog had followed and was looking up at him. He tossed him the rest of the bratwurst, quickly stepped back into the room, closed the balcony door, and tilted it open at the top. He bit a piece off another bratwurst, spat the bite into his hand, pulled his arm back, waited for Terry to raise his head, and then hurled it out through the crack. The dog's snapping catch looked like a circus trick. Terry burrowed and leapt in and over the crates and boxes, but never ventured too far out, although most of the meat landed on the lawn four stories below.

Edgar closed the apartment door behind him. Once downstairs, he unfolded the aluminum foil with the rest of the bratwurst, collected the scattered pieces, and laid it all in a heap on the lawn beneath the balconies.

"Come, Terry, come!" The dog barked, vanished, reappeared at the railing, his front paws in the flower box.

"Heel, Terry, heel, heel!" Edgar stressed each syllable just like Tino. He waited. Other balconies had plants, umbrellas, and antennas. The rain was falling harder. A small truck raced past honking. "Terry!" Edgar roared.

He walked over to the armchair, which was turning darker from the rain, and dragged it into the building. The spot at the edge of the seat was hardly noticeable. He set it down gently in the living room.

Edgar watched Terry jump up on the boxes, stretching his head forward, barking, and wagging his tail, as if he recognized something familiar down below. The dog turned excited pirouettes.

Edgar grabbed the balcony door by both sides, concentrated, closed his eyes—and slammed it shut. Terry was still standing on top of the boxes. Edgar heard the doorbell ring, and then came the sound of the door being unlocked. Standing on his hind legs, Terry slid down the door pane. Edgar let him in.

"Eddie, my love! You forget everything." Danny was holding a purple-labeled can in each hand, pumping them like dumbbells. "The dog food."

Edgar patted Terry's flanks. "Wet—it's all wet—wet!" His voice stayed calm, as if he were speaking to the dog. He went to the balcony and returned with a yellow and blue plastic box. "Soaked!" Edgar maneuvered around Danny, set the box down, turned back.

"Sorry," Danny called, following him out onto the balcony. "It hasn't rained all week."

"You two sure have some great ideas."

"We . . . the furniture's coming tomorrow, Eddie, and I . . . otherwise it'd all be such a mess, Eddie. . . ." Danny stepped aside to let him pass, picked up the next box herself, followed after him, and eased it onto the other two. Edgar was already outside again.

"Look here," he said, and just stood there. Terry's claws had not only left marks on the spines of the books, but had also poked little dirty holes in the pages. Danny shook her head. Edgar sat down in the wet chair. Terry jumped up into his lap.

"Want some pizza?" Danny asked. She was hunkered down on the rolled-up kilim, searching for a handkerchief in her left sleeve.

Edgar leaned back carefully. "Once the rain lets up, we'll bring up the rest," he said.

Danny sniffed. "By this time tomorrow it'll all be over."

"Day after tomorrow," he said, petting the dog. "*My* furniture's coming day after tomorrow." Responding to Edgar's touch, Terry closed his eyes.

"But we'll help, Eddie. And we'll take Terry with us today, okay, Eddie?" She stuffed the handkerchief into her jeans pocket. "Hey. Do you smell that?"

"The dog's wet."

"No, like French fries or something."

"I bought him a bratwurst."

"Oh, shit, shit! The little beast, look at this, on the kilim! He pissed on the kilim." Danny had leapt up and was now unrolling the carpet.

"He was alone too long," Edgar said calmly. "The whole building had to put up with his barking."

"Shit, what a mess!" Danny ran to the bathroom and came back with a blue plastic bucket filled with water. "Or did he throw up?" Edgar's forearms and hands were resting on the chair arms now. Someone closed a window nearby. Someone else was coming up the stairs, and stopped now on the landing.

"Eddie?" Danny raised her head. "Eddie?" She was still on her knees. "Good God, do you feel that, Eddie?"

"Spin cycle on a washing machine," he said. "Somebody upstairs is doing laundry."

"Spin cycle?" Danny wrung out the rag, rubbed at the stain, and then scratched at the wet spot with her thumbnail. A neighbor's door banged shut. Terry pressed his front paws against Edgar's stomach. More splashes in the bucket.

"What were you doing here the whole time?" Danny asked.

"I had to take Terry for a walk. The whole building could hear him barking," Edgar said. His damp, cold shirt was stuck to his back. "That keeper died."

"What?" Danny looked up. "The guy with the elephant?"

Edgar pulled his head back as Terry licked at his neck. "It all happened real fast, that same night I think. Leo had crushed some vital organs. They must have noticed something in the sand, afterwards, once they took him away."

"That's awful," Danny said, bending forward again to inspect the kilim. "I think it's vomit."

Edgar laid his head back and closed his eyes while Terry nudged him with his nose. The spin cycle had stopped, and there were no cars passing outside at the moment, so that all he could hear was a scratching thumbnail and the rain.

CHAPTER 12

killers

How Pit Meurer and Edgar Körner run into their competitor Christian Beyer in the outer office of Furniture Paradise. The secretary, Marianne Schubert, looks after them while they wait. Make haste slowly, it steels the nerves.

A knock. At the same moment two young men enter the waiting room. Both are wearing blazers, ties, and tan loafers. There's a sportiness to their movements. They both have their hands free. They stop side by side in the middle of the room. A fan rotates overhead.

"Something you want?" the secretary asks. She has short gray hair and a wide wedding band.

"Want?" Edgar crosses his hands behind his back and rocks forward. "What do you want, Pit?"

"I don't know. I don't know what I want really. A hefeweizen maybe?"

"With lemon?"

"With lemon." Pit fidgets with his tie clasp and stares at the glasses dangling from a thin silver chain at the secretary's breasts.

"I think," Edgar says, looking to his left, "that we want the same thing as that gentleman sitting there."

Beyer, who is holding a large white cup, doesn't budge.

"We were told to be here by six. It's almost a quarter to," Pit says, nodding to the clock in the wall unit behind the secretary. "Is he here?"

"It's five-thirty," she says without turning around, and points to the row of chairs at the window, which looks out into the sales tent. She sets her glasses back on with both hands, skims the page to her right, shifts it a bit, and begins to write.

"Can you tell me if he's in, or is that asking too much?"

"It's only five-thirty, Pit. She's right. Come on."

"I'd like an answer. We have an appointment and we're on time, ahead of time. So I'm allowed to ask if he's in, don't you think, Eddie?"

"Did he say when he's coming?"

"If you have an appointment." The secretary looks up but keeps on writing, then brushes an open calendar with the back of her hand. "There's nothing entered here."

"So he's not in?" Pit asks.

"Is there coffee at least?" Eddie motions toward Beyer. "Or did he bring his own?"

"Ask him when his paper has to go to press. Ask him. It's damn tight again. And then things get sloppy. Friday is always tight for Herr Beyer."

The secretary is on her feet now. Dishes rattle. Beyer sits there inert, as if intent on gazing through the open blind at people edging past one another in the narrow aisles between armchairs, tables, and corner ensembles. A line has formed at the checkout for gift articles. The saleswomen have white stickers on their red aprons that read: "Frau" and a last name "at your service." Apprentices just have "Anna" or "Julia" or "Suzanne."

"Regular coffee?"

"Both with extra milk," Eddie says, taking a seat at the window opposite Beyer. "Come on, Pit."

"I'm famished, Eddie. Given the fact that I'm not allowed to smoke in here," Pit points to the no-smoking sign beside the door, "I'd at least like something to eat. Or will the fire marshal make an exception in my case?"

"No," says the secretary, who is now standing in front of them, "he won't."

Edgar and Pit carefully take the full cups from the tray.

"He doesn't have anything against that fan though, does he?" Pit asks. "In a cubbyhole like this, minimum clearance and all? Well, thanks all the same, and cheers!"

"Here's to workers' safety," Eddie says. The secretary leans the tray against her desk.

Pit uses a hand to steady the cup on his knee. He points to the fan. "Fresh breeze is good for everybody. Competition stimulates business. Isn't that right, Herr Beyer?"

"Man, it's hot!" Eddie sets his coffee between his feet on the gray wall-to-wall. "But nobody can wait this long. Sure to ruin business. Don't you think, Herr Beyer?"

"He's managed to get the biggest cup again."

"Make haste slowly, it steels the nerves. We've got too many clients, Pit, just too many."

"Nobody even mentions targeted campaigns."

"Do you happen to know what Herr Beyer says about you?"

"People talk about me?"

"He told somebody that Pit has a rake on his ass."

"A rake?"

"'Cause you rake up all the ads. Nothing left wherever you've been, it's all raked up."

"A rake on my ass?"

"You clean the place out, he said. But he did make the comment about the rake first."

"What's a guy to do, Eddie. Truth is always so drastic, ain't it?"

"Sure. And when the man's right, he's right, Pit. Look how you raked Schmidt the lumberman clean. He lets Mr. Beyer take him out to dinner—and then signs with you, front page, where everybody can see."

"Beyer's business is dropping off pretty bad."

"Don't give away *all* our secrets, Pit."

"Am I talking too much?"

"Well, you know, he is a competitor."

"And stimulates business, Eddie, just like us."

"But he takes it personally."

"Something else I've noticed is——"

"Pit!"

"I was just going to say that magenta isn't pink or fire-engine red or orange. Magenta is magenta, that's what Herr Krawtcyk just told us. Herr Krawtcyk of Krawtcyk Building Supplies. And when Herr Krawtcyk says magenta, he means magenta. He doesn't mean pink or fire-engine red or orange. And when the yellow is smeary besides, that makes Herr Krawtcyk sad, very sad."

"What you're trying to say, Pit, is that it's not always just a matter of price when it's up to us to have to console somebody, is it?"

"I was trying to say that either Beyer was in too much of a hurry and his films stuck together, or they shifted during transport or his print shop does sloppy work. And so it's no surprise. He can get all the contracts he likes . . . that's what I was trying to say."

"A whole stack of good suggestions. . . ."

"I can come up with scads of 'em."

"Enough, Pit! I'll bet you won't hear a word, not one tiny little word of thanks. What do you think, Herr Beyer? How's it strike you?"

"I mean, we're not being nitpickers. It's all just constructive criticism."

"Just as you yourself wrote, Herr Beyer. One must hold out the truth like a coat, not like a washrag to slap people's ears with. That's why he's so sympathetic when it comes to letting people go, that's what Danny says at least. He can put himself in other people's shoes. That's why I cut out your 'Sunday Thoughts' column, too. We all really liked it, didn't we, Pit?"

"Did you know, Frau . . ."

"Frau Schubert," Eddie says, "Frau Marianne Schubert."

"Did you know, Frau Schubert, that Herr Beyer is a writer, too?—Hello, I'm talking to you!"

"Let it go, Pit."

"Everybody here sees right through us."

"Are you trying to say he sees through things?"

"Well, not exactly." Pit takes a sip. "I'm famished. And the moment I stop talking I feel even famisheder."

"We should do something about that. You've earned it."

"If it was a matter of what I've earned . . ."

"I'll go get you something, because it's Friday and because you have to live with a rake on your ass. And because nobody ever thanks you."

"Oh, Eddie, you're so good to me."

"And meanwhile you can tell a couple of jokes!" Edgar stands up and buttons his blazer. "Just to liven up the place a bit, for when I come back."

Pit waves to him as he goes, takes another sip, and sets his cup down next to the other one on the floor. "I think," he says with a quick glance at the secretary, "I think we can save everybody some time here." He pulls an envelope from his breast pocket and, propping his arms on his knees, fans himself with it. "I'll give this to you now."

The secretary shifts her left foot behind the shaft of her swivel chair. Beside it lie a crushed Nesquick four-pack container, the straw still in it, and a Beefie wrapper.

"He'll have all the time in the world to read it through," Pit continues. "Let him take his time, read it at his leisure, no rush. And you, Mr. Manager, will have more time, too."

Beyer leans back. Their eyes meet for a moment. "Raked up for good and all," Pit says, raising his eyebrows, then he stands up, walks over to the desk, holding out the envelope on both palms. "As good as a check. A sum in the high five-figure range, I'd say, that he'll save, maybe even more. Here you are."

"Just put it down." The secretary has stopped writing. She sits up straight as a rod.

Pit hands her the envelope and turns around. "And what shall we talk about now, Herr Beyer?"

Somebody bumps against the door from outside. "Chow mein or curry sausage?"

"Haven't you got anything for our friend Christian here?"

"Oh! Are you on a first-name basis with him now?"

Pit takes the paper plate with the curry sausage and starts eating. "He did give me a glance just now," he says, chewing.

"Wow!"

The secretary puts the envelope in a folder and takes it into her boss's office. She leaves the door ajar.

"Just look at you, Pit, you really dig in and scarf it down! Even if I weren't hungry myself—"

"You'd devour it with your eyes."

"Precisely."

"I told him he's wasting his time here, that we'll take over the job for him and he can start his weekend totally relaxed."

"While we rake up the countryside, Pit."

"No one can say we didn't warn him."

"Precisely. We've shown our cards. We have no secrets."

"Sure we have secrets!" Pit rubs the length of his thumb under his nose. "Thirty years old, nice curly hair, just can't take my eyes off of her. . . . Could you please . . ." His splayed pinkie points to his breast pocket. Eddie pulls out a crumpled tissue.

"Every time something tastes really good," Pit says, and blows his nose. Then he wipes the last of the bun through the curry sauce, puts the paper plate on top of his cup, and blows his nose again.

"Mr. Beyer has found himself a real girlfriend here. But there's nothing more Marianne can do now."

"You can tell Marianne that we're birds who've flown the coop, Mr. Beyer."

"Or even better, Pit. Let's go drink like fish."

They both stand up.

"At any rate, we'll leave you two alone." Pit feigns a bow. "When purple shades of evening fall, let's go get drunk and have a ball. You could give her a radio as a present and dance a little, do some gymnastics while you wait."

"Christian isn't even watching us leave."

"What do you suppose Christian is thinking? To judge from the way he looks . . ."

"Thanks a lot for the coffee, Frau Schubert," Eddie calls out, and gives Pit a nod.

"Thanks a lot, Frau Schubert. Have a nice weekend!"

"Ditto," Eddie says, and in parting sets two saluting fingers to his brow.

Cabinet doors slam shut in the boss's office. Beyer paces back and forth, then stops in front of the blind.

"There's no point," he calls out. "It's ten after six."

The secretary enters, rolls a sheet of white paper into the typewriter, and presses a button. "You wouldn't be the first person he's forgotten."

"The ad works well though, don't you think?" Beyer watches as the sheet is pulled in.

She sets a small watering can in the sink. When she turns on the tap, the jet sprays directly into the hole. She goes over to the philodendron and lifts the hydroponic inserts.

"You should pour the water over the stones," Beyer says. "Works better, they say."

The typewriter has stopped humming. The sheet of paper has vanished.

"I didn't think they were real." Beyer points to the flowerpots. "They can imitate ivy so perfectly—except for those black needles of artificial soil, you can't tell the difference."

The secretary refills the watering can.

"Does the name Körner mean anything to you?" Beyer asks, and returns to his chair. The strand of hair on his forehead flutters in the draft of the ceiling fan. "Do you know what Körner was, what he did, what Edgar Körner did up until November of '89?"

"I can never remember names."

"Didn't you ever read a paper? Anyone who hires him . . . I mean, everyone knows who he is! Intelligent, and he can be bought. I only know him in his Young Communist blue shirt."

"I'm closing up," she says, setting the watering can back with the hydroponic pots. She pulls the tip of a leaf from between the white slats and closes the blinds.

"Shall we go ahead and use the old ad?"

"Anything but that!"

Beyer tries to laugh.

"It's a good thing you weren't here on Tuesday. Doesn't anybody proofread your stuff?" The secretary sits down at the desk, opens a folder, and inserts the sheet of paper that has emerged from the typewriter. "People thought it was a trick to lure them in."

"Didn't you tell him we're not going to charge for it?"

"Very funny—not going to charge. What we ought to do is . . . If anybody threatens to sue, we'll pass it right on to you."

"Doesn't he have a car phone?"

"Sure. If you know the number. I don't have it." She pulls a cover over the machine and tugs it to rights.

"We have to publish something, don't we?" Beyer bends down to the two cups with the paper plates on top. "I was going to offer him an additional across-the-board discount of five percent."

"If he doesn't come in today, it'll be Thursday at the earliest. Best put it in writing." She locks the rubber-stamp holder in her desk.

"I'd rather do it in person. . . . Give me a call if he comes in, will you?" Beyer is standing at the desk, still holding the cups.

"I've got to go," she says, and bends down to pick up the fallen paper plates.

"Sorry, it was the draft," Beyer says, and looks up at the fan. "Can you give me a call next week, just in general I mean, if he comes in?"

"I won't be here then. Not anymore this year at least. I have no idea whether I'll be coming back."

"I don't understand. Did he—"

"I'm having an operation." She tosses the paper plates into the wastebasket.

"May I?" Beyer carefully sets the two cups in the sink.

She turns on the tap. She passes the sponge's scrubber over rims and handles.

"I'll write him that we didn't know exactly what we should do, and so we're repeating the same ad, the same ad with corrections. Here's a tray yet." He bends down.

"Goes there." With a nod she points to the corner of the desk in front of him. "Give me your cup." To make room for the tray along the edge of the blotter, Beyer rearranges a Scotch-tape holder, some paper clips, an orange highlighter, and a green eraser shaped like a VW Beetle. Then he carries his cup to the sink. "Should I dry?"

"You can turn off the fan—right behind you."

"Yes," Beyer says, "I'll write him. I think that's how we'll do it." He turns off the fan, sits down, tugs his briefcase out from under his chair, lays it on one knee, and takes out a ballpoint and a pad. Bending slightly forward, he starts to write.

While the secretary is drying and placing cups on the tray, she watches him. The fingers of his left hand are lying side by side along the edge of the briefcase, the thumb is holding the paper in place. He writes swiftly, line after line. All of a sudden his right hand comes to a stop. Eyes wander to the ceiling.

Although Marianne Schubert is looking right at him, she can't say whether he even noticed the last rotation of the fan. She is merely surprised at how young Beyer suddenly looks to her—almost like a student, who will soon need glasses but who still has everything, has his whole life, before him.

CHAPTER 13

yours now

Marianne Schubert tells about Hanni. Difficulty falling asleep,
accusations, and seductive calls. An important realization
puts Marianne Schubert in a good mood.

"At first I thought it was a man whistling, calling a cat or whatever, sort of like this—" Hanni lifts her head and whistles, then tries it once more, raising her long neck and sticking out her chest. "Yes," she says, "about like that, some kind of signal, nothing special at first." She takes a sip of her wine. Her silver bracelets jingle as they slip from wrist to forearm. "I lay there awake, listening to the whistles and arranging the moles on Detlef's back into constellations. All around the hotel—it wasn't actually a hotel, not a real hotel. We'd call it a workers' hostel. But they call it a hotel—four beds to a room. And outside the noise of fans and air conditioners, plus cars and people arguing or laughing, none of them Germans—and the streetlight right outside our window. And the worst thing, like I said, was this constant boo-bu-bu-boo-bububumbum right below us." With the edge of her hand Hanni hacks out the rhythm in the air. "Booo-bububoo-bububumbum." She shoves her glass away and lights a cigarette.

"Detlef has the Big Dipper on his left shoulder blade, and right next to it, along his spine, is Cassiopeia. The ladle of the Little Dipper is right above his butt crack. You have to cheat a little to make it work. Either the handle is too short, it intersects the Chi in Orion, or it's too long. If I don't use the bathroom first and then wait in bed for Detlef, he's already sound asleep. It was so warm, and he'd left me no room to move." Hanni sucks at her cigarette and blows the smoke up under the lampshade. "I was just thinking about moving to the next bed, and putting a towel over the pillow and bedspread. Wouldn't catch anything that way, I thought——Germans, all our kind, of course, paid as bad as Turks, but then, the desk can't even talk with any of the others. At any rate, there was the whistle and then suddenly this chuk-chuhoochukshookuk!" Hanni stretches out her neck again: "Chukchoochuk . . ." She breaks off and then crows a third time. She's had quite a lot to drink and acts as if we're all alone, as if we have the apartment or a whole house just to ourselves. All three candles have burned out.

"It didn't sound just like that, of course," Hanni says, and lays the palm of her hand to her cleavage, "but guttural and singsongy at the same time, some Bushman language, nothing you can just imitate. Now where did that get to?"

Looking around, she holds her cigarette perpendicular to the saucer with its nibbled sandwich. I go to the sink and dry off the ashtray. "Thanks," she says as I slide it her way. "I was amazed, totally amazed, because it was a woman's voice, truly beautiful. I didn't even mention that, Mariannchen, an alto, so easy, so effort-less. And that noise again, boo-bububoo-bububumbum."

"The bathroom's yours," I say as Dieter comes shuffling past the kitchen door. Hanni doesn't even hear him. The hall light goes out.

"So I was lying there in a strange bed. The sheet under me was nice and cool. And all I could hear was this boo-bububoo-bububumbum."

"Excuse me a sec," I say, and stand up.

"Sure," Hanni says, smiling and blowing smoke my way.

"Dieter," I say, closing the bedroom door behind me.

He points to the alarm clock. "Do you know how late it is? After one, look, after one!" His head is all red, as if he were screaming.

"The little bitch rattles on and on, won't shut up. She's ruined our entire Sunday, and wouldn't you know it'd be this Sunday," he says. "You haven't even packed your bag!"

"I know," I say, sitting down on the bed. "Looks like she needs somebody."

"You think maybe she'd want to know how *you're* doing? Or isn't she interested in a mere secretary for a furniture store?"

"She did ask about Connie."

"About Connie! And what did you say?"

"Not so loud . . ."

"The little bitch! Just because she's a museum director, she thinks can just do as she likes, is that what she thinks? Can she even think at all?"

"Hanni's not a director anymore. She's left the museum."

"What? They fire her?"

"She's not at the museum anymore."

"Was she with the Stasi? She one of them, too, you think . . . ?"

"You told her to stay."

"I thought she'd clear out then, realize we wanted to go to bed. Did she admit she was with the Stasi?"

"Where do you get that? This is the first time you've ever met her."

"Precisely! But in her tactful way she calls me Zeus, the little bitch. I should have thrown her out then and there. And forbidden her to call you 'Mariannchen.'"

"You were very nice to her," I say.

"She's your friend." Dieter lies down on his back, his arms crossed under his head.

"You gave her the eye," I say.

"Marianne," he says, "please."

"It's true!" I say.

"Nonsense," he says. "Any woman who does her makeup at the table, right in front of everybody . . ."

"That's not the point," I say.

"Aha," Dieter says.

"She has no idea where I'm going tomorrow," I say.

"Sure she does. When she told that stupid joke about feeling for lumps in the breast. I told her right off to can the jokes. Of course she knows what's up."

"While I was out of the room?" I ask. "You told her that?"

"Yes," he says.

We fall silent. Then I ask what he told Hanni.

"That you have to go to a hospital in Berlin tomorrow, for an operation, and that he's an authority who's listed you as 'research' so our insurance will pay for it," he says and looks at me. "That's all true, isn't it?"

"And then you suggested she should spend the night here, get a good night's sleep, that's what you said."

"Yes," Dieter says, "I thought she'd leave then."

I stand up. He wants to keep me here. "You mean you're going back in there?" he shouts, and slaps the blanket. I don't even look around, but turn out the light and go back to the kitchen.

Hanni has poured herself another glass. "You tired?" she asks. I take a fresh dish towel from the cupboard.

"It literally hurt, hammering at your ears: boo-bububoo-bububumbum." Hanni sticks out a pinkie and rubs it along the foot of her glass. "I even closed the window, something I never do, 'cause it always gives me a headache the next morning, at the latest. But now it's coming directly from my pillow, so to speak, boo-bububoo-bububumbum. The pauses in between were too short to rewind a tape, and too long for a CD. That was the worst part, really, that I could count beats between pauses. They'd stop, for two and a half beats, and then just when you hoped it was over, the bububumbum would start in again, really primitive stuff, nothing sophisticated about it. Come, sit down, Mariannchen."

I stay at the sink and dry the good glasses and silverware. Hanni stubs her cigarette butt around in the ashtray, which makes her heavier bracelets bang against the table.

"I was getting hysterical," she says. "It was awful, here was someone banging right on my ear. It's called the eardrum, you know, 'cause you can drum on it. And why wasn't anybody else upset? I shook Detlef awake. Usually he hears everything, the alarm, the telephone, usually wakes me when he's mad 'cause he can't sleep, so I can calm him down. There's nothing he's more afraid of than insomnia. 'I can't take it,' I say, 'I can't take it.' He pretended not to hear anything, just raised his head a little and asked, 'Can't take what?' and turned over. 'That drumming,' I said. 'Don't you hear it?' And he said, 'It's pretty soft.' 'It's banging away under my pillow,' I said. 'It's hammering in my ears, it hurts something awful!' I wanted him to do something about it. 'Jesus Christ,' I said, 'somebody has to do something. What kind of hotel is this,' I said, 'what kind of hotel is this, and how can the night desk just put up with it?'"

Hanni drinks her wine and lights another cigarette. "'You have two alternatives,' Detlef said." Hanni wags the match. "'Two alternatives,' Detlef said. 'Either you ignore it and concentrate on something else, or'—and he didn't even open his eyes while he was talking—'or you let it pass right through you and get rid of it that way.' 'Or, you finally get up and put an end to it!' I said. 'It's so loud it's massaging my feet.' 'Bullshit,' he said. Later he claimed he said nothing of the kind. 'Bullshit,' he said, 'they'd just laugh in our faces.' It didn't bother him at all. He tried to pull me back into bed with him. I thought I'd go crazy. I picture it sort of like the speed of light. Like light from a star. The star doesn't exist anymore, but it's not until now that we see it, and then someone takes credit as the discoverer and names it after his wife or girlfriend. When in fact the star no longer exists, it's gone out long ago, it's nothing but light. Did you know that?" She stares at me. "I forget where I was."

"Stars, the kaboom downstairs, Detlef," I say, spreading the dish towel over the radiator.

"Sometimes it seemed as if I must have slept a little. I went to the window and cried. And then I held my ears shut. It was right there. And whenever the boo-bububoo-bububumbum stopped for a moment, I could just reach out and grab hold of it again, dig it up from under us, so to speak. Mariannchen, I thought I'd go crazy." Hanni shakes her head. I put the good glasses on the tray. I ask her if she could open the door for me. She jumps to her feet. I carry the tray into the living room, where I've made her a bed on the couch. She waits for me in the kitchen.

"I couldn't go down there all by myself, the only woman. Evidently I was the only one it was bothering." She lifts the ashtray up while I wipe off the table. "The night before, I'd been thinking things between Detlef and me just might work out again after all, if only that boo-bububoo-bububumbum would stop. All I wanted from him was the truth, and then we'd see. I thought we could have a nice weekend in Frankfurt, and he'd show me the city. Just for once at least we'd have a nice time together—purest fantasy on my part, of course." She wipes the last drops of wine from the bottle on the rim of her glass. "Besides, the place is full of whores and junkies. Incredible. You can stand there and watch them do it, shoot up, I mean."

She tries to put the cork back in the bottle, keeps twisting away at it.

"Then it happened, Mariannchen," she says, laying the cork aside and grabbing my hands. "I was crying, Mariannchen, but then suddenly that same seductive call was right there in my throat. I controlled it. It was as if I could finally recall some ancient melody," she says grandly. "And I let that call out, softly, effortlessly, and in that same moment I felt it pass through my whole body, felt everything go calm, felt how my exhaustion stopped burning and turned gentle, lulling me. Suddenly I was at one with myself, at one like I'd never been before. I was in control of a call that can't be written down, that you have to hear. As if I had held out and was being rewarded for it, know what I mean? Maybe I'd gone to Frankfurt just for that, to learn that seductive call."

I pull my hands away. Hanni goes on sitting there with outstretched arms.

"When Detlef woke me up the next morning," she says, "I was dog-tired. But I was smiling. He headed for the bathroom, and I went over to the window. I prepared myself, closed my eyes—nothing. It was as if someone had stolen it while I slept, torn it out of my throat, as if someone had erased it. I looked at the window screen, but couldn't see anything beyond it, just wire mesh. I was so down, Mariannchen. Detlef touched my shoulder and kissed the back of my neck. I started sobbing. And that was when I knew it had all been for nothing, that Detlef and I were finished. Can you understand that?"

Hanni looks up. She's twirling her empty glass. She expects something from me. But I can't do it, not like her, just run off and tell people stories like that. We haven't seen each other for three or four years. We met in a women's gymnastic class. She was the youngest. But we never visited back and forth, just went somewhere afterward and had a little drink.

I get up from the table. I want a drink of water. Hanni slips off her silver bracelets and opens the clasp on her wristwatch.

"Mariannchen," she says, and comes over to me. She spreads her arms. She's about to give me a hug. I grab her hands and press them against my shoulder. Of course I don't even want that. I don't want to be touched at all.

I ask her if she misses Detlef. She shakes her head. I let go of her hands. She holds on to my shoulder. I try to dodge her breath. "You're all tight," she says. Her fingers massage me a little. From up close her upper lip looks blurry. There's nothing pretty at all about her face anymore.

"Yours now," I say, and when she looks at me with a scowl, I add, "the bathroom's yours."

I close the kitchen door and open the window. I empty the ashtray and wash it out, airing the room doesn't help much otherwise. Even the sandwich that she nibbled at has lipstick on it. I throw out both it and the cork, rinse the glass and the bottle, and begin setting the table for breakfast. I put her bracelets and watch between her eggcup and saucer.

I can hear her odd calls coming from the bathroom. I'm not sure if they're really so loud or I'm just imagining it. I dry the ashtray. I shove it in beside the wristwatch and wash my hands, letting water run over them a good while. I set the empty wine bottle on top of the wastepaper and pull out the TV insert from last week's paper. Sitting down at the table, I read my horoscope: "Virgo Aug. 22–Sept. 21. You'll be needed again. Put yourself in the shoes of someone in trouble, and you're sure to offer useful help." Then Dieter's: "Scorpio Oct. 23–Nov. 21. You'll rack your brains over an important decision. Wait for things to develop, and pass the time doing things you enjoy!" "Lipstick helps prevent cancer. Women have less lip cancer than men. Why? Because women wear lipstick, and the dyes in lipstick offer protection by blocking the sun's ultraviolet rays."

I can't get Hanni's heavy bracelet over my hand. Only a couple of the thin ones. The date on her watch has rolled only halfway into position.

I pour water for six cups in the coffee machine, but leave the top open as a reminder, so it doesn't run over in the morning. The box of filters is empty. I press it flat and slip it between newspapers. All we have left is a new box with filters that are too big—size four instead of three. It's a familiar sight, pushed back in the corner there between the baking powder and boxes of pudding. I open the box.

After I cut a little strip from the filter, it fits perfectly into the holder of our coffee machine. I use it as a pattern for trimming the rest. I don't know why I didn't do it long ago. I pull out the empty box again, squeeze it open, fill it with filter trimmings, and stuff it back in between the newspapers. I pick up the alarm clock with its oversized dial numbers and, holding it up to my eyes, watch the minute hand move. Feeling a chill, I get up and go to the window. There are no stars to be seen. No moon, either. I slowly wind the casement closed. It occurs to me again that I wanted something to drink. Taking a glass from the cupboard, I tell myself that we all have to die sooner or later. And in that moment the idea comes to me as a grand and wonderful realization.

I drink some water, scratch wax from the candleholder, cut the stubs out of the sockets, and put new candles in. Suddenly I'm no longer tired and would love to turn on the radio and listen to music, just some beautiful music. But I let it be. I don't want to take any risks. I want to hold on to this mood, for a few minutes at least.

CHAPTER 14

mirrors

What Barbara and Frank Holitzschek have to say to each other. A scene in the bathroom. The politician doesn't respond and is amazed at himself. A shoe lost in flight.

Frank touches his forehead to the bathroom door. "Everything okay?" he asks. His voice sounds muffled. He lays a hand on the door handle. "May I?" Despite the chewing gum, his breath is a souvenir of dinner, ragout in heavy cream, preceded by onion soup, with tiramisù for dessert. All he had to drink was beer. They left the rathskeller at midnight. It's one now.

"Barbara?" His fingers drum on the doorjamb. "Everything okay?"

He flinches as she unlocks the door, waits, and then opens it himself. "May I?"

She is standing in one of his shirts in front of the mirror, dabbing her left eyebrow with a cotton pad. Her skirt lies on the toilet lid, blouse and panty hose on the tiles below. She presses the cotton pad to a bottle, tips it briefly, and turns her head to the other side. As she raises her arm, he can see the sparse matted hair in her armpit.

"Babs," he says, and kisses her on the hair. "Does it still hurt?" Seen in the mirror, her face looks different.

"What would happen if I claimed *you* hit me, really beat me? What would happen then?"

His face relaxes. He smiles. "That'd be that. I'd be finished."

"Doubt it," she says, tilting forward again. "You'd claim the opposite, and everyone would testify that we're a happy couple. Then I'd be the villain again, the hysterical moneygrubbing bitch. That's how it works." She wedges the little clump of cotton behind the tap. "They wouldn't even revoke your parliamentary immunity."

"All the same," he says, and kisses her again, "some of the mud always sticks."

"And what if I were pregnant?" She looks at him in the mirror.

He pushes her ponytail to one side and kisses the nape of her neck. His fingertips brush her shoulder blades. "I'm so sorry," he says, and closes his eyes.

"You don't have to be sorry," she says.

"All the same," he says, laying his hands across her belly. "I should have acted sooner, a lot sooner. Nobody could've predicted it."

"Frank," she says. He gropes up under the shirt. He thrusts his hand higher and in the mirror watches his fingers fondle her breasts. Barbara tries to wipe off eye shadow. "Nobody could've predicted it," she says. Some fluff clings to her eyebrow. She says, "How could anybody have predicted it."

He kisses her shoulder.

She turns her left arm over and examines the scraped elbow. "Do you agree I'm an easy piece, Frank? Am I an easy piece?"

"Bull," he says.

"I'm just asking. Little women are easy pieces, aren't they? Tell me. Am I an easy piece?" He lets go of her. Barbara smooths the shirt down with one hand.

"How could anybody have predicted it!" she repeats, then gathers cotton wads from the edge of the basin and steps on the pedal of the little wastebasket. One wad misses. Frank bends down for it. He spits his chewing gum into his hand, presses it into the moist cotton, and tosses both in the wastebasket. "Fourteen-, fifteen-year-old schoolkids," he says, straightening up. "Flunked three times—poor bastards really, if you think of them as individuals."

"Not one of you lifted a finger, Frank, once they started in. Not one of you." She turns the tap on and holds her bent arm under it.

"You shouldn't do that," he says. "Wounds have a way of cleaning themselves."

"Five men," she says. "And not one of them gets up off his ass. Do you know what amazes me?"

"Okay," he says. "That's *your* viewpoint. But *I* think we did the right thing."

"Do you know what amazes me? That you guys didn't have the waitress tell—"

"They wanted to provoke us, all they wanted was to provoke us."

"Well, thank God we didn't fall for that, Frank, that was first-class work. And your friend Orlando . . . did they just want to provoke him, too? Is that why they stuck a knife in his back?"

"Oh, come on."

"They chanted their slogans for a good half hour. And you guys just sat there—"

"While you got sloshed—"

"You guys sat there in your Bavarian folk costumes, smacking your chewing gum. And when Hanni said she didn't want to stay here any longer, you told her, fine, and asked for the check."

"And ten minutes later the police were there and threw them out. Maybe fifteen. . . ." He straightens her towel out on the rack.

"And there they were waiting for us outside."

"Do you suppose they would have listened to me? If I had personally tossed them out, nothing would have happened then, of course. Is that your logic? Am I supposed to take a course in hand-to-hand combat?" She washes her face.

He says, "Not every stupid kid who's just showing off is a Nazi. Do you want to throw them all in jail?"

"What was that?"

"Don't pretend—" he says.

"Frank," she says. Her hands grip the rim of the basin. Water drips from her chin and the tip of her nose. "I still respect you, I always have. . . ."

"But? What should I have done? Can you tell me that?"

"Do you know what they called your wife? Did you stop listening when they told me what they wanted to do with me, Frank, wanted to do with your easy piece of a wife?"

"Stop it, Babs. . . ."

"I just took in the highlights."

"Don't shout like that. I heard them too."

"Then everything's fine. If you heard it too . . . I thought maybe you weren't listening. Looked that way to me. But I was wrong again. Forgive me for being so unfair."

"Am I supposed to get beat up in a brawl?" Frank takes a step back. "I might have been able to handle two of them, maybe even three. But there were ten or more. They would have beaten me to a pulp and then . . ."

"And then?" she asks, her wet face still above the basin. She gropes for a towel. "Go on, Frank. Beaten you to a pulp, and then? Then what?"

"Is that what you want? For them to beat me up?" He leans against the wall and crosses his arms. Her panties have slipped a little lower.

"Instead we ran like rabbits, Frank. Like rabbits. And when I went sprawling, you actually waited for me. I haven't even thanked you for that yet. I'm really being unfair. You waited for me, just a few steps up ahead, and offered advice!" She hangs the towel back on its rack. "You ever been in a fight, Frank? You would've been out of the hospital inside of a week, at the latest. I would've visited you every day, even cooked for you. Do you know what you are?"

"You're nuts," he says, gazing down at her legs. "All I'd have to do is just step outside. And that would make up for everything."

"Exactly," she says, then loosens her ponytail and, tilting her head to one side, begins to brush her hair. "I was going to ask you to do that. You could at least go fetch my shoe. It's just a few straps, but the pair of them did cost me two hundred marks."

"Babs," he says.

"Yes? I'm listening, Frank."

"Do you think I like the way I feel?"

"No, I don't think that. What makes you ask?"

"What do you suppose makes me ask!" He follows her movements in the mirror as she pulls the brush from her hair. "You can think whatever you like of me," he says, and puts his hands in his pants pockets. "We should've taken a taxi. But as for all the rest?"

"Your pretty democracy won't fail because of them. Not because of them."

"'Your democracy'! Very original, Babs! I can read that every morning at breakfast. Makes me want to throw up."

"Hey, I'm not deaf." She opens the flat oval jar of eye shadow.

"Of course not. You're not deaf, just drunk. Once again you managed that quite brilliantly." He unbuttons his shirt.

"You still haven't answered me, Frank." She applies some mascara now.

"Answered what?"

"My question." She dabs the outer corners of her eyes with her little finger. He hangs his shirt on the radiator knob and undoes his belt buckle.

"Are you going to fetch my shoe or not? I'm just asking." She snaps the jar shut.

He lets his trousers drop. "Can I get past?"

"Frank," she says, tracing the line of her lips. "That must mean . . . that can really only mean . . . that you're not prepared to go fetch my shoe. Right?"

Frank tosses his socks in the hamper, lays his trousers over the lid, and sits down on the edge of the bathtub. He splashes cold water from the spray on his feet. Barbara pulls her panties up, leaves the bathroom, and shuts the bedroom door behind her.

Frank spreads a little hand towel beside the basin. He squeezes toothpaste from the red Elmex tube onto both their toothbrushes, fills a glass with warm water, lays her brush across the top, and begins to brush his teeth. "Beauty Cosmetic—Pads Naturelle," he reads on the package hanging beside the basin. "Double pads of pure cotton, soft as a blossom, easy on the skin, multilayered, never shred."

Barbara knocks and immediately opens the door. "Can you hand me those?" She points to the toilet seat. He clamps his toothbrush in his mouth and hands her the items one by one.

"These are ruined, too," she says. She flings the panty hose under the basin and pulls on the blouse.

"What?" he says, his mouth full of foam. She steps into her skirt. "What're you doing?"

Barbara pulls up the zipper. Frank bends down to the faucet and rinses his mouth. He steps to one side so that he can see her face in the mirror.

"What's going on?" he asks, straightening up beside her.

"I can put up with a lot," she says. "But I'm not going to crawl into a hole . . . my only question is why I even have a husband."

Braced against the table in the entryway, she steps into her pumps and rummages in her purse.

"At least put on a sweater," he says.

"Where are my keys?"

"In the lock."

"You haven't even considered going, have you, Frank?"

"No," he says, "I haven't."

He follows her to the door. She unlocks it. He grabs her shoulder, pulling her back before she can press down on the handle. He drags Barbara by her upper arm back into the entryway, takes her by the waist with both hands, and spins her around. Now it's Frank in front of the door. "Babs," he says. "You're not doing this to me."

"No one would believe this either," she says. "Would anyone believe it, you think? What a dynamic man! Just look how he springs into action all of a sudden. My hat's off to you, hats off!" She tugs at her blouse. "Come on, Frank, let me out. Or do you want to stand here all night, hm?" She takes a step forward. "Come on. Don't give it another thought. I'm just going to dash out and get my shoe, and then we'll both hit the sack. You've got a busy day tomorrow."

"Why are you doing this?" he asks.

"That's what I've been explaining to you," she says, shifting her weight to the other foot. "So. How long are we going to play this game, hm?"

The doorbell rings. Two short rings, a long one, and after a pause that they spend staring at each other, a short one again. He signals for her to move back. "Babs," he whispers. "Babs!" Shoving past her, he heads for the bathroom. He turns off the light and steps to the window. He opens it soundlessly and leans out. The light at the door to the building goes out. After a while he calls out, "Hello?" At the same moment he hears the apartment door open. In the light streaming from the entryway, he spots a figure in the mirror, erect, in an undershirt, one hand on the window handle. He watches the face and waits for something about it to change. He can feel a draft on his legs.

"Frankie," she calls, and slams the front door. "Come on out! Someone brought it. It was lying here, outside the door. Come on, let's hit the sack!" Without taking off her pumps again, she runs into the bedroom.

He observes himself, still standing erect, his left hand on the window handle. And then he watches the window close slowly.

big mac and big bang

What Dieter Schubert and Peter Bertram have to say about two women. Hunting carp—a new sport. Problems with the object of their success and its documentation. Pains in the region of the heart. Fog and morning sun.

"Big Mac!" Bertram yelled, pressing the giant carp to his chest and groping for new handholds at every step up the bank until he was at the top, being greeted by the flash of the camera. "Huge!" he cried, thrusting the fish and then grabbing on to it again.

"Damn!" Schubert shouted. "Jammed, something's jammed!" The tail fin slapped back and forth. "Don't squeeze him to death, Super Carpman!" Another photo flash. Bertram's fingers pressed into the fish flesh. Schubert came toward him, but after only a few steps pointed back over his shoulder. "The scales . . ." he shouted, and turned on his heels.

Bertram sat down in the grass in front of the tent and crossed his legs. In his left hand he grasped the mirror carp under its front fins, balancing it with his right at the spot where the whitish flabby belly ended and the tail began. The lowest fin batted against Bertram's dirty shoe tips.

"Look out!" Schubert said, and crouched down.

Bertram smiled. "This is the one, Dieter!" He balled his fist. "Comes in at fifty-five, I'll bet you anything." His chin brushed the dorsal fin.

"Stay right like that," Schubert said. "Goood," he said, "real good."

Clasping the fish to his chest, Bertram crawled forward on his knees and laid it carefully on the modified bathroom scales.

"Fifty-six and eight ounces!" he shouted. "Damn it, hold still, you bastard, fifty-six nine!"

"My God," Schubert said.

Bertram grabbed the writhing carp again under its jaw. "The scale's too small, that's all, too small for such a bruiser. Fifty-six ten, fifty-six pounds ten ounces!"

"Holy shit!" Schubert said, bending over deeper until the pointer and the fish filled the viewfinder, then flashed the shot.

"He liked the taste of our boilies," Bertram said, extending the tape measure between his arms, "better than the smarties. Three foot one. Got it?"

"Just a sec," Schubert said. They had to wait until the flash recharged. He poured water over the fish from a big Coke bottle.

Bertram held the tape measure to the dorsal fin and then wrapped it around the belly. "Nineteen."

"Shiny as beetle wings," Schubert said. He took the camera back to the tent and returned with a medicinal tube.

"Big Mac," he whispered, patting it. "A potbelly like that and with hardly any scales. Amazing he can even move." He carefully stuck a finger into the mouth and rubbed salve over the spot where the steel hook had been. "Holy moly, roly-poly," Schubert sang out. "We ought to take another shot, he's earned it." He wiped his hand off on the grass.

Bertram emptied the Coke bottle over the gills. "Let me." He lifted the carp and climbed down the embankment. He walked a little farther along the canal, waded out into the water, and let the carp go.

"Ahoy, Big Mac!" Schubert shouted from up top, and made tooting sounds like the horns in "Yellow Submarine." "You still see him?"

Bracing his hands against his lower back, Bertram gazed out into the fog across the water's smooth brown surface. Then he checked their other lines. Schubert ran parallel to him along the top of the slope, doing a few knee bends and moving his arms in circles, and then took off at a slow jog for the next power pole. About halfway there, he turned back.

"Well, Super Carpman," he gasped, "how does it feel?" His lower lip was shiny.

Bertram walked to the tent and took a chug from his flask. He held it out to Schubert, who shook his head and began rotating his hips.

"The next one's yours," Bertram said, and started undressing. "You can spare yourself the gymnastic antics. You're out of your tree, Dieter—new running shoes, a jogging suit. . . ." In underpants and thongs, he flip-flopped over to the line strung between the tent and the power pole, threw his shirt, socks, and khakis over it. He set his wet shoes next to the open tent flap and then rummaged through his backpack.

Schubert shook his arms and legs, loosening up. "That's a lot of bull, that you have to feed 'em first for three days," he said. "By day two they don't suspect a thing."

Bertram pulled on a sweater and, fresh socks in hand, balanced on one leg.

"Hey, Super Carpman! What time is it?" Schubert asked, and went into his breathing exercises.

Bertram set his bare foot in the grass, then wiped the toes off on his other leg before pulling the sock on. Then he slipped into the tent. "You should have gone to see your Manka rather than coming here," he shouted from inside.

"What's wrong now? I'm bright-eyed and bushy-tailed," Schubert said, flinging the entrance flap back. "You hungry, Peter?"

"I thought you bought a new pack of film," Bertram said. "You said you were going to buy film."

"I did." Schubert crawled over the top of his sleeping bag.

"It took almost an hour. I battled with him for almost an hour and there's not one single snapshot of it. Just because you were snoring away in here."

"You should've said something." Schubert smoothed out his sleeping bag. "I'm not a sports reporter."

"All you're interested in is your . . . you just don't care about this anymore. Not even this much." There was less than a half inch between his thumb and forefinger.

"Sure I do," Schubert said.

"Don't give me that. All you've got in your head is that woman and getting certified as a victim of political discrimination. That's all."

"If I didn't want to come along, I wouldn't be here. You should've seen the look on your face"—Schubert laughed—"those bug-eyes you made when the bobber started beeping." He pulled up the zipper. "Did you ever sound the alarm, bellowing for all you were worth!"

"Just like on the border," Bertram said.

"Were there beeping alarms there, too?"

Bertram snorted and crossed his arms below his head. "We had everything there, rabbits, foxes, roe deer, stags, wild boar, badgers—everything."

"And all I got was this," Schubert said, and tapped his glass eye.

"What amazes me is that the animals never caught on. They could see the others all got ripped to shreds. They have a nose for everything else, even earthquakes."

"Is that why you lost your job?"

"What?"

"You were pretty high-up, weren't you?"

"When they called you up from the reserves, they'd always award a star, so what? Can I help that? The others were with the combat unit."

"Why was that?"

"I thought we were here to fish, Zeus."

Schubert laughed and gave his glass eye another tap. "The last guy who called me Zeus didn't do so well." He poked at the roof of the tent. It dripped. "Not well at all."

"You're like a little kid." Bertram reached for Schubert's hand.

"Yes," Schubert said, "old and childish."

"And sentimental."

"Whatever. At least you're not mentioned in my files. You need to get more joy out of life in general, at least when you go fishing."

Bertram let go of Schubert's hand. "A whore," he said, "who's bleeding you dry. That's what makes you happy, huh?"

"She's . . ."

"A . . . a little hooker, even younger than your Connie."

Schubert poked at the roof again.

"Zeus," Bertram said, and rolled over. He pulled at his sleeping bag until it covered his back. "Doesn't Marianne wonder why you go to Berlin so often?" Bertram bolted upright.

"No bites," Schubert said after a while. He hummed a few more bars of "Yellow Submarine." They heard cars honking across the canal. "Oh, Peter," he said. "We know each other pretty well." He pushed his hair back. "Maybe it's all not that bad for us."

Bertram burst into laughter. "I think you've got some screws loose!"

"You talk like an old man," Schubert said. "Instead of finding somebody, you sit there drudging away at that smut nobody wants to print."

"Oh, so now it's suddenly smut, is it?"

"I mean, you should go out and find yourself a woman."

"So now it's smut?"

"Damn it, Peter, don't get pissed off. . . ."

"I'm just asking whether the stuff I write is suddenly supposed to be smut. I seem to recall a totally different reaction, some real enthusiasm, don't I?"

"You have to admit it's . . ."

"Yes?"

"Not quite normal."

"Not quite normal?" Bertram propped himself up on one elbow. "So why did you want to buy my smut from me then? Why'd you make copies for yourself? Why'd you say reading it gave you a hard-on. Can't you get one otherwise?"

"Bullshit," Schubert said.

"Maybe it's Zeus who's not quite normal here. So why do you pay your little whore, then, if as you say she doesn't ask you for money?"

"It's worth it to me," Schubert said.

"Want me to tell you why it's worth it, why you have to pay her?"

"I just want the situation kept clear, that's all. She's there, I'm here, and then we meet. She gets her money, and we go our separate ways."

"I'd love to have your imagination," Bertram said. "First, the kid wants to earn some pocket money, second, you ask her to do some things, a few little specialties, if I know you. Isn't that right, Zeus?"

The wind thrust against the roof of the tent. Bertram raised his head again.

"The things you come up with, Peter," Schubert said.

"What else do you expect me to think of you, to think of a guy who reads smut."

"Damn it, Peter!"

And in that instant, they both bolted upright.

"Let's go!" Bertram shouted. The bobber on the farthest line was beeping.

Not much later, Schubert was following the fish as it moved upstream, heading for the power plant.

"Give him some slack, he's getting away! Hey, hey, heeey!" Bertram shouted and clapped his hands. He heard the line hum off the reel. Everything was quiet except for crackling in the power lines and the sound of a car or two on the other side. When he turned around, Schubert was already running toward him.

"What's wrong? Here I am running toward the power plant . . . damn it, Dieter," Bertram shouted, "I want to see white water, I want to see whirlpools! I want to see you play him!"

In the next moment, the carbon-fiber rod twitched as if it had come alive. Schubert extended both arms, and the line hummed off the reel again.

"He's a sneaky bastard!"

Bertram fetched the landing net. Schubert crouched on shore, arms outstretched, the tip of the rod almost in the water. He reeled in line.

"Can't be! No fish is this easy. Or did I lose him?" Schubert got up from his crouch and let himself be pulled farther downstream. The air was no longer so chilly. Slowly the far shore became visible—guardrails and car headlights.

Suddenly the line went taut again, the tip of the rod dipped into the water. Schubert pressed his lips together. The veins on his forehead and arms stood out, so did the tendons under his chin.

"Now we're in business!" Bertram shouted. "The fight's the thing! He needs a name!"

Schubert was breathing hard and buckled over with exertion.

"That's the best part, Dieter, to feel him, feel his power. What you gonna call him?"

"Big Ben," Schubert squeezed out the words, and took little steps trying to move back from the water. The carp darted back and forth, but Schubert played him, and the pliant rod gave with each violent tug.

"Big Ben's old hat. Call him Big Bang," Bertram shouted, without taking his eyes off the water. "Big Bang's a great name, don't you think? So it's Big Bang."

The carp surfaced. "Whoa!" Schubert yelled.

"Damn, Dieter!" Bertram shouted. "Cleared for landing. Get ready!"

It looked as if the fish had given up the fight. Little waves splashed the shore.

Schubert pulled the carp out. He tried to wipe a strand of hair from his damp brow with his arm, but ended up with his nose in the fish. "Yuck," he said. The camera flashed.

"What's wrong?" Bertram asked, "why the face?"

Schubert didn't reply. The carp fell with a slap onto the scales. "Fifty-six nine, fifty-six ten," Schubert said, and stepped aside to make room for Bertram. He watched him bend down over the pointer, lift the fish a little, look under it, then lay it back down.

"Fifty-six nine," Bertram said. "Can't be. Fifty-six ten."

They stood side by side, gazing at the carp. Bertram took one step forward. "Fifty-six pounds ten ounces. He can't be that stupid. It can't be, but it is. Big Mac!"

"I'm feeling kind of shitty," Schubert said. "Must be the stink he gives off."

"Don't give me that," Bertram said. "Come on, get over it." He extended the tape measure along the fish. "Three foot one. Can't you at least take a snapshot? Three foot one. What's wrong with you?" Bertram picked up the salve. "We forgot the water." He pointed at the gills. Then he stuck his finger into the carp's mouth.

Schubert massaged his heart. He was holding the camera in his left hand.

"Nobody's gonna believe you, Dieter, really. Anyone seeing the picture will think you borrowed this guy, borrowed him from me."

"Or vice versa."

"How's that?"

"There's no time coder on this camera." Schubert winced and turned away. "Shit," he hissed.

"You mean . . ."

Schubert crouched down.

"What is it? What's wrong, Dieter? You sick?"

Schubert lay down on the grass. "I need to stretch out," he said, and turned over on his back. "It's like a sharp stab."

"What?" Bertram pulled the carp off to one side. "What is?"

"I'll be okay," Schubert said. He bit his lower lip. His hand rubbed back and forth under his shirt. "Get him out of here, Peter, please. He really stinks."

Bertram ran down the embankment with the fish. He stumbled once or twice, but caught himself each time.

Up to his knees in water, he dropped the carp, which sank to the bottom in front of him. Bertram kicked at him with his toes. He bent down, then immediately straightened up again. "Dieter!" Bertram shouted. All he could see was the tent with the clothesline and his wet things. "Zeus!"

Downstream the sun was coming through the fog. You could make out the colors of cars on the other side now.

"Hey! Mountaineer!" Bertram shouted. "Mountaineer!" Suddenly he bent down and with both hands shoved the carp off like a little boat. He felt muck and stones underfoot, and the water around his hips was like someone grabbing at him. He yelled.

The current took the fish. Bertram turned around and struggled toward shore, his arms flung wide. As he waded the last few feet onto land and turned around, he thought he spotted the carp's white belly one last time in the morning sun's reflected light.

Bertram rubbed his hands dry on his sweater, shuffled across the gravel to the other lines—his flip-flops squishing softly—and then up the embankment.

He knelt in the grass beside Schubert for a long time. He finally managed to cradle the man's head in his lap, to close his eye and his mouth. His upper teeth had left deep marks in the lower lip.

"Damn it, Zeus!" Bertram said. With one hand he kept caressing the forehead and cheek, and covered the glass eye with the other.

CHAPTER 16

beer cans

How Jenny, a student nurse, and her patient Marianne Schubert meet near the Virchow Clinic in Berlin and talk about a dead man. Maik, a young waiter, waits on them. Jenny's cigarette is left in the ashtray. Transient and eternal values.

"Why are you telling me this?"

"I thought that if you knew—"

"I don't believe you."

"That's up to you," Jenny said.

They were sitting side by side at the bar. The young waiter behind the counter had made coffee for them, plus a gin and tonic for Jenny, and then taken the chairs down off the tables. He had vanished into the back through a curtain and only came out now and then to empty the ashtray. He had strawberry blond hair, looked pale and despondent, or simply just exhausted. Almost no light came in at the window, because outside the building was scaffolding draped with canvas. It was close to nine in the morning.

"Although you really ought to," Jenny said.

"What?"

"Know that what I'm saying is true."

"No."

"He said that as far as you two went—"

"Now listen here—"

"Nothing was happening anymore." Jenny put out her half-smoked cigarette. "That's really why I told you, so you wouldn't worry that somehow you were——"

"I want—to stop talking about all this. I've never talked about such things. With anybody. It's none of your business. You're simply being rude."

Jenny drank. "Sorry," she said. There were still some ice cubes in her glass. "I just thought——"

"You're making all this stuff up. . . ."

"So why'd you call me then? You could've slipped the letter into a mailbox and that would've been that."

The woman closed her eyes a moment, then gazed over her shoulder into the empty room.

"The police gave me his things, number one." She thrust her right thumb up. "Two, I found the letter in his travel bag, no stamp on it. I didn't know a Jenny Ritter in Berlin. The address didn't mean anything to me. I got out the phone book and called you."

"You wanted to know who Jenny Ritter is."

"No." The woman stared at her nails. "I didn't want a dead man sending a letter."

"But after that . . ."

"You don't talk about things like this on the phone. As a nurse you should know that. I wanted to tell you what had happened to my husband."

"Didn't my voice sound familiar?"

"So what? Who'd suspect a thing like that? Besides, I didn't know your last name."

"Aren't you the least bit curious what's in it?" Jenny pulled the gray envelope from her leather jacket and laid it between the coffee cups. "I would've wanted to know. I always want to know the truth." She lit a cigarette and blew out the match.

"I've heard all I want to hear," the woman said, looking aside as the waiter appeared.

"Another," Jenny said, and shoved her empty glass forward.

"What about you?" he asked. "Coffee?"

"No thanks. Wait, some water, no fizz or anything, tap water, is that a problem?"

"No problem," the waiter said. For a moment his face brightened. They didn't say a word until he had served Jenny her gin and tonic and retreated again with the empty glass.

"What else do you know about me?" the woman asked softly.

"Your first name . . . Marianne."

"Did you like that, a man with a glass eye? I would've thought that if you wanted . . . you could . . ."

"I would never even have noticed Dieter—what's wrong?"

"Nothing. You would never even have noticed him. . . ."

"He was trying to be so elegant, scooting across three chairs to the window, instead of just pulling a chair back. But then stood right back up again, on account of his coat. Which he wadded up on his lap, but then didn't know what to do with when the menu arrived. He kept shifting around—making all sorts of needless extra motions, you know? And besides, he spoke so low that the waitress had to keep asking him to repeat himself. He ate carefully, staring at his plate so that our eyes wouldn't meet. When he was done, he paid at the counter and took off."

"Here you are," the waiter said. "It's not ice-cold, but it's cold." He spoke with a light Swabian accent.

"Thanks," the woman said.

"Anything else?"

"No, that was very nice of you." She rummaged in her purse. The waiter stood there irresolute, exchanged ashtrays, and then turned away.

Jenny crossed her arms, clasping her elbows. "We ran into each other again the next Wednesday. I thought he came here often, and he figured I always came here. He invited me to join him. It was pure coincidence." Jenny turned her left wrist until her watch touched her gin-and-tonic glass. "Whenever I took out a cigarette, his lighter was lit. If I went on talking, it went out, and he waited for the next opportunity. And he helped me into my coat and held the door open for me. . . . When I saw what was up, I said that I'd grown up in East Berlin, in Friedrichshain."

"Saw what was up?"

"He thought that because we were sitting here in the West, that everybody had to be from the West, too. Which is why I mentioned it. But either he didn't know where Friedrichshain is or—"

"He didn't like Berlin. We never came here, not even to Sanssouci. He liked Dresden better, all that Italian Baroque. And then he had his cliffs there, too, the sandstone along the Elbe. I'm sure he told you he was a mountain climber." She pulled her glass toward her and, tearing open a little packet, dropped an Alka-Seltzer in it.

"I decided it wasn't important, either," Jenny said. She scratched both forearms at once. "We had a drink, and suddenly he offered me three hundred marks. All he wanted, he said, was to lay beside me and wake up that way again."

Both women watched the Alka-Seltzer flop like a flounder at the bottom of the glass.

"He knew I was training to be a nurse."

"We used to call them the carbolic girls. Everybody in the hospital reeked of it."

"I told him I was a student nurse. But he just smiled, as if he didn't believe me."

"Apparently he didn't. Weren't you offended? Why didn't you refuse?"

"Yes," Jenny said, "I should have." She gazed at the curtain, at the shelves with the bottles of grappa and the mirrored wall behind, and then at the glass with the Alka-Seltzer that was still wobbling round in circles and then stood up almost vertically.

"You liked him?"

"When he saw I was thinking it over, he upped it to five hundred. I wasn't afraid."

"But then the last time—"

"That had nothing to do with being afraid." Jenny's hand groped for her gin and tonic.

"You don't want to talk about it?"

"I already did. You didn't believe me."

"You just said that he got brutal."

Jenny sipped at her glass. "Perverse, not brutal."

"Beg your pardon?"

"You know, perverse."

"What did he . . . what happened?"

"Like the fizz powder we had as kids," Jenny said, pointing her chin at the Alka-Seltzer. "After that, all I wanted—was to see his face. Whether it was when he came to visit you and we'd run into each other at the nurses' station, or when I'd opened the door to your room and there he was sitting on your bed, when I'd ask whether you wanted cheese or cold cuts for your evening snack. I just wanted to see his face."

"Were you trying to blackmail him?"

"I just kept imagining what must be going through his mind."

"And?"

"Panic."

"So you wanted him to . . ."

"To panic? Yes."

The woman nodded, then shook her head. "Little Miss Carbolic as a . . . hm, yes."

"I'm not like that. And you know it."

"You take money."

"That was incidental. He wanted it that way. Why won't you believe me?"

"According to you, you were together five times. So you cashed in five times."

"No," Jenny said, "not the last time."

"You took money."

"It had nothing to do with that. You don't have to insult me."

The Alka-Seltzer floated to the top. A few pieces broke off and drifted to the edge. The spray was landing on the envelope.

"Yes, and now he's got away. It happened while he was fishing. It was already too late when they found him."

"I know," Jenny said. "They told us at the nurses' station. He talked about that a lot, about fishing. He was always talking about something. He could tell good stories."

"He was a teacher."

"He wanted to explain the whole East thing to me."

"He was a bitter man."

"I know, because of his eye, because they never put his glass eye in right."

"What?"

"Why sure. He hated the GDR because they could never manage to make a decent eye, at least not for him."

"Because of his eye?"

"And then his nickname, too."

"It happened right after the war. They found some munitions. . . . But that's not why he—"

"I know his stories, all of them, about night school, about the art society, about his student years, and how they threw him out. . . ."

"For nothing, for less than nothing!"

"Sure, right, and how they put him to work mining soft coal, on probation, and why they didn't want to let him be a teacher, or at least not right off, and how your daughter was discriminated against, and how, all the same, Connie was the first to realize how things would turn out, and then the story about the cans, the whole shebang."

"What cans?" The woman was holding the glass with the dissolved tablet in her hand.

"He called it his beer-can story, because of the altar of cans. . . . When Dieter would spend the night here, in your nephew's apartment, on Liselotte-Hermann Strasse, with the altar of beer cans in the living room. My brother was the same way. A can like that was the greatest. He would have traded anything for it, even money."

"An empty beer can?"

"Sure. Didn't you ever talk about it? He rummaged through the garbage bins at the Michendorf rest stop. That's why he can't let go. Every can has its story. But now they're just trash. You can buy them at any corner kiosk. He admitted that himself. But apparently it never really sank into his head."

"Into my husband's head?"

"Maybe not into his either."

"You talked about things like that?"

"All night long. Sometimes he'd say: 'Look at that, isn't that wonderful?' It would be getting light outside. We hadn't slept at all. He took my hands and kissed them all over, very carefully, a kiss here, a kiss there, down to the fingertips. All of a sudden I had to yawn. I could feel my mouth opening wider and wider, but I couldn't do anything about it. And he was looking right at my mouth. The whole time. I couldn't put a hand across it, he was holding them both tight. I apologized, and he said, 'You can do it anytime you want,' and went on kissing my hands. He liked everything about me."

"Why are you telling me this?"

"So you'll believe me. So you'll realize that I could never have expected anything like that. Maybe I should have known that when somebody talks and talks and nothing else happens—that it's bound to turn out bad."

"Sometimes he'd kind of short out," the woman said.

Jenny laughed. She picked up her glass, set it down again.

"I just mean that . . . why are you laughing?"

"The way you put it. . . ."

"What?"

Jenny shook her head.

"If he told you all that—what more do you want?"

"You don't understand." Jenny laid one hand on her other forearm. "There was a Turkish woman sitting across from us in the subway, twenty years old maybe, with five or six shopping bags stuffed full. She had huge hands, real shovels. And Dieter turned it into a tale of indentured slavery, there was no calming him down. That was so typical of him."

"Did you ride the subway with him?"

"Sure, why not?"

The Alka-Seltzer had left a narrow white stripe on the rim of the glass.

"Watch out!" the woman said. "Look, it's falling off."

Jenny removed the cigarette from the edge of the ashtray and stubbed it out. "Does it still hurt here?" Jenny pointed a thumb at her breast.

"I have to be there at ten, radiation. I have to go."

"Yes," Jenny said, and nodded. "We don't have to say any goodbyes." She leaned to one side. "I always break the counters down on my shoes." Her fingers fished for her shoes, and her head touched the woman's shoulder. Even when Jenny's cheek pressed against her hip, she still sat straight up, never budging.

"They're good shoes, too," Jenny said as she popped back up. "But I break the counters down on all my shoes. Pure laziness. You walking?"

"It's not far."

Jenny nodded. "Are you feeling better—did the Alka-Seltzer help?"

"Good God," the woman said, shifting her weight to one side of the bar stool. "This wasn't made for me." She had to brace herself briefly on Jenny's thigh. "You're about to lose a button . . . there, the top one."

"Thanks," Jenny said as they stood facing one another.

"You shouldn't smoke so much," the woman said. "Or better, not at all."

Jenny nodded again and watched her until the door closed after her.

"Well?" asked the waiter, who was suddenly standing there. "Feel better now?" He wiped the counter, lifted up the ashtray, and set it back in the same spot. Jenny sat down on her stool.

"I don't get it, what's the point? What'd you get out of it?" He bent his upper body forward and lowered his head to look her in the face. "Hey, Jenny, I'm talking to you. She didn't believe a word you said. So why all the shit?" He watched her tap a cigarette out of the pack, and quickly offered her a light.

"You thought I'd tell," Jenny said, and blew smoke to one side. "You never budged from behind that curtain, because you didn't want to miss anything."

"You're nuts," the waiter said. "Did you at least offer to pay for hers?"

"Do you know what they call that, Maiki? I call it a Peeping Tom." Jenny laid the cigarette on the edge of the ashtray, tore open the gray envelope, and peeked inside.

"You're not cut out for the job," the waiter said. "I told you right off. You're not cut out for it."

"It's not my job," she said.

"You're really nuts," he said without looking at her. His face was red, his forehead and the tip of his nose were shiny. "Either you deal with it, or you quit. Then it won't be your job anymore, got it? And why did you sit here at the bar if you didn't want me to hear?" He put a new gin and tonic in front of her. "In her condition she would've rather sat out there, at a regular table."

Jenny counted the bills, shifting them from one hand to the other. "Want to know what he did?"

The waiter turned the empty envelope around on the counter. "Is that his handwriting?"

"Probably. Probably it's his." Jenny yawned and counted the bills a second time. "So, do you want to know, Maiki?"

"Very generous," the waiter said. "Five hundred? For that much you could have waited until she buried him, you could have at least waited that long."

Jenny put the money away. "I need new shoes," she said, and yawned again.

"Christ, Jenny! You can't be serious!" the waiter shouted. "I'll buy you twenty pairs, as many as you want." He wiped his hands off on the dish towel. "You sleepy?"

"No," she said. "But it just doesn't get light in here."

"Should I make some coffee?"

"No," Jenny said, and nudged the cigarette with her fingertip until the filter no longer stuck out over the edge of the ashtray. "I'm okay. I feel really good." She carefully brought the glass to her mouth and began to sip. Putting his hands on his hips, the waiter watched.

d e b t s

Christian Beyer tells about a summer vacation in New York with Hanni, his new girlfriend. An unexpected visit. Men, money, and water.

We've been in the city for five days and haven't seen anything except the Statue of Liberty, the World Trade Center, and the Museum of Natural History. At eleven in the morning the TV says the temperature is 101 degrees Fahrenheit, and according to the conversion table in my Baedeker, that comes to 38.33 degrees Celsius. Everything's way too hot and damp, including the toilet seat, and books are starting to get wavy.

The air conditioner isn't working. It's set into the window on the left, right above our double bed. It looks like the back side of an old TV, but it means 25 percent off the rent for the apartment, which belongs to Alberto, a Spanish architect. The wall on the left is done in floor-to-ceiling mirrors. Which means we're forever watching ourselves on the way to the bathroom or the apartment door, maneuvering around the big table and past the little galley kitchen.

Hanni is lying on her tummy, her head turned away. She's using her right hand to hold her hair away from her neck. Her butt and a thin stripe under her shoulder blades are white. With both pillows behind my back, I've been reading to her from an issue of *Geo*— about the Jews in Crown Heights.

"You asleep?"

Hanni's head moves, and then she says, "No."

We've both been having crazy dreams. Last night it was more a feeling, a situation. What's underneath me, my bed, is a port city somewhere in Asia, it's evening or night, with lots of lights. Everything below is in motion, no matter where I put my head there's life down there, a world teeming with voices and messages, some of which are directed at me. I couldn't shake the dream even when I got up to go to the toilet. I didn't calm down until morning, when it was as if the bed beneath me finally fell asleep too.

"Should I open the window?" I ask. Hanni's head shifts. "Does that mean no?"

"No," she says, her mouth half pressed to the sheet. Night after night, when the street sweeper comes by, some car alarm goes off. I've learned the sequence of signals and the brief two-second pause before it starts all over again. Besides which, the fire escape rattles sometimes. The water tower on the roof across the street leaks. In the morning water drips onto the air conditioner. Someone above us is probably watering flowers. You can't lean out the window because of the screen.

"Want something to drink?" I ask.

"Read me some more," she says.

"I'm done," I say. "Should I make some tea?"

"I don't want any tea. You had to pour it all out yesterday."

"Not all of it," I say.

"Okay, then not all of it," Hanni says, turning her head to look at me. "Why didn't you say something when it happened?"

"It's pretty unpleasant," I say, and thumb through my *Geo*. "You feel incomplete somehow, like something's been amputated."

"Jesus! Just imagine what people might think!" she cries, rolling onto her back and sitting up. "Is this so awful for you? A whole week with no stress, and you want to live on bread and water."

"Yes," I say. "It's like I've been exposed."

"That's your problem," Hanni says. She curls her hair around one hand and fishes under the bed for her barrette with the other. The bottom halves of her breasts are white. "Sorry," she says, "but it really is your problem. My credit card's still good at least! I've got a little bit saved up. And for as long as that lasts I'd like to enjoy things with you, pull up someplace in one of those stretch limos. And I want to eat in a restaurant where the waiters explain the menu and there's candles on the table. And a view. And I want to ride in a helicopter too, and go to the Met. And I'll have you in the bargain too. And Italian mineral water."

Hanni has stood up now. She crouches in front of the fridge, holds the door open with one elbow, and drinks. She's chugging, tipping the bottle higher and higher, until I can see the pale blue label. She lets the door click shut and sets the bottle on the floor next to the others. "And then"—Hanni's eyes brush past me—"I want to be happy again. Don't say anything, please. I know you're not a machine. I just wanted to say that. I'm allowed to say it at least." She picks her straw hat up off the table and gazes at herself in the mirrored wall. "Anyway, it's not as expensive here as it looks. Besides, it's Manhattan!" She tugs at the brim with both hands. "Well?" She slips into her sandals and stares at me. "Any other objections, Mr. Universe?"

"You don't have any money, either," I say.

"I'm going to buy you a bow tie. A bow tie and maybe that tux, too. It was dirt cheap and with a real designer label." She pulls Alberto's baseball bat from under the TV table, props it on her right foot, and sets the back of her left hand to her hip. "What was that guy's name, Donatello?"

"Come here," I say. Her tummy has left a damp impression in the bed.

"Donatello," she says, shifting her weight to the other leg. "All you need is the socks."

"We'll go everywhere, anywhere you want," I say, "if you—"

"He had long hair and such a sweet little belly. . . ." Hanni pushes her own belly out. "Like this. Not like yours, but like this."

When I stand up she shakes her head. "Excuse me a sec," she says, and hands me the baseball bat. "Business calls, gotta pee."

She hastily shuffles in her sandals to the bathroom. She keeps the hat on. In the high window across the street is a white plastic chair with a fanned back and a bunch of green bananas on the seat. I shove the bat back under the TV and stretch out across the bed. I can hear her stream splashing the water in the bowl. The door is ajar.

We hardly ever make it out before one or two. When it gets too bad, we slip into a store. The evenings aren't any cooler. The heat stays in the asphalt, in the stone. Subway stations are pure hell. And there's a smell everywhere. I hear the flush and then, after a pause, the shower.

I first met Hanni when we were looking for someone to give advice about pets, and who knew all sorts of astounding stuff about the animal world in general. Hanni writes a double column for us every week. Sometimes about cats, sometimes about earthworms, or maybe migratory birds or spiders. I told her I wanted to go to New York, and she said, "Me too."

There's a knock at the door, and she turns the shower off. There's total silence for a moment. At the second knock, I pull on my sweatpants, and on the way to the door I check the bathroom. Hanni is standing all soaped up in the little tub, eyes squeezed shut. "Close the door," she whispers. I keep one hand on the bathroom doorknob, as if I don't want to let Hanni out, and wait.

"Sir? Excuse me, sir?" A high clear male voice. "I'm Robert Vanderbilt from Palmer Real Estate, sir. Would you open the door, please?" The peephole has been plugged. "Mr. . . . Mr. Beyer," he calls out, "I have to take some pictures of Mr. Sullivan's apartment, sir. I'll slip my card under the door, okay, sir?"

The business card of Robert D. Vanderbilt appears at my toes.

"Sir, would you please open the door, please?"

I have trouble removing the chain because the spool slips off its track. You have to move it slowly, steadily. One little mistake, and it sticks and has to be pushed back again. I try a second and finally a third time. I assume that only I can hear the sound of metal rubbing against metal. Then I let Robert D. Vanderbilt in.

"What the hell were you two doing?" Hanni blinks. She pulls a T-shirt out of her suitcase. She has a towel stretched around her hips, clamps it between thumb and forefinger. She has wound a smaller one around her head like a turban. "What was that about?"

"Robert D. Vanderbilt," I say. "He's selling this studio for Alberto."

"What's he doing?" She sits down on the bed. Her eyes are red.

"He's trying to sell the apartment," I say.

"And you believed him?" The towel falls away from her lap. She pulls it back up over her thighs.

"He shoved his card under the door," I say. I can feel the sweat beading on my back and under my arms, even on my feet.

"Why didn't you call and ask to see if he's allowed in, if you can let him in? What do you know about what Alberto's doing with this place and what sort of guy he was?"

"What's wrong?" I say, and sit down. "He was a friendly guy who's managing the sale of the apartment. That's all."

"We're in New York, and you open the door to some total stranger—and leave me standing in there as if I didn't even exist. You two chat away and . . ." She closes her eyes and presses her fingertips to the lids.

"Hanni," I say.

". . . don't even ask if I need anything." She pulls the towel from her head and tosses it behind her. "Don't even ask . . ." She pulls her T-shirt on and looks around, searching for something. Her panties are on the floor at the foot of the bed. "You could at least have knocked and asked if I was okay."

"What could've been wrong?"

"Who knows! Everything's lying around out in the open here, money, underwear, your socks. . . . You could at least have waited till I got dressed."

"Mr. Vanderbilt is gone," I say.

"With you everything's gone, over and done with. And what if he comes back? What if he was casing the place? What if that's why he was here?"

"Then he didn't find anything," I say.

"Jesus," she says, and looks up briefly at the ceiling. Then she stares at me. "You could at least have called someone to check."

"Alberto sent him. How else could he have known my name? You heard it all."

"How do you always know stuff like 'Alberto sent him'? What if he didn't? Why didn't he take pictures of the bathroom? If I were interested in an apartment, I'd want to know what the bathroom looks like." She stuffs both pillows behind her back and draws up her knees. "You can't even describe him! A child would wonder. But not big Mr. Manager here."

I bring her his card and the Polaroid shot lying on the table. She rubs her hair with the towel.

"Have a look," I say, and dial Alberto's number.

"At what?" she asks.

"He forgot this one. Or couldn't use it," I say. "He couldn't deal with the mirrors."

"What? You let some Chinese guy take snapshots? No, can't be."

"He said that right off, while he was still standing outside, that he wanted to take pictures. He has to do it. If he wants to sell the place he has to be able to show people something." Hanni is now holding the Polaroid in both hands. Alberto's line is busy. I go to the fridge. I put a new bottle of Pellegrino on the table, find two clean glasses and a bottle of apple juice. "Besides the fact that he's Chinese, or whatever, do you notice anything else?" I ask.

"You forgot to suck in your gut."

"He's wearing a dark suit, a white shirt, and a blue tie," I say, handing her a full glass.

"Sure. You two had a nice chat, got to know each other. Thanks. Shame he left, huh?"

I put the bottles in the fridge. I take a sip as I walk back and sit down at the phone.

"He was in Texas for two years. There's a water shortage there."

"In Texas? What's a Chinese guy doing in Texas?"

"Why not?" I ask, and dial the number. "They're even burning cactus so the animals'll have something to eat. People borrow saints from the churches and walk around the fields with them to show them how bad it is. The animals are down to just skulls, and the farmers are all ruined."

"Listen," she says, "you think a Chinese guy is going to become a farmer in Texas?"

"I didn't claim he did. I'm just saying he comes from Texas or was there for two years and that a drought is ruining the farmers. And when land dries up it's harder to sell real estate. A drought like that at least makes things clear."

"What things?"

"It makes everything clear," I say. "Nobody can help it. Nobody can blame you. Either you get hit by it or you don't. But nobody accuses you of being totally naïve or being a failure. If people get mad, then they get mad at God, or a Virgin Mary if they have one. But somehow it makes things nice and clear."

"Did he say that?"

"He spent the whole time taking pictures and talking. It was difficult, because of the mirrors. They give you the wrong idea about a room, about its size. I didn't know how to get out of the way. I always ended up in the picture."

Hanni and I finish our glasses at the same time. My thighs are stuck to the chair, my forearms cling to the plastic tablecloth.

"Did he keep trying to shoo you off?"

"No, he didn't do anything. Just waited. Then I realized I was only in the way. They're a lot politer than we are. I think he left Texas because of debts."

"Debts?"

"Sounded that way." Wedging the receiver between my ear and shoulder, I dial a third time. Hanni has the Polaroid shot on one knee, the business card on the other.

"What's the D in front of Vanderbilt stand for? Ding or Dong or Dung? Can't be Dung. Maybe Deng?"

"Or Detlef," I say. We look at each other. "Presumably Alberto's selling because of debts. They won't let it go for under $220,000. Bound to sell for more. That'll put his books in order again."

"Didn't you say the Chinese guy was in debt?"

"He thought at first he could live with his debts, that's what he said at least. When an overdue statement landed in his mailbox, he just tore it up. But one fine day he suddenly woke up thinking about all those overdue bills. And the next morning, too, and the one after that. He felt defenseless. The first thing he thought about was his debts. Especially when he was alone. He couldn't get the money together. And so he bailed."

"Who you talking about? The Chinese guy?"

"Every government auditor costs the taxpayer sixty thousand marks a year. And do you know how much a guy like that brings in every year? One point four million marks. Just imagine. One point four million!"

Hanni fans herself with the Polaroid shot. I wait until the female voice on Alberto's answering machine has finished, then hang up.

"Hey! You have to say something," Hanni cries. "He never picks up."

I look out the window, across to the green bananas, and dial again.

"The Chinese guy told how he left Texas because of the drought and how he's selling Alberto's apartment for him here in New

York? Is that right?" Hanni asks. "And that's gonna get them both back in the black? I think you misunderstood or got things mixed up. Or the guy *was* just a gangster with a stupid story." She takes a glance at the photo and then goes back to fanning herself. "Or by water does he maybe just mean money."

"Why money?"

"Yes, that may be it. Maybe there's a turn of phrase here like when we talk about the water being up to our necks. Or you think maybe somebody turned his tap off, your Mr. Ding Dang Dong?"

"We can always give him a call." I wait for the beep after the female voice. Then I say that Robert Vanderbilt has been here and took pictures of the whole apartment and that we hope that that was okay.

"Satisfied?" I reach for my glass, but it's empty.

"Was the least you could do," she says. "Really."

"Vanderbilt is a very friendly, nice-looking man," I say, and go back to the fridge. "He didn't do anything to us, not one thing."

"If you say so," Hanni says.

"If I were a woman," I say, "he'd have a real chance with me."

"But you wouldn't with him," Hanni says, without taking her eye off the Polaroid shot on her knee. "Donatello, maybe that's a possibility? D as in Donatello."

Out of the corner of my eye, I can see my reflection. I should ask Hanni why she told me to close the bathroom door if she didn't want me to let anyone in. After all, she could just as easily have said, "Don't open up." But maybe it's just a sort of luxury to argue like this over nothing.

Hanni has fluffed the pillows and stretched out. The Polaroid is now lying beside her. She pulls her T-shirt straight. It reaches down to her thighs. One arm across her head, she puts her other hand inside the short sleeve and wipes the sweat from her forehead. This tugs her T-shirt up a little.

"Christian?" she says.

"Yes," I say.

"That's okay," she says. "I just wanted to know if you're there."

"Just a sec," I say, then put my glass in the sink and go to the bathroom. Her hat is on the toilet lid. I don't know where to lay it, and put it on. I flush so Hanni can't hear me splashing.

Then I use both hands to turn the shower head, but hold my head slanted to one side to keep the hat from getting wet. All the water you want, hot or cold, whenever you want it. I even drink some.

CHAPTER 18

the morning
after

Frank Holitzschek tells about a morning at the end of February. Barbara and the latest development in her nightmare. Frank's attempts to cheer her up. Enrico Friedrich, Lydia, and snapshots.

Barbara's talking wakes me up. She's lying on her back, an arm across her forehead. It will be light soon. Barbara had another one of her nightmares. Maybe I blinked without noticing, or rolled over, and that's what made me think I was awake. Or she just started in talking. She always has to talk after one of these dreams. If I'm not here, she phones me, no matter where I am. It goes something like this: She's at the wheel of a car and passes a woman on a bike, and when Barbara glances to the right again and checks the rearview mirror, the woman is gone. Barbara doesn't think anything of it, until she reaches the next town, where a screaming man with bloody hands pulls her out of her car. His arms saw at the air and flail at her. Barbara sees herself lying beside the tailpipe. She tries to lift her head, not out of curiosity or fear, but so the man can land his blows better. She wants to start the day all over, doesn't want any of this to be true. "Please, please," Barbara whimpers in her dream, "it's supposed to be a dream, just a dream," although she knows perfectly well that it's not a dream and that of course the day can't start all over again. Everything stays just as it is. And the man screams "Murder!" and "Murderer!" They're taking pictures of her—passersby, the police, people in passing cars. She sees herself on a billboard-sized wanted poster, and has to wait there under it until she's arrested.

I've heard it so often already it's a wonder I don't dream it myself. Whenever I see little crosses beside trees at the side of the road or a wreath attached to a streetlight, it reminds me of Barbara's nightmare.

She crooks her other arm now and lays it across her eyes, too. I slide closer and tug at the sparse hairs in her right armpit with my lips. Her deodorant leaves a bitter taste on my tongue. We got to bed late, something neither of us can get away with anymore, at least not during the week.

"And then you claim it doesn't matter, things like this just happen," Barbara says. All I can see is the tip of her nose and her mouth, the lips slightly open. She softly clears her throat.

"If we hurry, you say, no one will notice, we just have to hurry. You tell me to sit on the luggage rack of your bike. You keep on trying to convince me, without ever once bothering to"—she sucks her lips in—"to check on the corpse."

"And what about the guy who's hitting you? Where's he?" I watch her pulse in an artery on her neck.

"I don't know," Barbara says. "He's there somewhere. He knows everything." There's total resignation in her voice.

I rub my tongue across my teeth to get rid of the deodorant taste. "And do you come with me in your dream?" I kiss her right breast. When Barbara doesn't answer, I say, "It's not a great feeling, appearing in your wife's nightmares. Not that I'm blaming you," I add, because in this mood she has no sense of humor. "Maybe I symbolize help of some kind. Isn't that possible?" She says nothing and doesn't seem to notice as I caress her ribs, then brush down across her hips to her thighs.

"If you're lying in a hospital," she says, "stuck in a cast maybe, from your head to your feet, staring at the ceiling, and you know you've killed somebody . . ."

"You don't even drive anymore," I say. "You haven't driven for two years now." Ever since Barbara ran over a badger, nothing anyone says can get her to sit behind the wheel. Her refusal to drive has complicated our life. It's an hour and a half to Dösen for her, that's if she doesn't miss her bus. I'm annoyed that Barbara is covering her eyes. That's not good. She always gets caught up more and more in this dream.

"You ran over a badger," I say, "a badger! Maybe you only just grazed it, and it's a grandpa by now, fully recuperated."

"If you say so," Barbara says. "If you say so, then it's probably true."

I run my hand along the inside of her forearm, circle her elbow, and then return to the wrist, where I switch to the other arm and my hand makes a swift arc and lands in her left armpit, my forearm brushing her breast. My hand moves lower now, returning to my side by way of her knees.

Barbara says, "You're lying there staring at the ceiling, time stands still, or passes so slowly that it's not worth mentioning, even though it's the only difference you can think of, the only thing that separates life from death."

"You were dreaming, and now you're awake," I say, laying my head on her right breast and letting my finger trace a circle around her left.

"What if I can't really wake up, what if it turns out it isn't a dream?" I can feel her body resonate as she talks. She asks, "What will you do with me then?"

"I'll marry you all over again," I say. "Or what should I do, in your opinion?"

I lean across, belly to belly with Barbara, to the alarm clock. The blanket slips. Alarm clock in hand, I raise myself up again, pull the blanket straight, and stretch out on my back. My temple bumps her elbow. I want to ask her to move her arm. I want to shove it away. Barbara's lack of consideration angers me. But I don't say anything and slide farther over to my side.

If we got up now, it would be a normal morning with a shower and hard rolls for breakfast. Our bedroom door is closed. Otherwise I could hear Orlando hang the bakery bag on our apartment door. I reset the alarm for seven and hold on to it. That's a good twenty minutes. If we rush we should manage.

She says, "Before you realize you're not going to wake up, you think, Maybe I'm somebody else, maybe it's all a mistake that *I'm* stuck in *this* role. But then you realize you can't wake up, you can't get out of this body."

"Babs," I say, "what are you talking about?"

It's never been this bad. The cracks in our ceiling run in parallel, like borders on wallpaper, but zigzaggy. The irregularities in the white plaster form patterns, sometimes dash-and-dot faces, or steel springs or lathed columns, and growing out of them are inverted flowers with huge petals, long folded leaves, and a short stem, just like the ones in our speckled wallpaper. Then the flower twists open, or it can even be a cherub, a curly-haired plump cherub—with a mouth contorted in a scream.

"I'm getting up," I say. "We've got to get to bed earlier." We spent yesterday evening visiting Enrico Friedrich, an old friend of Barbara's. Barbara wanted me to find Enrico a job as a speechwriter, so he could get back on his feet again. But that's out of the question. He's a lush and a windbag, a wannabe poet, who even writes on the walls so he won't forget any of his precious ideas.

"Where do you know his wife, this Lydia, from?" I ask.

"She isn't his wife," Barbara says after a while.

"But she lives with him."

"No," Barbara says. "We just happened to meet one time, by accident, at the Natural History Museum."

"And what was it you two argued about?"

"Who says we argued?"

"It was just in the air. While I was in the bathroom, you two got into it."

"You sure know a lot, seeing as you were in the bathroom. . . ."

"I don't understand," I say, "how the woman puts up with Enrico. Given how he carries on and the way he looks, it's nothing short of a miracle."

"There are worse," Barbara says.

She has always defended Enrico. According to her, society is to blame for everything. We've been to visit him together now twice. Both times I've had to look at old snapshots, Enrico and Barbara on a pier out into the Baltic. I hate all that posing. Which is why there are hardly any pictures of Barbara and me, except a couple from our wedding and the official stuff. Which can't be avoided.

I don't even want to know if there was ever anything between Enrico and her, or if so, what. But I can't hire a lush as a speech-writer just to please Barbara. I'd just be adding to his list of negative experiences and making a hopeless ass of myself.

"Do you know what Enrico's problem is?" I say. "It's that he can't find any problems now to write novels and poems about, not real problems. The whole world envies us, envies us for the problems we have. They'd all love to change places with us. And a guy like Enrico can't deal with that. He wants to suffer."

Used to be that when we got home after being out, Barbara and I would fall into each other's arms the moment we were alone. Used to be that we'd sometimes tell each other that we had things good, that we didn't even know how good, and that we were healthy and very lucky. If I'd wake up in the night and didn't hear Barbara, I'd reach out for her or turn on the light. I was even jealous of Enrico at one time. Yesterday it was Barbara who was jealous. Which is probably why she wants all this attention today.

I would love to talk about something to get her mind off her dream. But I can't think of anything to say about our situation. I look at the ceiling, where the cherub has turned back into a steel spring. I try to make out a map of the world in the plaster, there in that rough spot. India faces Florida, not to scale but quite clear, underneath is Scandinavia, and Australia lies in the Baltic.

"Do you remember Candelaria?" I ask. "The foghorns echoing softer and softer off the mountain terraces? And how every morning I thought it was going to rain. But it was just the mountain hiding the sun. And in the evening you couldn't tell where the ocean stopped and the sky began, everything silver gray, no difference at all."

"That wasn't Candelaria," Barbara says.

"Well then, where was it?" I ask. When she doesn't react, I say, "I'm sure the place we stayed was called Candelaria."

We end up arguing about the simplest things. Last week I cleaned out my sock drawer. And Barbara thought that I'd thrown out one of her new Relax socks. I didn't throw out any single socks, just pairs, I said, pairs I hadn't worn for years, that had shrunk or had holes, or were just ugly or faded. That's the funny thing about Relax socks, she interrupted, they look old even though they're new. A single pair cost fifteen marks. I asked what a Relax sock is. And she answered, How could I claim not to have thrown one out if I didn't know what I was talking about. I repeated that I had only thrown out socks in pairs and simple shoe size would have told me that they couldn't be my socks. I found this note on the bathroom windowsill: "Relax Socks—NO [then smaller] ELASTIC, PERFECT FIT, Durable Fabric, Checked for Flaws, meet Eco-Tex Standard 100." The next day I decided to tell her that if she couldn't find her socks, then in fact the only possibility was that I was the culprit, although I had trouble understanding how I could have put her socks in with mine. After all, she's the one who always puts the laundry away. Barbara said that her sock had reappeared. When I asked why she hadn't told me before, she gave me an incredulous look, as if she couldn't fathom how I could ask such a question, although her expression might also have meant: "I told you, you just weren't listening again." That constitutes at least half of our misunderstandings, where she says I haven't been listening, although I could swear we'd never discussed it. I'm not deaf!

The alarm rings. I turn it off. The only sound now is that of a helicopter. Finally I say, "Babs, we gotta get up."

"Frank," she says—her right elbow is pointing at me—"what happens if it's not a dream, what if suddenly you can't wake up again and you've grown old in just a few hours and can feel you've lived long enough and have finally waited long enough, too, and don't want to wait any longer, and so you step to the window and look out and it makes no difference if you can see or not, if it's day or night, and you know that differences no longer exist, none, and that you've experienced the one miracle you might still be able to hope for. Then you can jump."

"It's seven," I say. "We've got to move, Babs, you hear?" I sit up, slide down to the foot of the bed, slip into my house shoes, and go to the window. The canal is frozen. Blue, yellow, and pale green plastic bottles are trapped in the ice, along with low-hanging willow branches. The street on the other side has been closed off. So you can't see cars anymore. The real estate agent said you don't just rent an apartment, you rent a new life: new neighbors, new traffic, a new view.

I press my forehead to the pane in order to see the street in front of our building. It's empty. Just two magpies are hopping from branch to branch in the chestnut tree across the way. I try to concentrate and think through the next few days. Saturday evening is the theater ball, and on Sunday Barbara's father is coming to coffee with his new girlfriend.

"Either you call in sick, or you get up now," I say. "I'll run your bath, okay?" Barbara doesn't answer. Evidently she's not even listening.

"Will you stay with me?" she asks.

"I've got to go to Erfurt," I say.

"That's not what I mean," she says. "Would you stay with me no matter what?"

"Babs," I say. "What else could I possibly do?"

"Who'll vote for you, with a wife like this?"

"Good God," I say, "what's wrong? You're awake, awake!"

"Don't shout," Barbara says. She spreads her arms. The left one extends beyond the edge of the bed, her hand drooping low enough for her fingertips to touch the carpet. I can finally see her eyes. Barbara raises her head, looks at me, and then lets it fall back again. I don't know what to say to make her get up and use the bathroom. I don't even know what I should do next. The magpies fly away. First one, then the other. The branches they were sitting on bounce for a bit. Then nothing moves, like in a photograph.

CHAPTER 19

a miracle

How Enrico Friedrich is given a bottle of vermouth. He tells
Patrick how Lydia suddenly appeared and then disappeared.
Meanwhile he drinks himself under the table. Patrick is
silent, but as he leaves he asks the crucial question.

"Those two women must've known each other from somewhere,"
Enrico said. He unwrapped the bottle of Martini, smoothed out
the gift wrapping, folded it off-center, and pulled open the bottom
drawer that held plastic bags. "You've taken hundreds of pictures
of Frank. Of course you know him." The paper jammed against the
top. Enrico stuffed it in deeper and shut the drawer. "Before the
last election he strolled around the market passing out roses. He's
stopped smoking, but he can't give up chewing gum." Enrico's
hand slipped trying to unscrew the cap. He grabbed a dish towel.
"Snap!" he said and opened the bottle. "Great sound. Ice?"

"No," Patrick said. He read some of the notations scribbled all
over the wallpaper and tipped the back of his chair against the
fridge. Enrico poured both glasses half full.

"Lydia was talking about some birds that need only fifty hours
to make it from Alaska to Hawaii. I've gotta get in there," Enrico
said, pointing to the fridge. "At first I thought Barbara belonged to
the Friends of the Museum, what used to be called the Cultural
Alliance or Urania or whatever. They collected shrews, dead
shrews. Who the hell knows what they were trying to prove."

Patrick leaned back again.

"It's a habit," Enrico said from the sink. He banged the tray on the inside rim and upended it into his palm. "But never more than two." Most of the cubes fell on dirty dishes. Enrico gathered the cubes up, piled them on a plate, and kept his hand over it until he had set it down in the middle of the wooden table. "I inherited this whole set of dishes from my grandma."

Patrick topped off his glass with mineral water. "Cheers," he said.

"Cheers," Enrico said, and dropped in an ice cube.

"And what's this?" Patrick asked.

"A double pack of black panty hose, a Duro toothbrush, nail scissors, a nail file, four tissues, a used bus ticket, and two marks and five pfennigs." Enrico snapped his fingernail against the glass bowl between them. "This is all she forgot." Enrico looked past Patrick to the house across the street, where lights had gone on in two windows.

"Frank wanted to toast to being on a first-name basis, said to call him Frank. Maybe he figured that because he's in the state parliament at Erfurt, Lydia wouldn't feel at ease. Cheers again, old man. Let's toast."

Patrick stretched out his arm.

"He kept looking up her sleeve. Whenever she passed something around, he'd stare up her sleeve. She was wearing her black dress with the wide . . ." He traced a quarter circle under his armpit. "And later, when he left to go to the bathroom, he said, 'She's all legs.' He whispered it." Enrico turned around to the door. "Well come on, Kitty, come on, what's wrong? Now he'll just sit there and watch. I call him—good boy! sit right here—I call him Kitty. He snores when he sleeps. But he never purrs." He chucked the pale ginger tom under the chin. "Have you noticed the days are getting longer?"

Patrick shook his head. His tongue passed over his teeth behind closed lips. He took another look at the scribbled wallpaper.

Enrico poured himself a second and held up the bottle. Patrick toasted him with a half-full glass.

"Well then," Enrico said. "You have to picture it. First, there's Lydia standing at my door, then she's turning the place upside down, then Frank calls and offers me a job. All I have to do is write whatever I think, the personal point of view. That's what matters, he said. Well, Kitty?"

Enrico rubs his nose from side to side. "He's learned to do Eskimo kisses." The cat sniffs and backs off.

"I ask him what it pays, right in front of Lydia and Babs, so it's all out in the open. And he tells me. And I say, 'See, I'm a real man after all, can earn some real money.' And then Lydia gave me a kiss."

The moment he stopped petting it, the cat pressed its neck against Enrico's hand or put out a paw to touch his arm.

"So, now Lydia's gone just like she arrived. Stood there with her suitcase, that green thing she kept on top of your bedroom wardrobe. The plan was to share rent, for the time being. And that was that. I made tea. She bought bigger pots for the plants, a spray mister, and that palm tree. I call it a palm, but it has a real name too. I had to make an extra trip to the cellar for that overgrown twig, find an old molding rod to tie it to. She knew how much water each plant needed and how often. She'd turn the pots every other day. Should I turn on a light?" Enrico kissed the cat between the ears. "Just imagine, old man, if Lydia had picked up the phone. Not that it had to turn out any different. But what if *she* had answered. I don't know, but what would you have said?" Enrico laughed and finished his drink.

"That would've been even better. I'm just saying, not that it matters to me, I'm just talking about the situation. Picture the situation. Really absurd. Sorry, old man, but I can't help it." He unscrewed the cap with one hand and lifted the bottle. "Or do you think that maybe I can? Want another?" Enrico poured himself a new drink. The cat lay cradled in his left arm. "It was really nice here, a state of purest harmony. Some guy came to repair the rattle in the apartment door, then there was a plumber. And the radiators got bled. Suddenly everything's working. I write, Lydia reads, Kitty dangles his paw over the chair and snores. I can smell a cake baking in the kitchen. No need to tell you, a real miracle, I thought. And can I tell you something else? Don't get me wrong, old man. Lydia was the first person, absolutely the first person, who ever thought my stuff was good. I waited a long time for someone to tell me whether it was good or bad. Not blaming you, old man, I'm just saying. But I needed somebody to say 'I think the stuff you write is good.'" Enrico brushed the palm of his hand along the scribbled wallpaper. "All just ideas," he said. "Then when Frank and Babs got here—those two women must've known each other from somewhere. They both get around a lot, because Frank is making it big as a young lawmaker, the next generation so to speak, and they have a special program for young lawmakers, send 'em all the way to Australia. I asked him what the point was. He thinks it's good for him, a change of perspective if he can see the whole thing from the other side now and then, what with Asia and Japan, or whatever. He talked about all sorts of stuff. He thinks I can make something out of it, stories or something, whatever it is that Frank has in mind." Enrico runs his thumbnail down the vertical ribbing of his glass, turns it to the next rib, and repeats the motion.

"While they were in Australia, one of these young lawmakers swallowed an inlay, a tooth inlay, while he was eating. And so for three days he didn't go to the toilet, because he was afraid of stirring around in his shit looking for that inlay. And then he had to go while they were on the road somewhere, nothing but red dirt and some scrub grass. He sent the bus on ahead. And when they came back to get him, there he was actually stirring around in his turds. Frank has all sorts of stories like that. One about a teacher who broke off all the angels' wings before a Christmas pageant, because he was a materialist and considered angels an affront to reason.

Those two women must've known each other from somewhere. See, they argued while Frank was in the bathroom. They thought I didn't notice. I would've figured jealousy. But that wasn't it. Lydia said she could understand Babs—didn't call her Babs, of course, but Dr. Holitzschek, kept everything real formal. Lydia said she could understand Babs, but that she shouldn't claim she'd been looking for a badger, it definitely wasn't a badger. And that if a person did run over somebody, and there was no chance of saving a life or anything, then that person didn't have to ruin their own life too. Lydia said she understood Babs. And then Babs started shouting that Lydia was a liar." Enrico giggled. "Lydia-lie-lie-lie. And when Frank came back everything was fine again. Lydia-lie-lie-lee. They didn't say a word. Should I turn on a light? What's wrong. You pissed, old man?"

Enrico watched Patrick take a sip of vermouth, then poured himself some more.

"Sometimes you turn to look at a woman because you notice the legs or the profile or the hair. But then when she turns around and says something . . . with Lydia, with her you can look at the whole package, the longer the better. Hey, say something! Anybody'd be happy to have a woman like that standing at his door, wouldn't he?" He finished his glass, no ice, no water. "I can imagine how you're feeling, old man. But you don't have to be pissed at me. Hey, come on, Lydia left you. And moved in with me. That's how it was. I'm just asking if that's how it was—if she left you and came to me. All you have to do is answer." Enrico thrust his head farther forward. "Am I right or not, yes or no?"

Enrico put the empty glass to his lips, slowly tipped it higher till the last few drops trickled into his open mouth.

"You think I have to drink. If I don't drink, I'm nothing, is that what you think? If there's anything I have to do, it's write, old man, and if I'd wanted her to, she'd've stayed." He clasped his glass with both hands and pulled down the corners of his mouth. "Want me to tell you why she left? I know why, I know exactly why."

The cat shifted on his lap. Enrico bent forward till his nose touched between its ears.

"She didn't see it happen, the miracle, that's all, that's the problem." The cat jumped off Enrico's lap and sat down beside the half-open door. Enrico crossed his arms on the table and stared first at one elbow, then the other. "She just didn't see it happen." He pressed his lips together and slowly shook his head. "I hadn't put the bottle away. It was standing just under the towel rack. I'd been cleaning the bathroom and had poured some Mr. Clean in the bucket. I'd wanted to empty the bottle, didn't figure there was much left. Then I forget about it. Can't see it, either, when you're standing at the washbasin, you can't see the bottle, because the towels are hanging in front of it."

"Don't understand a word you're saying," Patrick said, and sloshed what was left of his drink around in his glass.

"We'd cleaned house, on account of Frank, Lydia did the kitchen, and I did the bath. From the washbasin, if you're standing there and washing up, you can't see the bottle."

Patrick edged closer.

"Interested now, aren't you, old man?" Enrico poured himself another. "I was standing in the bathroom at the washbasin. All her stuff was gone—toothbrush, cold cream, hair spray. Lydia took a bath first. She'd packed it all after taking her bath, even her wet washrag. All I asked was if she had to go just yet, had to leave in the middle of the night? She'd written a list of when and how each plant was to be watered, and put the keys on top. She opened up the fridge and said, 'Here's the bell peppers, here's the sweet herring' . . . tsss." Enrico giggled. His saliva hissed between his teeth. "Sweet, in cream, not pickled—tsss. I let water run over my hands, to calm myself down, while she stood leaning in the doorway. I turned off the tap and slowly dried my hands, slow and methodical, like a surgeon. I don't have to drink. If I don't want to, I don't have to. And when I put the towel back on the rack, next to the other towel, I was paying close attention, but I still didn't get it symmetrical, it fell on top of Mr. Clean and toppled him over. And that's when it happened, old man." Enrico yawned. "All ears now, aren't you, like a lynx?" He drew big pointy shapes above his ears. "Strange, really incredible. Not even Copperfield could pull it off, not every time, 'cause it's a matter of pure luck." Enrico drank. "I bend down, pick it up, pick the towel up, and believe it or not, old man, Mr. Clean stands up too. Somehow it pulls him along, he totters, I stop. Slowly I lift the towel higher and higher, and pull it away just like from a magic hat. And Mr. Clean has stopped tottering. I wanted to say something, something full of hope, because it was a good omen, for Lydia and me, a miracle in fact, that put everything in a new light." Enrico took hold of his glass again and rubbed his thumbnail along the ribs. "'Did you see that?' I ask her. But there's no answer, just a draft, the door handle moves, softly, the way she always closes a door, then the front door, thump, and her footsteps down the sidewalk. Then I hear a crackling sound. I've never heard that before. The foam was melting, the foam that hadn't gone down the drain was melting, or whatever you call that, you know what I mean. She could never have enough foam. And I just had to check it out, the way the little bubbles burst. Hundreds of bursting bubbles each second, crackle, crackle, crackle," Enrico said. "That's the last I heard from Lydia." He finished his glass and set it down on the table, hard.

When he raised his head again, he could only see the curve of Patrick's left shoulder and the beginning of his arm silhouetted against the light from the windows across the street and the glare from the streetlight. He saw outlines of the plants, the molding rod in the pot with the palm, and to the right, in profile, the spray mister.

He tried to make out the items on the table: Lydia's glass bowl looked like an ice cream sundae, with the toothbrush as a plastic spoon, and the ribbed glass in his hand was a gear or a wheel of fortune with his thumb as the brake. The lines written on the walls tangled, formed thick ropes, long labyrinthine strands.

Enrico noticed it had suddenly become even darker. But, he thought, that's really only because Patrick has positioned himself between me and the window, because he's sitting there all full of himself, showing off. This train of thought proved to him that his mind was still working very precisely and that he could establish connections with playful ease and could write about anything he wanted. He saw the cat beside his chair, how it repeatedly licked its paw and ran it over its head. He wanted to describe that, the way a cat cleans itself, and how somebody stands in the light and you tell them to move a little to one side, you're blocking the sun. Enrico giggled soundlessly. He patted his pocket for a pencil. All he needed was a pencil and paper. He wanted to write about everything, about the whole world. Step aside, that's what he'd write, that's all I want. If I didn't have to giggle like this, Enrico thought, I could write: "Don't block the sun." If I had a pencil and paper I could write it down now. Enrico heard his own name and he heard Lydia's name. The wheel of fortune under his thumbnail vanished. If only there were still some empty space on the wall . . . he didn't know what sort of question the words formed, the question someone kept shouting in his ear, over and over, and whether that was the smell of aftershave or just of the breath he felt on his face. Of course I slept with Lydia. Everybody has to sleep sometime, even Lydia, even me, you die if you don't sleep, he thought, but I have to write, too, above all I have to write. And even when Enrico felt the pain at the back of his neck and felt his forehead strike the table, he couldn't stop describing the world. He simply could not stop writing.

CHAPTER 20

kids

*Edgar Körner tells about a trip with Danny on an old stretch
of autobahn. Women behind the wheel, or, when both like to
drive. True and invented stories. Real love can wait.*

Danny wouldn't let go of the steering wheel again. From start to
finish she sat behind the wheel, and even when we stopped for gas
she only did a couple of knee bends beside the open driver's-side
door. Earlier in the week she'd had her hair cut really short without
asking what I thought of the idea. She was edgy because she hadn't
found a job and because of Tino, who was getting more difficult by
the day and had thrown a temper tantrum when we left and tried
to kick her. He didn't want to stay with his father for even two
weeks. I'd used all my savings for our new Ikea kitchen. We were
barely managing to squeak by each month. All the same, she wasn't
about to give up her old Plymouth with its undivided front seat
and cupholder. She called it "Jimmy Jr."—to distinguish it from
"Jimmy," her old Skoda.

Danny wasn't a bad driver, liked to wind the gears out a little
too far maybe. But I usually get sick as a passenger. And this old
stretch of autobahn was hell, a jolt at every seam, pure torture. It
was like watching a training film: the wheels hit the edge of each
tar-smeared slab, the impact is transferred to the seat, then the
spine. The worst damage is to the neck vertebrae, where it hurts
most. And the next instant the back wheels heave, a couple of
nerves get pinched, and you're half an inch shorter. Plus Danny

was back on the pill, although we'd decided we wanted a kid of our own. At thirty-four or -five she still wouldn't be over the hill, she'd said. And I'd replied, "Whatever you think, Danny." What was I supposed to say to her putting it off again. There're always reasons, that wasn't the point. But Danny started in again about how it would probably be best if we just gave up on the whole idea.

"Who knows if we'll still be in love in two years, Eddie?"

Later she cried and said she was sorry, and I took her in my arms and asked, "Sorry for what?"

She was reading too much psychological crap, that's all. First there was the Miller woman and then C. G. Jung. She was constantly coming at me with some new example, one that really settled the issue. I'd told her she shouldn't waste her time on such hocus-pocus. But there was no talking to her, she'd have to come to that conclusion herself.

I had just bent forward—for a second I thought I'd spotted a plane flying parallel to us off to the left, but it was only a smudge on her window—when she asked, "Have I told you the latest about Lucas?"

Lucas is her godchild, one of Tom and Billi's twins. The other twin is Max. Lucas had nailed his teddy bear to his bed, and Billi had slapped him—for the first time ever. The next day Lucas made a grab for the parakeet. But it got away, and now they'd made signs and tacked them to the trees in the village, asking if anyone had seen Herbert, a yellow-green parakeet. So Billi explained the story of Jesus to the kids one more time, and Tom helped them build a birdhouse that the kids pounded full with every nail in the house.

Since Danny didn't even smile, I expected her to come up with something from C. G. Jung or the Miller woman. I said I thought the birdhouse was a good idea.

She pushed in the cigarette lighter and explained to me how important those earliest years are for a kid, because if they didn't go well it was incredibly hard to straighten things out again—if you ever did. And a lot of people wearing themselves out as teachers would be better off if only more parents were better parents. I asked who she meant by that. She just wanted to make sure we both were completely aware of these things, in case we should ever have a kid of our own. I patted her just below the hem of her shorts, Danny laid her hand on mine. Then she said that Tino had been handled badly.

"Because they spoiled him rotten," I said.

"No," she said, "not because of that." But then we dropped the subject.

Although Danny had let up on the gas, the jolts suddenly got worse. You felt totally at their mercy. A little apple rolled out between my feet from somewhere—when I picked it up it felt like a baked apple, wrinkly and warm—then the papers for the car fell out from behind the visor. I said she should go ahead and pass that slowpoke up front and then stay in the left lane. But then traffic backed up behind us. We had to switch back to the bumpy lane. I laid the baked apple in the indentation where the passenger's can of Coke is supposed to go.

Danny fumbled with her pack of Luckies, held it up to her mouth, and snagged a cigarette with her lips. With the filter clamped in her teeth, she asked if I wanted one too, and cracked her window a little.

"I'm not feeling all that great," I said.

"We certainly picked the day for it," she said and slipped her thumb along the inside of her seat belt, stretched it, then let it snap back. I don't suppose that at that moment she was the least bit aware of how much I liked to watch her do it. I gazed at her right hand, which was holding the cigarette. You could see the veins on the back, but not too clearly, and you never noticed the blond hairs on Danny's forearm until she was really tanned.

I asked her again to keep left as much as possible and then stop at the next gas station. We slowed down, and it felt as if ours was the only car that never passed anyone. Of course there's no point in passing right before you stop for gas. Danny stubbed out her cigarette, rolled her window all the way down, and dangled her left hand out, as if inspecting her nails in the sideview mirror.

Actually, at that point it could have turned out to be a fine vacation.

These concrete slabs had to come to an end sometime, and our exit was coming up soon besides. I figured I'd take the wheel after we got gas, and if I were driving I wouldn't feel sick, either. Danny would then cuddle up next to me, slip off her leather sandals, press her toes to the windshield, but keep her left leg crooked for me to caress. I hoped she would find a new job in September or October. I also said that before putting out money for new shocks, we really ought to get a different car.

But then I could only sit and watch as Danny drove right by the gas station. We drove past, and she said that with German cars you were helping to pay for the workers' swimming pools, that French and Italian cars weren't any good, and that the Japanese have no sense of style. Suddenly she let up on the gas, causing the car to lurch, and then lurch again as she shifted down.

"'Swimming pools' sound more like America to me," I said. I was annoyed by the way she thrust out her lower lip and set the can of Fanta to her lips at such a steep angle, as if there were hardly anything in it. She wiped the back of her hand across her mouth, pressed the can to her neck, rolled it around in her cleavage, then held it up to her shoulder.

"Doesn't make any difference." Danny spoke with a studied casualness, and I thought how being a passenger is always a stupid position to be in and that it wasn't good for the car to downshift so abruptly. Besides, she held the turn signal on much too long, and the next gas station was evidently forty miles ahead. The windshield was speckled with exploded insects and needed to be cleaned, I was feeling sick, and the right lane was a catastrophe. I wanted to do something, say something, but was determined not to ask if it would bother her if I took the wheel. The fun was ruined in any case.

So that's about how you have to picture the situation that caused me to tell a stupid story that I knew would upset her. And if she started in again then with C. G. Jung's *Synchronicity and Acausality*, I decided I would make it clear to her once and for all that I considered that stuff pure lunacy and would refuse to hear any more such nonsense. And in its place I'd suggest she take up music. Something real, at any rate. Or maybe astronomy.

"Did I tell you about the train?" I asked. I could tell from the way she said "No" that I'd surprised her, since it was close to a week since I'd taken the trip. In any case, I started to tell her about a boy and a girl who were running up and down the aisle. They belonged to two different women, who had laid the kids' stuffed animals— a penguin and a giant frog—on empty seats catty-corner ahead of me and then gone back to their own seats at the other end of the car.

Just thinking of Tom and Billi's twins and their antics was all I needed to embroider the whole thing perfectly.

"The kids ran around screaming the whole time," I said. "A bald guy with a high voice tried to calm them down. His wife had fallen asleep, or at least pretended she had. They both left the car shortly after that. Other people followed when the kids began to bang a wastebasket lid. A fat older man, who had stayed in his seat, scolded them. At first the kids stopped, but then they were soon back at it, and the old man looked down the aisle to the women, shaking his head."

"How old were they?" Danny asked, and I said that I always have trouble guessing kids' ages, first-graders maybe.

"I meant the mothers," Danny said.

"Mid-twenties," I said, and fell silent for a while.

We were bouncing along behind a huge dump truck, trapped in a fog of exhaust.

"Finally the kids started playing 'ambush,' as they called it," I went on. "The girl had to walk down the aisle and the boy leapt out at her from behind and dragged her to the floor. They traded roles, and when it was the boy's turn again, the old man broke it up. The boy explained how he wanted to join the army when he grew up so he could strangle his enemies. He was mouthing off like that and the old man laid into him saying he wouldn't be able to do whatever he wanted in the army, that it was just the opposite, the army was all about rules and discipline. He grabbed the boy by the arm and shook him. And then I heard the old man ask, 'What would you do if you were in Yugoslavia?'"

I added a little pause here. Danny glanced my way, for the first time in the whole trip.

"What would he do there, the old man asked, and the little boy repeated, 'Strangle my enemies.'"

"And then?" Danny asked.

"The old man let him go."

"What about you?" Danny had passed the dump truck now and was changing back to the right lane, which was as bumpy as ever, although we were doing eighty K at most.

When I realized what was going through her head, I said, "The kid was only six or seven. . . ."

"And can do whatever he wants . . . ?"

"Danny . . ." I said, and didn't know what else to say. She had twisted the whole thing around in a different direction.

"Incredible," she whispered, exhaling slowly, letting air hiss between her teeth. I adjusted the back of my seat upright, just for something to do. "The boy wasn't all that wrong, that's how things are," I said. "And for as long as nobody intervenes, the slaughter will go on, until everything is ethnically cleansed and tidy. You can't just stand aside and watch." And I explained my views to her at length and in detail. It sounded reasonable to me. I still wanted to ask her to stop or to switch to the left lane, because I was feeling sick as a dog, but one car after the other kept passing us. And then we were at our exit.

Danny was driving along at a good clip now. I put a hand on her knee and asked if she wanted a cigarette. She didn't budge. There was a blister on the back of my hand that I'd got trying to warm some hard rolls, just a red dot by then. At some point Danny would lay her hand on mine. Gliders were doing corkscrews high above the open fields.

The last nice thing I remember is that I suddenly spotted the shiny insole of her leather sandal and then saw her bare foot and polished toenails on the gas pedal. For a moment I thought that was the reason we were going so fast.

When we started speaking again, all we could do was argue. She said she didn't even recognize me anymore, couldn't believe the stuff coming out of my mouth. She was appalled. I thought she was about to burst into tears. Instead she got nasty. "Can I hear all that one more time?" she asked. I told her she made things too easy for herself, way too easy. Danny stared stubbornly straight ahead. She'd thought the same way I did for far too long. That had been her big mistake. "You never would've talked like that back in '89, never!" She kept taking one hand off the wheel and getting a new grip, like a gymnast at his bar or a weight lifter, and repeated how she couldn't believe it was me talking like that.

We stopped for gas. Danny did knee bends while I took care of the rest. At supper, we read the paper or stared at the butter between us. She left for home the next morning.

I stayed on alone in the cabin on Scharmützel Lake for two weeks. We wouldn't have got our money back in any case. I'd make my bed first thing when I got up and wash the breakfast dishes right away, so that a mess couldn't even get started. I never left the little yard except to go for a swim. I even bought flowers twice, because I'd found a vase in the kitchen cupboard.

I tried to think through my relationship with Danny and Tino. But all I came up with were things I'd already known for a long time. It seemed to me it was normal to want a kid of my own. That didn't mean I wouldn't take good care of Tino. Up until the very last day I figured Danny would at least come to pick me up.

First all three of them—that's including Terry—moved in with Tino's father, with her brother-in-law, I guess you'd say. For a while I hoped that Danny would give me a call on my birthday. After all, she still had a lot of stuff in the apartment: her Walkman, a couple of books, her Callas CD, the gray monster—her favorite chair— and all sorts of things we'd bought together—the everyday dishes, straw rugs, two floor lamps, the chaise longues for the balcony. I couldn't just call her up and say, "Hi, Danny! Today's the day. Don't you want to wish me happy birthday?"

I was pissed at Billi and Tom, because I couldn't help thinking they were the ones who'd advised her to leave me. Six months later, at the end of January, I lost my job. No one at the paper had expected I'd get the ax. I was the only one who knew that when they talked about staying competitive, it was me that was foremost in their minds. Every layoff, even that of a bad ad rep like me, was made in the interest not just of the staff as a whole, but also of the nation's economy, and so ultimately in my own interest as well.

That was the last piece I needed to complete the jigsaw puzzle of misery that I'd become since Danny left me. And it was all exe- cuted in such proper form that I didn't even bother to file an objection with the Labor Court.

At first it wasn't so bad, my stint at polishing doorknobs was over. I was also tired of the smirks I got from people I'd known from before. The only thing I was sorry about was Pit. Working with him had even been fun sometimes.

I decided to make good use of my time and began reading Störig's *Brief History of Philosophy,* but hung it up before I even got to Plato. Then I planned to have a go at *The Man Without Qualities*—those four blue volumes of the *ex libris* edition had been on my shelf for an eternity—and ran out of gas after eighty pages. I joined the Fitness Studio, six months for 449 marks, and never made it past week two. I even gave up on my daily routine with the *Langenscheidt's Basic English Vocabulary* that always lay beside my bed. I couldn't think of anything I might want to talk about. Looking back, I can't really say what I did for those nine months, except buy a new vacuum cleaner and get together with Ute now and then. Whatever it was I needed, I simply couldn't get a handle on it.

I thought I was the only person who realized that the world turns. No one understood what I was talking about. Even though I'd given a lot of thought to that phrase. The world turns, and you just wait for it to go on turning and change perspective on things, so you can see them differently again at some point, too. Until the cosmic window appears and you can finally start your rocket. Somehow I just went on seeing the same things over and over.

But then suddenly I had a job again, got it with just a standard application, the kind you forget as soon as you've mailed it off. Friedrich Schulze, Berlin-Mariendorf, International Transport— they've opened new branches in Crimmitschau and Guteborn near Meerane. I'm in France now twice a week, delivering Altenburg vinegar and mustard to Lidl Markets there. Which leaves me enough time to dream of Danny, of a Danny who hasn't had her hair cut short.

She's living with a former coworker now, a photographer from Beyer's newspaper, whose wife ran off. I saw him once at Tom and Billi's. He's not right for Danny.

It probably had to turn out this way. I only wish someday Danny would notice that no one has taken her place, that I really love her, her and nobody else, even when I sometimes think that I'd have no idea what we might do together, what we'd even talk about. At any rate, I don't think it's unnatural to love just one person and nobody else, even if you don't live with that person, never even get together with her.

A few weeks ago I saw her Jimmy Jr. in the Kaufland parking garage. Nobody was around, so I peeked inside. Nothing had changed. It was as if I were just about to get in. Except the apple wasn't there anymore.

I pictured what would've happened if *I'd* been driving and hadn't invented that story about the two kids. . . . Danny would've slid over to me, laid her head on my shoulder, slipped off her sandals, snuggled her heels up to the dashboard on the right. Her hair would have fallen over my arm and her polished toenails would have been pressed against the windshield. Tired as she was, she would've fallen asleep. And that evening I would've driven the car to the edge of the lake, kissed her eyes, and whispered, "Hey, Danny, look where we are."

CHAPTER 21

n e e d l e s

How Martin Meurer receives the first visitor to his new apartment. A man for Fadila. Fish in a bottle and a bowl. Life stories. Cleaning a balcony roof. Who are you waiting for?

"Veni, vidi, vici," Tahir says, and laughs, throwing his head back. He stands on the top stair and hands a one-and-a-half-liter bottle of Bonaqua mineral water to Martin, who is holding the apartment door open with his back.

"What are you doing here? The move was more than a week ago."

"Look," Tahir says.

"Wow! Two? No, three!" Martin watches the fish through the space separating the two blue labels.

"You put them in a bottle and they get very big. Nobody knows how they get in." Tahir is wearing a faded shirt with a little crocodile on the chest, black pants shiny around the pockets, and scuffed loafers. A jacket is draped over one arm.

"Dead ahead, Tahir, just follow your nose." Martin closes the door. "Like the place?"

"Give here," Tahir says. He carries the bottle over to the wall unit, pushes aside some Matchbox cars and stones and pulls a ship-in-a-bottle to the front. "When fishes get bigger, you put it like this."

"Fish get bigger . . . the plural of fish is fish, Tahir. Not fishes."

Tahir lays it on its side. Its blue cap touches the cork of the other bottle on the shelf.

"How am I supposed to feed them?"

Tahir turns around and sends his forefinger hopping along the back of his left hand. "What you call it?"

"Yes," Martin says, "fleas, but until Monday? Is the pet store open on—"

They both jump back. The bottle slowly rolls off the unit's lower shelf and lands almost soundlessly on the carpet.

"Nothing broke," Tahir says, and bends down. "Nothing broke."

Martin, in his stocking feet and jeans cutoffs, is standing on some newspaper spread beside his sneakers. He strokes a paint-brush along the windowsill and then washes it in a half-full glass, pressing the bristles hard against the bottom.

"I could've used you," he says. "Wanted to introduce you to Steuber. He knows of some other opportunities, some completely new and different opportunities."

Tahir lets the bottle dangle between two fingers. "I had to play chess," he says.

"You could've earned better than fifteen marks here—or what are they paying for a game of chess these days? My brother, Pit, was here too, the only guy whose clothes might fit you."

"What's that?" Tahir asks.

"Paint thinner."

"No. Tick-tick-tick. A clock?"

"Awful, isn't it? Like a ticking time bomb. I thought you were the electrician."

"I'm no electrician."

"Not you! I'm waiting for an electrician to fix it for me, and I thought . . ."

"Okay," Tahir says, and nods.

"Hums like a transformer station." Martin tries to reproduce the exact noise. "And then that ticking. If that's the latest in technology . . . if they don't fix it, we don't pay, not a cent, simple as that." Martin dries the brush on a torn pair of undershorts. "This is just the super's apartment. You should see what it looks like downstairs. Genuine art nouveau, two stories, one-of-a-kind splendor. Was all a kindergarten once, got completely run-down. And up here under the roof, the super's apartment, with separate stairs."

Tahir tosses his jacket over his shoulder, one finger in the collar loop, and follows him into the entrance hall.

"For Tino, if he ever comes. This door's just been painted, too."

Martin pushes on the door handle with his fingertips. The curtains are caught in the window. "A little small, but better than just okay." He opens the window, straightens the curtains, comes back out, pushes open the door opposite.

"I sleep in here. Nothing much to see. Steuber doesn't say much, but he can't possibly have got his two floors for under a million. Window fixtures, all redone, beautiful, aren't they? Steuber is in constant fear that the old guy, the old super, is going to blow the whole place sky-high. He never let anybody in. You can't imagine what this looked like six weeks ago. You have no idea. You gotta look in here." In the bathroom now, Martin puts down the toilet lid. "Biggest tub we could fit in, main thing, it's a tub. Here, press on this, extra lights. And the mirror! I collected bids and just put the bills in his mailbox. And he's paying me besides. And now for the best part. Pull that shut behind us, okay?"

In the kitchen Martin opens the balcony door as far as it will go and wedges a piece of wood under it with his foot. "Once this is finished . . . more like 'balcony with apartment,' wouldn't the gentleman say?" He takes the bottle from Tahir. "Just so you don't drop it on somebody's head," he says, setting it on the table.

Martin has to pull all three translucent plastic bowls out of the cupboard to get to the biggest one. He rinses it with cold water, empties it, and then unscrews the Bonaqua cap. "The only noise here comes from the birds," he shouts. "Fir trees are pretty rare in this area. Moss, too, firs and moss." Martin holds the bowl at a tilt, like a beer glass. The water flows down the side. He tips the bottle up slowly.

"I think maybe Fadila is here with you." Tahir is still standing at the balcony door.

"Fadila? She's your fiancée, not mine." Martin lowers the bottle. "I don't even know her. How's she supposed to know . . ."

"I say about you a lot." Tahir throws his head back and laughs. "He and I say about you a lot, man."

"She, if you mean her. She, her, hers." Martin shakes a fish out of the bottle and screws the cap on. "This bottle's worth something, thirty-five pfennigs."

"We are speaking about you and Fadila—why not?" Tahir hangs his jacket over the back of a chair. He takes a color snapshot from his wallet, wipes his hand across the tabletop, and lays it in front of Martin.

A young woman, barefoot, in faded jeans, flannel shirt, and a pageboy is leaning against a stucco wall. Fadila has high cheekbones and a serious look.

"She look like someone?"

"Who?"

"I'm asking you, man."

"Going by hairstyle and height," Martin says, "Mireille Mathieu."

"Juliette Binoche. She doesn't need makeup to see good."

"To *look* good."

"You see? They're this little, like this!" Tahir demonstrates a span of about four inches. "Well, like this!" His fingers move apart like pincers. "No more."

Fadila's right foot rests on top of her left, the knee bent.

"Tiny shoes, like Juliette Binoche."

"Does she have little shoes?"

"Don't know." Tahir laughs.

"I thought Fadila is in Berlin, isn't she?"

Tahir stares at the photograph. "We live on Leipziger Strasse. Mother is in Berlin."

"The last time it was the other way around." Martin opens a cupboard door. "And your father?"

Tahir bursts into laughter.

"Is he here too?"

"Butchered."

"*Your* father? How'd it happen?"

Tahir laughs, sets his fist at his navel, draws it up to his chin and says, "Cut open."

"I thought . . . I didn't mean . . . sorry." Martin shoves a package of rye crisps, Glocken noodles, and a bag of berry muesli to one side. "Where'd it happen?"

"In the hospital, in Brčko."

"We'll go out for a bite afterwards, okay, Tahir? Or would you like something now?" Martin shows him a package with a picture of chocolate pudding dripping with a yellowish sauce. "Instant."

Tahir shakes his head.

"My treat. You're my first visitor. We'll go out then, okay?"

"Yes," Tahir says.

"Hungry?"

"Yes."

"When this is all finished there'll be a housewarming party. You can bring Fadila along, okay? Wonder if this would work—dried basil?" Martin taps the bottom of the bag.

Tahir kicks a table leg, the water almost sloshes over the rim. "Why not marry Fadila—why not?" he asks.

The two orange fish run their mouths along the bottom of the bowl. The blue one swims around slowly. Martin stirs the basil around in the water. "So you're not looking for Fadila at all?" he says, and looks up.

"I'm looking for Fadila. Fadila . . ." Tahir snaps for a mosquito with his left hand. He slowly pulls the tips of his fingers back from his palm.

"Missed," says Martin.

Tahir spreads his hand open and points to a spot between his middle and ring fingers. He flicks the mosquito into the bowl.

"I thought you were engaged? You said you were engaged, and now here you are asking me if I want to marry her." Martin puts the bag of basil back in the cupboard. "Do you really think she's coming here today, that Fadila's coming here?"

"I think," Tahir says.

"Where did you really get these fish?"

Tahir puts the snapshot back in his wallet. "An aquarium was broke, then was a big argument. Everybody took the fishes that were still . . ." He moves his finger.

". . . still alive, still wiggling?"

"Yes, wiggling."

"A broken aquarium?"

"Yes." Tahir puts the wallet away in his jacket. A few crumbs of basil cling to the edge of the bowl.

"This ticking is driving me nuts, the ticking from the circuit-breaker box. Or am I just being an idiot, Tahir? What time is it?" Martin points to his wrist.

Tahir takes hold of his left wrist and turns his watch around until the face is visible. The second hand jerks back and forth.

"You need a new battery," Martin says. "It needs a battery. Can you give me a hand outside here? It's too dangerous just by myself. I have to sweep the balcony roof."

"Are you him?" Tahir picks up a photograph from the bread box.

"Recognize me? On the far right, in a crouch, was twenty then." Martin comes around the table. "That's me. I found it during the move. And this guy"—he gives it a tap—"forgot it and left it behind—Dimitrios, a Greek." Martin takes two bottles of Clausthaler beer from the fridge. "You can forget about all of us, every person in that picture. Nothing ever became of any of us."

"What never became?"

"Art historians, curators. Want a Clausthaler? Three or four years ago he was suddenly standing at the door, no notice, no phone call. The doorbell rang, I opened up, and he tucked his head between his shoulders. That's how he always laughed, with his head tucked in." Martin imitates it. "He had a huge suitcase with him, and there were two shoulder bags on the landing, big suckers." With a Clausthaler in each hand, Martin draws large circles in front of Tahir's face and holds out a bottle to him. "Our seminar group was helping with the apple harvest. Dimitrios had fingertips like a guitarist's, or a violinist's, thick calluses. He's a nibbler." Martin bites at his fingernails. "A nibbler, understand? He spoke English, Spanish, French, Italian, and after a year at the Herder Institute in Leipzig, German too. Greek goes without saying. And as is only proper for a Communist—his father had been on Makronisos, in prison there—Russian as well. We'd last seen each other in '88, when he got his diploma. He was going to get married, a Danish girl, and take her back home with him to Athens. He wanted to study the early Italians in the museum here, Guido da Siena, Botticelli, and so on. And then he asked for a glass of water. He would've only asked for half a glass in the old days. Cheers, Tahir."

"Why?"

"Cheers. Because he wanted to suffer, for Communism, for science, for . . ." Martin took a drink. "For everything. His suitcase and the shoulder bags were crammed with material, as he called it. He said he was instructing revolutionary comrades, everywhere, anywhere they were to be found. He didn't know anyone here except me. I told him I didn't think a revolution in Germany was either probable or desirable. So he started suffering again and said, 'Too many think like that, but that is not right.' The next day we went to the museum, then the train station. We took turns carrying his luggage. Might've been a bomb in one of them. Never heard from him again. Don't you like the beer?"

"And this guy?"

"Our spy. He showed up two weeks after Andrea, my wife, was buried, to ask how I was doing. We'd stopped talking back in Leipzig. I couldn't tell you now why I let him stay the night. Not here, in my old apartment in Lerchenberg. It really made me mad back then that he didn't even change his sheets. Never took a bath, either. Mainly I was pissed with myself for doing him a favor. I'm just not fast enough on my feet. I never wanted to see him again, ever. And if I ever did, I wanted to confront him and say: 'There isn't room here for both of us.' I even practiced, so I could be pre-pared." Martin drank from the bottle.

"And did you?"

"He left Leipzig a long time ago."

"Martin is Jesus Christ now and loves everybody."

"And Tahir fasts for Allah and has bad breath."

"I have bad breath?"

"Yes. I even offered you a Fisherman's Friend, in the car pool. Just to freshen the air." He put his hand to his mouth, then to his stomach. "Not to fill your tummy. Would you rather have mineral water?"

"And this guy here?"

"He lost his job and started drinking, or lost it because he was drinking. He was divorced even before that. We ran into each other in Berlin a year ago. He hadn't changed a bit, I mean, he said the same things he always used to say, and read the same things as always. Except he got drunk every day. 'Berlin's a tight-ass town,' he'd say, 'a tight-ass town.' That's a turn of phrase, means cold, unfriendly. They renovated the building he was living in, on Knaack Strasse, the back building. Everything new, even the plumbing. There were holes in the floors everywhere, big holes. And drunk as usual, he stumbled into one and fell to the floor below and froze to death. All the other tenants had left long before that. We're really not much to boast about." Martin goes to the sink and rinses out his bottle. "The girl next to me even snagged a tenure-track position—our princess. She ate with a cloth napkin in the dorm cafeteria. The new faculty brought their own people with them. She's a tour guide in Erfurt now. And the beauty, with the dark hair, is divorced with two kids and lives with her mother somewhere near Templin. Nobody has ever heard from the others, either. Here, stop torturing yourself." Martin takes the Clausthaler away and presses the cork cap back on. "These guys don't like the taste either," he says, bending over the bowl. "Have to get used to their new environment."

Martin goes to get his sneakers. Returning to the kitchen, he sits down on a stool, tugs at tongues and loosens laces.

"There were some professors and instructors who really took an interest in us, or at least in the subject, who wanted to salvage something and pass it on. They only knew Greece or Hildesheim from pictures, too." Martin crooks a leg, sets his heel on the edge of the stool, and ties a bow. "It's them I feel sorry for, that nothing ever became of us. I feel sorry for them. Understand?"

Tahir puts the snapshot back on the bread box.

"Want to help now?" Martin walks to the balcony, carrying the stool ahead of him. He points up. "That's corrugated plastic or whatever they call it. You can see through it when it's clean. There's crud in all the troughs. Twigs, needles, and crud. Comes down like dandruff from those fir trees there. You ought to see the moss Steuber collects every week—he's proud as a peacock of his moss. Nobody's done anything around here for years now. You just have to hold me, hold on to me." Martin shakes the railing, which still has hooks for flower boxes, and pushes the stool forward. "Take hold of me here." He grabs at his belt. "With both hands is best, right. Now first this . . ." He pulls out a toy shovel and a whisk broom from behind a bucket of clothespins. "First this and then this."

Martin bangs the flat of his hand against the roof's supporting beams. "They'll be next. Paint's completely gone." He scratches a leftover white fleck with his thumbnail. "Can we get started?"

Tahir laughs. Martin first kneels on the stool, then slowly

stands up. His hands work their way up the corner post. He takes a step out onto the railing. "Hold tight, Tahir!"

Martin pulls the other leg after him. "Tahir! Come on, hold on to me!" Martin goes into a slight crouch and turns around very slowly on the railing.

"What's wrong? Give me the shovel."

"It's raining," Tahir says.

"The shovel!" Martin puts the handle between his teeth and sticks his head up over the roof.

"It's like topsoil. All caked together. Look at it! Regular muddy ditches!" With a dull thud the first sweep falls to the garden below. "Real topsoil!"

Tahir follows Martin's movements. He watches the play of calf muscles and the sneakers as they slowly shift along the railing.

"It's raining," Tahir says.

Martin stands on his tiptoes. "I'm making it rain crud and needles. You'll see how it brightens the place up. It's the icing on the cake." His right hand reappears under the roof and grabs at the empty air. "Broom!"

Tahir puts the handle in his hand.

A while later Martin's head appears under the roof. His hair is wet, bits of mud are stuck to his nose and chin. He jumps from the railing onto the balcony. "Well? That makes a difference, doesn't it. Didn't get it all though, did I?" He bangs the toy shovel on the underside of the roof. "Now you'll be able to count the needles as they fall, every single one!"

"Very loud now."

"Only when it rains," Martin says, and wipes his sleeve down across forehead and nose to his chin. "I like the sound of rain on the roof. Check the living room, the window, see if it's raining in, understand?"

When Tahir returns, Martin is hunkered down against the wall. Someone is flinging children's toys around among the trees in the garden below. A woman's voice is shouting loudly over and over: "Filthy! Every single toy, filthy!"

Then Thomas Steuber appears. He is moving carefully over the moss, gathering toys. In one hand he's holding both a tricycle tractor and a dump truck. With the other he picks up various sandbox molds, but each time he bends down he bangs the tractor's rear left wheel against his ankle. The woman raises her voice again.

Suddenly Steuber turns around.

"Keep off the moss!" he bellows, raising outstretched arms. He drops a red sandbox mold. His wet shirt is pasted to his shoulders. He bends down and tries to pick the mold up with one finger. He makes several stabs at it. He has no luck. He stands up, hauls one arm back, and flings the tractor onto the veranda steps, then the dump truck. He hurls the rest of the toys after them, picks up the mold, and throws it over the fence.

"He's nuts," Tahir says, "really nuts."

From his crouch Martin squints up at the roof, where the rain is pounding now, drowning out every other sound. A single fir-tree needle jumps to one side, just the least little bit, and back again, the needle twitches back and forth, and now there's another needle and another and another. They're all twitching in the rain.

"Good God!" Martin says. "Do you see that?"

The roof is covered with needles. It's a teeming mass of twitching needles.

"Don't you see? Tick-tock, tick-tock." Martin demonstrates with his forefinger.

"Yes," Tahir says, "jump like little fishes." He leans in the doorway. "When does electrician come? You going to wait?"

"No," Martin says after a while. "We can leave now." And then, with his back to the wall, he slowly pushes himself to his feet.

let bygones be bygones

*A conversation in the sanitarium at Dösen. The story of
Ernst Meurer as told by Renate and Martin Meurer. Dr.
Barbara Holitzschek takes it all down. What becomes of love.
A wife killed in an accident and a hitchhiker in love.*

"But why?" Renate Meuer asked, taking a deep breath as if to con-
tinue, then holding it—her hands pressed together between her
knees. "No, not surprised. I even expected it. You don't have to be a
psychic for that, you really don't. Except..." She looked to one
side. "Well, you know," she said, "it's funny how something has to
happen before anybody does anything. Laws like this..."

"I know," Dr. Holitzschek said. "But we have to obey them.
Besides... how else would you have us handle it?"

Martin smiled. "The horse has to escape so somebody can close
the barn door."

"Well," Renate Meurer said, "we've learned that lesson." She
pulled her shoulders back and sat up straight. "I just didn't know
what *kind* of trouble he'd get into, but that something was going to
happen, that was certain." She sipped at her mineral water and set
the glass back on the desk in front of her. "It all seems logical now.
It had to be something totally idiotic, something that didn't really
matter to him. Nothing else fits, fits the order of things—I don't
know, fits the law. Nobody's going to react otherwise. That's why

I'm glad Ernst did something so stupid. And that nobody was hurt. He was a good man."

"*Was* a good man?" Martin asked.

"He really was!"

"You said he *was* a good man. Ernst is alive."

"I know that. But I can still say Ernst was a good man. What's so awful about that?"

"Nothing," Martin said.

"A real *chelovek*, as the Russians say. Does that suit you better? Martin's not pleased with me of late."

Without turning aside, Dr. Holitzschek took her cardigan from the back of the chair and pulled it on over her short-sleeved medical smock, which was a size or two too big for her.

"I was twenty-seven when I married the second time," Renate Meurer said. "Ernst really liked kids. Martin was eight, Pit six. I didn't want any more children. He accepted that, even though his son from his first marriage had died by then. Ernst had only one condition, that there wasn't to be any connection to my first husband. When Hans wrote us a letter, we sent it back, packages too. I thought I owed that to Ernst. He wasn't allowed to have contacts with the West."

"Your first husband is . . ."

"He assumed," Martin said, "that once he'd gone over, we'd follow."

"If you stay away like that, you've decided to turn your back on the children, too, that was always Ernst's opinion. At first I thought, Ernst only wants me because he's been ordered to, to keep us from going over. But I didn't want to leave. And I liked him. And he wasn't all that wrong, either."

"Not wrong about what?" Martin asked.

"You know what I mean. Don't start in again. . . ." She stared at the desk in front of her. "Money is worse than the Party sometimes. It certainly wasn't the fault of people like Ernst. And if you want to change things, he always said, then you can't just stand back, you have to join the Party. And it might've been the right thing too. . . . Can't I say that?"

"Your mother—"

"Sure you can," Martin said. "I didn't mean to . . . I'm sorry but—"

"As a school principal you're not a private person. That's true the world over. There are some things you have to make sure get done even if you don't like them."

"Nobody's arguing that," Martin said, and turned to Dr. Holitzschek. "What did you mean just now about how he first has to . . . Have you—calmed him down?"

"We haven't done anything yet. He was brought to us last night just as he was." She tugged at her cardigan.

"And what do you think he—"

"I can't say anything yet."

"But—"

"Not a thing. This first has to go to the health commissioner and then be forwarded to a judge. And then we'll see. I only know that he's not the only case. That's all."

"He'll be staying on here?"

"For a few days, certainly."

"Days?" Renate Meurer asked.

"And then? Can we . . ." Martin fell silent when she shook her head. "I understand," he said.

"It's all really very clear," Renate Meurer said. "We shouldn't delude ourselves. I know what's wrong with him. That's what makes it so difficult. The worst thing is that I know exactly what's going on inside, in here. I know exactly."

"Excuse me," Dr. Holitzschek said, responding to a knock. She opened the door, which had been slightly ajar, and spoke softly to someone, nodding. Her ponytail, held in three velvet rings spaced at regular intervals, swung to and fro at her back.

"What do you think of the place?" Renate Meurer whispered.

"It's been renovated at least," Martin said.

"Yes, whole thing's in tip-top shape."

"I'm sorry," Dr. Holitzschek said, sitting back down. "I interrupted you. . . ."

"I lived through it all, step by step." Renate Meurer drew a set of stairs in the air. "Day by day. I just assumed it would end at some point." Her hand dropped. "Other people managed, after all."

"They stuck him out front," Martin said. "He always let them do that to him. He never said no when they wanted something."

"He did too say no, Martin. That's not so. If he hadn't said no—"

"But he let them stick him out front, again and again."

"When things started up in '89, he was given the job of writing a letter to the editor," Renate Meurer said.

"And Comrade Meurer wrote," Martin said.

"Only what he thought. He wrote about Hungary in '56 and about Prague in '68 and how demonstrations don't change a thing and provocateurs shouldn't count on leniency. When they started running around here, too, with their candles and their slogans, there was a poster that read: 'No Leniency for Meurer.' And then, wouldn't you know, a photograph appeared in the paper, with that same poster in it. I was afraid. I admired him for going to school the next day. I thought, at some point they'll be on our doorstep. When Martin asked if I wanted to come to Leipzig, just to have a look at it all, Ernst threw him out, banned him so to speak. And so what does Martin do, what do he and Pit do? They give us a bus trip to Italy. In February of '90, we took an illegal trip to Italy."

"For their twentieth anniversary, five days in Venice, Florence, and Assisi," Martin said. "Just to get their minds on other things."

"And?" Dr. Holitzschek asked when they didn't go on.

"You've got to tell that part, Mother."

"Without that trip to Italy, without that letter to the editor, things would have turned out different. At least that's how I see it at times. He let a teacher go once because a student had written '*Ex oriente Bolshevism*,' on his homework notebook. They accused the teacher of knowing about it—because in the same notebook his signature was on an invitation to a recent parent-teachers meeting. That was in '78, or thereabouts. Our Christian Democrats had just had a convention in Dresden, and their slogan had been: *Ex oriente lux* or *pax,* or whatever. And so Ernst had to act, on orders from the top, from way at the top! He wasn't a firebrand. And who was on that same bus but this Schubert."

"Zeus?" Dr. Holitzschek asked, squinting one eye.

Renate Meurer nodded.

"Ah," Dr. Holitzschek said. "Didn't he die a year or two ago?"

"He never even got hurt by all that back then. He found a——"

"What do you mean didn't get hurt, Mother? Three years mining coal. On probation, serving the national economy."

"Other people work there their whole lives. . . . He found a job at the museum afterwards, education department. It's what he always wanted, you said so yourself. He and Martin knew each other."

"I saw him now and then. He was always around, at every gallery opening. Everybody knows everybody in this town."

"Excuse me, but what actually happened to Zeus, to Herr Schubert?"

Renate Meurer shook her head.

"Outside Assisi," Martin said, "the bus broke down. And Zeus went bonkers. Giotto was his idol. And there was Assisi within his grasp, and he had to turn back. He just lost it, I'd call it culture shock. There is such a thing, right? The GDR mentality—the feeling he'd never ever get there again."

"He really laid into Ernst, both barrels, in front of everybody. It was so pointless." Renate Meurer gingerly rubbed her inflamed right earlobe. "The worst thing was, though, that Tino, his grandson, wouldn't have anything to do with him. Ernst was such a doting grandpa. Tino is difficult, very difficult."

"My son," Martin said.

"Tino's mother was killed in an accident, in October of '92. And since then—since then Tino only talks to other kids, to kids and to his aunt. He doesn't respond to other people, not even to Martin. And now that he's going to start school—that could be a real problem."

"On a bike? Is she . . . is your wife the lady on the bike . . . ?"

"You remember it?" Renate Meurer asked. "It was in the papers, hit-and-run."

"She'd just learned to ride a bike," Martin said.

"Martin blames himself, you see. . . ."

"Mother . . ."

". . . I say, you break your neck, you're dead on the spot. But he keeps worrying and wondering if maybe she could've been saved. . . ."

"If your wife's neck was broken, then she died instantly."

"You see, dead on the spot."

"And if it is a cause of worry . . ." Dr. Holitzschek said, and twirled a button on her cardigan. Then she pressed a hand to her chest, at the neckline of her smock, leaned out over the desk, picked up her rimless glasses from on top of a journal, put them on, flipped to a new page in the ring notebook in front of her, and began writing.

"Martin gave Tino a dog, a fox terrier," Renate Meurer said. "Ernst thought that we were trying to turn the boy against him, that that was why we'd bought the dog, because he's allergic to dog hair."

Dr. Holitzschek went on writing.

"Tell the story in order, Mother. All that happened a lot later."

"The newspaper threw mud at him," Renate Meurer said. "And Zeus was behind it, I'm certain. They rehashed the whole story about Zeus, but as if the Party hadn't even existed, as if Ernst had contrived the whole thing, made the decision all on his own. The article appeared in '90, the week before Easter. Then came the

Committee of Inquiry that he had to appear before. The worst scoundrels were on the committee. People were forced to resign, one after the other. We got anonymous letters. The worst part was the declarations of solidarity, all anonymous too."

"He made a mistake," Martin said. "You see, he resigned on his own. After the article in the paper, he wrote a letter of resignation, in hopes—I guess—that somebody would try to stop it, that someone would say what really happened. Of course nobody lifted a finger. Surprise! Ernst just lost control of himself for a moment. If he'd 've put it to a vote of confidence—he would've squeaked through, I'm pretty sure he would. But this way they all figured he'd worked for the Stasi. Why else would he resign, voluntarily? And bang, there he sat, with no job and everybody going out of their way to avoid him. He resigned from the Party too, because they hadn't uttered a peep either. Perfectly logical, they're not going to incriminate themselves. All he would've had to do was wait. The new district superintendent of education would've bailed him out, and if not, would've given him early retirement. Ernst made a mess of it all by himself."

"That's not so, Martin. You know what it was like once that article appeared. They even threatened you too. Why would you say such things? They gave it to Ernst with both barrels, he was easy game. Nobody took his part. Nobody said a word."

"Did he defend himself? Did your husband do anything on his own behalf?"

"What was he supposed to do? It all happened so fast, and suddenly it was over. Suddenly nobody was interested anymore. Main thing was money and a job, an apartment and a Eurocheck card, getting a handle on new forms and laws. Didn't care beans about anything else. That's what did him in. That and Tino." Renate Meurer blew her nose.

"Would you like another sip of water?" Dr. Holitzschek asked. "Or you?" Without laying her pen aside, she unscrewed the cap with her left hand and filled both glasses, by turns, until the bottle was empty.

"Thanks," Renate Meurer said. "After I was let go by Textima, I worked for a man who up until the very end . . . I'd rather not say what he was, but an apparatchik in any case—and now he has an accounting and tax-consulting office, not the sole owner, but he's the boss. He's intelligent and he rolled up his sleeves, really dug in. His motto is: Chickenshit's manure too. Neugebauer just grinned when people talked about cronyism when he hired me—because actually I'm a statistician. He hired me and grinned them down until Ernst started blackmailing him. Ernst put together a report about himself, about Neugebauer, and a couple of others, he knew them all. Everybody was supposed to sign, with a copy to be sent to all the papers. I learned about it from Neugebauer. I didn't understand what Neugebauer wanted me to do, what it was I was supposed to put a stop to. The embarrassing thing was that he offered us his weekend place in the Harz for the whole summer, free of charge. What a nice thing to do, I thought. I thought: That will get Ernst out again. He was just sitting around the house. When I was home he dogged my every step. We took a bus out to the place, I had to go back—and the next day there he was at the door, grousing and playing the victim, as if I were trying to get rid of him. Then he gave up our garden, it was under his name. We should let nature take care of itself, he said. I cried, because of the strawberries, it had been an oasis. By then I absolutely knew he had a screw loose. But I thought, Time heals all wounds."

"I have to interrupt here," Dr. Holitzschek said. "There was nothing in the papers back then?"

"Why should there be? When the last Free German Youth boss gets rich arranging contracts for construction firms, he's already in bed with the devil. They're all successful businessmen who create the jobs and place the ads. Why should the papers open their mouths? Let bygones be bygones," Renate Meurer said.

"Neugebauer wanted to know if I'd lodge a protest if he laid me off, giving downsizing as the official reason. That way at least, I could start drawing unemployment right away. Ernst met me at the door with champagne. At that point I was ready to sue for divorce. Two months later I found a new job, near Stuttgart. Ernst called me a traitor. Not in the political sense. He phoned me twice, three times, every day—the bill came to six, seven hundred marks a month, totally crazy. Even though he was offered a job himself. Tutors for Kids wanted him. He'd always been a good teacher, no doubt about it, nobody ever claimed otherwise. But he thought filling out applications was beneath his dignity. He was suddenly all concerned about dignity and pride. I filled out all the forms for the Welfare Office. New ones every year. They can strip you naked, let me tell you, absolutely naked. They even wanted to know what his father had earned—he never came back from the war. Ernst never even knew him! They end up knowing more than the Stasi."

"Mother," Martin said. "Just because the offices are in the same building as—"

"Well, that just makes it worse. Sitting there in the big Stasi villa. And then there's his health—rheumatism, ringing in his ears, fevers. When he came home from the doctor, he looked at me like he'd taken a bullet in the gut. Cancer or the like, I thought. No wonder it's taking its toll on him. And Ernst says, 'Healthy. Not even a spot on my lungs.' He was insulted when I wanted him to see a psychiatrist." Renate Meurer stared at the tissue in her hands.

"We play chess together," Martin said, "once a week. All he wants to do is play chess, nothing else."

"Doesn't want to talk?"

"Just small talk. I don't want to upset him, and he's the same with me, although there's nothing that could. Except when I decided to be baptized. For him that was like joining the CDU or whatever, like deserting to the enemy—to 'history's winners.' "

"You've never asked him anything?"

"About what?"

"What crime did he commit?" Renate Meurer asked. "In the stairwell at the Unemployment Office, where they have that safety net stretched—with a red scarf in it, so everyone can see it and not even be tempted to try—we ran into one another, Schubert and Ernst. I usually went with him when he still had to report to the Unemployment Office. He won't go to the Welfare Office alone, period. I always have to go with him there."

"Your husband spoke to Herr Schubert, did he?"

"There was no chance. Schubert ran away. He wanted to be certified as a 'victim of political discrimination,' with official title and documents. We didn't know that. He didn't even want to talk. Really funny, the people you run into there. I always think of that stairwell whenever I hear the phrase 'social safety net.'"

"Social hammock," Martin said.

"Afterward we went to the in-store café at Volkstädt for coffee, a strawberry torte or gooseberry meringue. Volkstädt was our one luxury. And then straight home. All the same, Ernst started keeping an appointment calendar. He wanted to know everything a month ahead. I would sit down with him as if he were a child going over his class schedule with me. And if I asked him anything, he first had to pull out his calendar and check it. 'Got it,' he'd say, and write in a time, an address, and both first and last names, even if it was only to visit Martin. I once asked Ernst if there wasn't at least something he liked to remember that had happened after '89. He looked straight at me and said, 'I've never liked to remember anything I experienced all alone'—as if the children and I, as if we all didn't even exist."

"Is he interested in anything on television? Does he read, go for walks? What does he do?"

"He used to read Fallada's books with the kids, the *Tales from Murkyland* or *That Rascal, Fridolin*. I gave him two parakeets for his birthday. He tried to teach them to talk. They're probably too old for that. He took it personally. He takes absolutely everything personally. Once some tulips I brought home didn't open up. I secretly bought new ones, because otherwise he'd think it was his fault. And he got so meticulous. No sooner had we finished supper than he'd set the table for breakfast, and there was hell to pay if I didn't wash a glass the minute I was done with it. And the noises he made eating . . . He slurped and snorted. He never used to be like that. And then there was the renovation. The renovation is probably what pushed him over the edge. We draped sheets over everything. It looked like Lenin's study. Ernst even made jokes about it. For the first few days he just stood around in the way. But as soon as the project went over the budgeted time, he started to complain. Ernst demanded that the workers take off their shoes, kept cleaning up behind them every five minutes, and finally wouldn't even open the apartment door to them. They were already done with their next job, and we were still missing three window frames. I had to use some of my vacation so they could get into the apartment. And when it was over, he claimed that the people who'd moved into the building after the renovation were using our welcome mat. He would stand at the peephole and then fling open the door whenever anybody went past. Kids threw garbage and dead mice through our windows or onto our balcony. They were afraid of him."

The telephone rang. Dr. Holitzschek said "Yes" several times and "Fine" and "Sorry" when she hung up.

"The people upstairs don't mean to be unpleasant," Renate Meurer said, "but they're home all day, they're young, you know. They even invited me in. The music wasn't all that loud. It's the bass that does it. If you lay your hands on our dining room table, you can feel it. Ernst sits there in his cave the whole day and reacts like an animal that's being teased. It's bound to exhaust you at some point. I can understand that. You don't have to be a psychic for that."

"All I've seen is the police report," Dr. Holitzschek said.

"They stormed the apartment. Five men in bulletproof vests and all the rest of it. They stormed it, in a regular assault."

"Just because they couldn't tell the difference between an air gun and the real thing," Martin said.

"Didn't anyone call you?"

"Only afterwards," he said.

"And you?"

Renate Meurer shook her head.

"The police didn't call you?"

"No," Renate Meurer said.

"What does it say in the report?" Martin asked.

"He fired a shot with an air gun in the stairwell, threatened to use force to get some peace and quiet if he had to, and then holed up in the apartment," Dr. Holitzschek said. "Fortunately he didn't offer any resistance."

"I can't give up everything just for his sake. I'm going to have to work for at least seven years yet, maybe even twelve. If I'd come home from Stuttgart, I'd be admitting Ernst is right. I can't quit my job on his account. That's what he wants. He must realize it won't work. No one behaves like he has, no one. I'm his wife, not his kindergarten teacher. If he can't get that into his head, I'll divorce him."

"You said you understood him, didn't you, Frau Meurer?"

"Of course, yes. I understand him, that's my point. But we've got to move on from here."

"Which means," Dr. Holitzschek said, "once he's released—"

"When will that be?" Renate Meurer asked.

"—he'll be living alone during the week, at least for now?"

Renate Meurer stared at her tissue and said nothing.

"Fine," Dr. Holitzschek.

"He can move in with me," Martin said.

"No, Martin. That's stupid. That would be really stupid. You won't help him that way. You have to worry about work. You can't sit around the house and look after Ernst. Besides, he wouldn't even want to, and Tino would never come to see you then."

"A lot of people live alone," Dr. Holitzschek said. "That doesn't mean no one looks after them. He wouldn't be left all alone."

"I was just saying that Ernst can live with me if he wants."

"Fine," Dr. Holitzschek said, and wrote.

"Martin . . ."

"Everything's in here," he said, and pointed to a bag. "Toilet articles, underwear, bathrobe, wallet, and so on."

"No belts, scissors, files, pocketknives, no razor blades?"

"Will he have his own room?"

"No."

"He mustn't know I was here. The flowers are from Martin." The telephone rang. "You won't tell him I've been here, will you?"

"If that's what you want."

"And when can we talk to him?" Martin asked. He laid the manicure kit and razor on the desk.

"Tomorrow, maybe the day after. But you need to call ahead."

Martin nodded. He crumpled up the flower wrapping paper lying beside his chair. The telephone went on ringing.

When neither Martin nor Renate Meurer got up, Dr. Holitzschek said, "Fine, then," and stood up. She pulled back a curtain concealing a washbasin, washed her hands, dried them slowly, and dabbed a little perfume behind her earlobes.

The soles of Martin's shoes squeaked on the flooring. The two women's footsteps were inaudible. Patients in street clothes and slippers or sneakers were seated around tables. A smock-clad attendant had joined them for a game of Parcheesi. Dr. Holitzschek pushed the ward door open with her shoulder and stood in front of it.

"We'll see you soon," she said, letting the other two past.

"Thank you," Renate Meurer said, and held out a hand. Dr. Holitzschek shook first her hand, then Martin's. "I'm needed up there," she said. Hands in her smock pockets, she hurried up the stairs. The heels of her shoes echoed off the stone treads. The ward door closed with a soft click.

"You shouldn't have said that, Martin, that part about history's winners. Her husband is in the Landtag. . . ."

They walked through the hospital park toward the main entrance.

"People here are either young or old," Renate Meurer said. "There's no one in between, is there?"

"Your parakeets chatter the whole day long," Martin said. "'Good morning, Renate.' 'Bon appétit, Renate.'"

"Really?"

"Hello, good night, sweet dreams. What shall we do today? Renate, Renate, Renate. They go on like that all day."

"Funny," she said, and stopped in her tracks. "What else?" She took a ruby red earring from her purse and attached it to her inflamed earlobe.

"You have to listen for a while to catch it," Martin said, who had wadded the flower wrapping paper into a ball the size of an egg. A woman with a black-and-red-checked bag was coming toward them.

"The next bus isn't until five-fifteen, we don't have to run," Martin said. He threw the wad of paper into the air and caught it with his other hand.

"Do you despise me?" she asked without looking at him. "You've become so stern—is it because of this?" She tugged at a strand of hair.

"The dye job?"

"Because I didn't tell the Holitzschek woman anything . . . about . . . He gave me these earrings."

"Look good on you. And what is the name of this great unknown admirer?"

"Who? . . . Hubertus."

"Do you really want a divorce?"

"I keep thinking I'm making a mistake. I feel so uncertain when you look at me like that. Do you think I'm being ridiculous?"

"No need to run. The bus isn't for forty minutes."

"Martin?" She linked arms with him and tried to fall into step. "There's something I have to ask you, Martin." She looked up at him. "Are you—gay? Don't laugh! I'm allowed to ask, aren't I? Why aren't you looking for a wife? You're the only man I know who doesn't at least give it a try, and Danny—"

"Danny?"

"I thought when she left that Edgar fellow . . . that the real reason was so she could move in with you, I'm sure it was. That's why she had her hair cut short, because she thought you'd like it better that way. And that woman there in her flimsy smock, Dr. Holitzschek. She was making eyes at you, too. Didn't you notice how she blushed when I was talking about Andrea's accident, didn't you see her eyes? It's really abnormal for someone like you . . . whereas Pit is so different." Martin laughed. She squeezed his arm against her. "Pit tries at least. You don't even give it a try. When there's nothing more beautiful than falling in love, absolutely nothing!"

"I know," Martin said.

"Do you think I'm being foolish? For some reason I react to the metal in this earring. Love is a power sent from heaven, he always says. That's more along your line, isn't it?"

"Who . . . oh, you mean . . ."

"Let Ernst stay where he is, Martin. You have no idea what you're getting yourself into. Who would even want you then? Volunteering for a ball-and-chain like that. And stop laughing!" She clasps a hand around his crooked arm. "Is he supposed to live in Tino's room, or where? We're not some big clan, an extended Stone Age family." She rested her head on Martin's shoulder.

"Maybe I'll get married soon," he said as they walked through the gate.

"Are you joking?"

"Nope. Let's sit down over there." Martin pointed to the covered bus stop opposite the entrance. They crossed the street.

"Well then . . ." Renate Meurer said, and pulled him along.

"Where to now?" he asked.

She let go of him. He stood there at the bus stop. She stepped back out into the road. "I thought since there won't be another bus for—"

"Mother!" Martin shouted as she began to wave her outstretched arm. The car, a red four-door Audi, slowed down, but then picked up speed again and raced past.

"Stop it! We'll wait!" Martin bent down for the wad of paper that had fallen at his feet.

"Want to bet?" Renate Meurer shouted without turning around to look at her son. "Bet you anything this one stops." She walked slowly along, waving her arm, staring at the onrushing dark blue car, and whispered, "Please, please!"

CHAPTER 23

sign-off

*How Christian Beyer swears that Hanni has misunderstood
his plans. Everything is suddenly different. A tortured entrepreneur and a corrupt civil servant. Just because receipts are
missing. Close your eyes—maybe it will be fun. A train trip
in a silent night.*

"It's not true," Beyer said. "It simply isn't true, Hanni, please." He
threw his coat on the couch.

"Come here, Hanni, stop crying. There's no reason for tears,
absolutely no reason." He slipped out of his jacket and put it
around her. She had stopped at the living room door, was standing
there in her black cape, her feet close together, one hand to her
mouth.

"All I can tell you is that it isn't true, that you've completely
misunderstood. That's all. That's it, the end."

Her handbag was still dangling from the crook of her left
arm.

"It isn't true! How many times do I have to say it? *I'm* the one
who ought to be angry. *I'm* the one who ought to hit the ceiling,
because *you* assume I'd do such a thing. This is all backwards. Why
don't you believe me?"

Although Hanni's hand was pressed to her mouth, her sobs
were louder now. She took a few steps back, and as she turned
around, her handbag fell onto the runner in the entrance hall. She

charged for the bathroom, slammed the door, and locked it behind her.

Beyer immediately heard the sound of water splashing in the basin, then the toilet flushed. He picked up the handbag, pushed the telephone and the little lamp to one side of the end table, and laid it down there.

He got a pack of cigarettes and some matches from his jacket. Before he sat down on the couch, he hooked one finger in the ashtray and slid it across the glass coffee table toward him.

Beyer asked himself what tie he was wearing. Sometimes names would slip his mind, or a whole day in the previous week. As if someone else had taken his place in the boss's office at the newspaper. He fingered the knot, slid his hand down to the tip of his tie, and lifted it. Actually, he didn't like this blue one with the yellow squares. But he couldn't wear the same tie every day.

He thought of Hanni, of her trembling chin and her little scream that had begun like a sigh, or a moan. He tapped the bottom of his pack of Marlboro Lights. He held the match right below the head. Elbows on knees, he began to smoke.

Beyer picked up the remote. The Dow Jones and the DAX were on the rise again. For every dollar he now had to pay forty pfennigs more than he had during their trip to New York. He wedged his cigarette in a notch on the ashtray and stood up. He squatted down in front of the bathroom door and peered through the keyhole. All he could see was a bright spot, but nothing that appeared to move across it.

"Hanni," he called. The water was still splashing in the basin. She must have turned the tap on full-force. He waited, his head lowered, and then returned to the couch. He took another drag on his cigarette, stubbed it out, and sank back, spreading his arms and laying the back of his head against the top of the couch. The cold leather on the nape of his neck made him shiver. He could feel goose bumps even on his thighs.

Beyer looked at the ceiling and at the souvenirs on the top shelf of the wall unit. He gazed for a long time at the big-bellied wooden bottle he'd bought in Plovdiv, and tried to reconstruct how the flower-petal pattern had been executed with a compass. Next to it was a blue-and-white Romanian jug which actually belonged in the kitchen but wouldn't have fit on top of the cupboard. The brass candelabrum had been given to him by the children of a neighbor after she died—a thank-you for late-night runs to the emergency pharmacy. He had accepted it with its seven dust-covered red candles already burned halfway down. Farther to the right was a white globe-shaped vase with a tiny gaudy lantern dangling over its edge, a glass mug with a pewter base and lid, and finally the right-side speaker. Beyer closed his eyes. With his right heel he nudged off his left shoe, wanted to slip the right one off, too, but was afraid the shoe heel would soil his sock.

Beyer started at the sound of a key turning in the bathroom door. He wasn't sure how long it had been quiet now. Hanni was carrying her cape draped over her arm. Her shoes hung from two fingers. She pressed her thumbs on the bottom bin beside the hall wardrobe and put the shoes away. Then she took a long time arranging her cape on a hanger.

"Hanni," said Beyer. He was standing just at the threshold to the living room, the remote still in his hand. The only thing moving was toes inside the blue sock on his left foot. Hanni walked toward him and halted right in front of him. He took her in his arms.

"Sweetheart," he whispered, "my dearest darling sweetheart." She leaned against him, so that he had to take a step back. He had turned the television off.

"Why should we be spared really?" Hanni asked now. "We've been spared until now, that's all, simple good luck, incredible good . . ."

He pressed her to him.

"We both lead charmed lives, you know," Hanni said when she was able to speak again. "We thought this sort of thing just doesn't exist anymore, at least not here with us, that it was extinct, like feudalism. We've just been spared it, that's all."

"Come here," Beyer said, and kissed her forehead. He walked to the couch. The remote fell to the carpet. "Come here." He took Hanni by her wrists. She let him pull her sideways onto his lap.

"It'd be crazy not to do it. It's no big deal." She threw her arms around his neck.

"Don't talk," he said.

"I don't know why I'm so upset. You can turn the TV on every night and see a story like this. Really. Maybe not every night, but almost."

"What are you talking about?" Beyer looked at Hanni's painted white toenails. There was a run in her right stocking that started at the middle toe and came up over the instep.

"There was a great movie about it, an American movie, way back in the deepest GDR days. Some kids, college students, started speculating in pork bellies. And of course it went sour right off, and he had to drive a cab. She stayed at home and decided she had to do something, too. That's how she got started. The gag was that he drove one of her johns to their place, and he thought, Okay, why not check in at home. That was the real gag. But it turned out in the end that pork bellies were the right tip after all. A great comedy." She leaned to one side and tugged at the cord of the table lamp. "Do you know what I always think back on when things get bad? To last Christmas, when we were in the supermarket and there was that blackbird perched in the vegetables. And those guys came along with a landing net and tried to catch it." She ran splayed fingers through her hair, making it stand up. "I thought, Why doesn't somebody do something? They'll chase that poor panicked bird around till it dies of exhaustion. We just left our shopping cart where it was, and you went to the manager's office.

And he didn't even know what was going on. And when he asked you what you thought he ought to do, you said, 'Turn off the lights, open the doors, but leave a light on at the entrance, it's that simple.'"

"But he didn't do it." Beyer brushed a strand of hair back behind her ear.

"I don't know anyone who would've knocked on a supermarket manager's door to help a bird. That's why I love you. And when I think that all your hard work could be for nothing. You don't even know what it means anymore to spend a quiet evening at home."

"That's going to change, Hanni. Believe me. And I'm not just saying that."

"Do you know what else I've been thinking? Power leads straight to blackmail. And it seems perfectly normal to people with power."

He held the strand of hair in place behind her ear. His other hand brushed along her calf.

Hanni pushed his tie up over his shoulder and pressed her middle finger to the buttons of his shirt, one after the other. "He just scribbles his signature. And once he's done that, he'll be gone, won't he? That'll take care of it. That'll end it, for good and all."

"Just forget about it now, Hanni. . . ."

"And he's alone. He is alone, isn't he?"

"Of course."

"And he's the only one who has to sign his name?"

"The only one."

"You see! Then we've got him. Then it's actually *us* who've got him. . . ."

"Hanni! It's not my fault. If only he hadn't gone over the ledger from '91. He's not even allowed to do it now. I depended on other people. I didn't know anything about keeping books, you know? And nothing really happened, nothing illegal, no fraud. But nobody believes me. What with all the chaos, nobody will believe me that it was all on the up-and-up—because the receipts are missing. The receipts aren't there, but that's the only thing that's wrong."

"I know," she said. "You don't have to justify yourself to me."

"It's just my own incompetence, Hanni. I shouldn't even have taken it on. That was my mistake, taking it on. I never should've got involved in an enterprise like this. I even offered him money."

"Gamblers love to gamble," she said. "I know what all you do for me. Everything you do you do for us. Without you . . ."

"Hanni," he said, and leaned back. Beyer could feel his eyes moisten.

"Come on," she said. "You once explained it to me. You said you feel like a fly, a fly caught between the window and the curtains. I thought it was a funny way to put it at the time. You said that the fly can save itself only by accident, by doing something counter-intuitive, because its own logic says that it can get through the win-dowpane. And it doesn't stop until it's dead. Remember?"

"Yes," he said. "It never stops, and everybody's watching you."

"I wanted to shoo the fly away and was amazed it wouldn't budge. I don't know why you always find dead flies lying on their backs. This one was lying on its stomach, or standing, I guess, propping itself up with its proboscis. And that's when you made the comparison."

"I want to fly away somewhere with you, Hanni, anywhere it's warm. For a week at least. Let's do it, what do you say?" He sat up.

"When's he coming?"

"He's here. He's been back since Monday—and is staying till Friday, at the Park Hotel, Room 212."

"And when would we get a flight?"

"Tomorrow, Friday, or Saturday, at the last minute, whatever we can get."

"On Saturday?"

"If you want." He stroked the back of her neck.

"Yes," Hanni said. "Once it's all over, I'll just close my eyes and think about you." She sat up straight. "Maybe it'll even be fun—if I'm thinking about you." She smiled and slipped off his lap. "Room 212?"

"Yes," he said, "The Park Hotel."

"And what's his name?"

"Room 212."

"I'll be right back," she said, giving the lamp cord another tug, and returned to the bathroom.

Beyer bent forward, took off his right shoe, and picked up the remote. He watched an oompah-pah band with the mute on, men dressed in green knickers. The audience sat at long tables and raised their beer glasses to the panning camera. Two large-eyed women smiled at each other as they sang.

Beyer walked over to the wall unit, picked up a brandy bottle between his thumb and forefinger, and hooked a cognac glass with his pinkie. He poured as he walked, chugged the brandy, and exhaled loudly. He fetched a second glass and poured them both half full. Then he took his shoes and coat out to the hall wardrobe.

Reentering the living room, he loosened his tie and pulled it off over his head. He took off his pants and, holding them by the crease, laid them over a chair. He hid his socks under the pant legs. He hung his shirt and undershirt over the chair back.

Beyer gave his underpants a glance and took them off. He tossed them in the air with his right foot, like a juggler with a ball, and tucked them between his shirt and undershirt. He turned off the lights in the living room and laid his watch on the coffee table.

The cold leather upholstery excited him. He watched his penis in the flickering light of the TV and carefully fingered his testicles.

Beyer surfed the channels, came back full circle to the folk music, and started around again. There was a soccer match in black-and-white on the local channel. He turned the sound on, watched the green volume bars multiply, but heard nothing. He took out a cigarette, but made a broad gesture that sent it rolling across the glass coffee table.

"Roland Ducke," someone said very loud. "No tiring him out today, either." Beyer now heard stadium background noise. The players' shorts were very short and tight, the crowd was barely visible in the shadows. "Well, sports fans at home. We're getting close to the end of the first half here at Central Stadium." Beyer recognized the voice of Heinz-Florian Oertel. "GDR–England 0:0" was superimposed in white letters across the bottom of the screen. From a chair Beyer picked up the blanket that Hanni always wrapped around herself when she watched TV at night, shook it open, and pulled it over his shoulders as he lay down.

The telephone rang. Beyer knelt on the couch, a corner of the blanket in his left hand, the receiver in his right. "Hello, Beyer here," he said automatically. He could hear guitar music in the background. He said "Hello?" again, then whoever it was hung up. He had slept for almost two hours.

On the TV screen Jürgen Frohriep was bent over a desk, his arms extended wide. He was looking up at a young woman who slowly raised her head and said something.

Beyer turned on the light. Hanni's handbag was gone. He walked through the apartment naked. The bedspread was turned down, a nightie lay on her pillow. The bathroom door was ajar. He looked everywhere, even in the pantry.

Beyer emptied one of the glasses. His feet were ice-cold. He surfed the channels. He was looking for an empty screen of snow, like those that always used to light up the whole room after sign-off. For a while he watched a train move through a summer meadow. The camera must have been mounted on the engine. He waited for something to happen. He surfed on and landed at the train again. The train kept going across a flat landscape, a few trees, no houses, no people either. The only sound was a kind of rumble, low and hollow, as if someone were trundling a huge barrel. There was no sign of the locomotive. A few railroad ties lay on the embankment.

Beyer emptied the second glass, too, and stretched out under the blanket, his head turned away from the television. It was still warm where he had been lying before. It was cold only when he tried turning over completely on his stomach or back. He thought he could hear the panting of the steam locomotive, the rhythmic banging of the wheels at each joint in the tracks.

Beyer suddenly wanted to see what landscape his train was moving through at the moment. He was about to roll over and look out the window when it occurred to him that it was the middle of the night, black as pitch out there. He had to sneeze, so he pulled the blanket up and wiped his nose with it. He moved his toes a little now and then. But otherwise he lay perfectly still.

CHAPTER 24

full moon

Pit Meurer tells about the end of an office party. Peter Bertram and he look up Hanni's skirt. Plans for getting home. Marianne Schubert appears in the role of an Amazon. A knight is born, a love affair begins, and an attempted payoff fails.

Kuzinski, who owns the advertising weekly I work for, had rented the family party room at the Toscana and was playing DJ again. His wife had shown up in a white wraparound with silver trim and started dancing right off, but usually alone. And all the while she made a face as if she were doing a guitar riff and wiggled her hips, snaking her arms upward and running her fingers through her hair.

There was no easy way to ignore Kuzinski's coaxing, so we practiced the duck dance he'd played several times the year before. The five women from layout and reception downed three bottles of Baltic Fog, then ordered two bottles of batida de coco and vanished with them.

Bertram arrived very late and was greeted over the address system as "Lucky Thirteen." When Kuzinski called out a polonaise and his wife made steam locomotive motions with her arms and started running around in circles, Bertram showed real character by slipping off to the john. I didn't understand why Eddie had been fired and Bertram, an out-of-work teacher, had been hired. The vertical crease between his eyebrows gave him a look of perpetual concentration. Kuzinski handled him like a raw egg.

I was trying to get drunk so I could make a try at sleep later, despite the full moon. The later this goes, the better, I thought. Kuzinski had demonstrated several times with deadly seriousness how you're supposed to drink tequila, slurping his thumb vigorously with each swig. Later he shook everyone's hand and had his wife drive him home.

By twelve-thirty only Bertram and I were left behind with an almost full bottle of calvados that somebody—I didn't know who—had ordered. We moved up front to the restaurant, where I often ate my lunch. Half an hour later, the last guests there had left as well. Only the woman at the table for two near the kitchen door was still sitting alone. She was slim and stylishly dressed in a short black skirt and blazer. Propping her arms on the table, she stared into her empty wineglass. Her purse was hung over the back of her chair.

When Bertram came back from the john, he went over to her and fed her some line, pointing at me twice. She barely raised her head.

"She's crying," he said as he slid in beside me to keep a better eye on her. Franco served her a large shimmering blue brandy glass of grappa, turned around with her empty wineglass on his tray, and gave us a wink.

Bertram made a couple of remarks about Kuzinski and his wife. To change the subject, I asked him about fishing. Bertram took an evening train every Friday to get to the banks of the Rhine or the Neckar or the Twente Canal in Holland by morning, to spots where power stations draw off their water for cooling. In the middle of his story he asked, "You like the looks of that chick?"

"She'd do," I said, and he nodded and went on talking. Bertram explained how you go after carp, talked about boilies, about real action and the fight at the net, about white water and how to play carp, and didn't stop until the woman stood up. She was in her mid-thirties maybe. She stalked in high heels to the telephone— she must've already put away quite a bit. All she had on under that blazer was a silk blouse.

Receiver in hand, she fed it her coin, dialed, and without saying a word hung up again. Maybe she'd misdialed. Her money was gone at any rate. She looked again for some coins in a small black purse. And then it happened: she dropped a fifty-pfennig piece or a mark. She paid no attention and dialed. This time she talked, but what with the music—Franco loves guitars more than anything else—and the fact that she had her back to us, we couldn't understand any of it. After she'd hung up, she bent down to the coins at her feet without going into a crouch.

"Wow!" Bertram said. We stared at her pink panties. "Wow!" he said again as she stood up. "Tasty stuff, huh?"

With the bottle of grappa in hand, Franco followed close behind her to her table, waited till she sat down, and poured the big-bellied glass a quarter full.

She held Franco back with one hand and demonstrated with thumb and forefinger of the other that he should pour more. But he stuck to his standard shot. She chugged the grappa. Before pouring any more, he made a mark on the beer coaster in front of her.

"She drinks like a fish," Bertram said, "like a fish."

Franco held the bottle up and made another mark.

"Pit," Bertram said. Then he began to lay out his plan to me. He spoke very calmly and looked me straight in the eye. Although I didn't answer or nod, the idea seemed plausible to me, or relevant at least. Every now and then he would say, "If it works, it works, if not, then not." He said, "It'll be fun, for all three, just plain fun, Pit, you'll see. But if you don't want to . . ." He said, "She doesn't drink, she guzzles. Like a fish."

Neither of us was sober by then. I listened to Bertram talk and watched Franco and the woman in the pink panties, those tiny pink panties under her skirt. Bertram held his hand over his glass when I tried to give him a refill. It was a really dumb situation.

"*Finito,*" Franco said. The woman turned around to him and got up, or rather braced herself on the table to stand up. She managed the first few steps more or less steadily, then brushed against a chair, bumped into the next one, and halted. She looked around, gave her skirt a tug, and stalked in the direction of the phone.

"See those lips?" Bertram asked. "Powerful lips." He pursed his own as if imitating a carp and waved to her. "She won't even remember that," he said.

She laid the receiver on top of the phone and thrust several marks into the slot.

"We've spoken before," Bertram said, "years ago, when she was still head of the Natural History Museum."

"And what if she calls a cab?" I asked.

Bertram beamed at me. Even that didn't smooth the crease between his eyebrows. "Then *we'll* play taxi for her." He laid his hand on my forearm and squeezed. "Know how they used to do it, during the war? The skirt up over the head, and then someone sat on it, on the head, that is." Before taking his hand away, he gave my arm another squeeze.

She waited, the receiver at her ear, her left arm propped on her hip, but turned away as she started to talk. It could've been only a few words. In the next instant she slammed the receiver down. Change fell into the coin return.

She used the backs of chairs as a railing as she walked, but suddenly lost control and plopped down into a chair at an uncleared table two tables away from her own.

Franco turned the music off and added up the bills. The only sounds came from the kitchen.

"Closing time," Bertram whispered, and pushed his glass toward me. I doled out the rest of the calvados. "Kuzinski's a generous guy," he said, "you gotta hand him that much."

Then everything happened very quickly. Hanni laid her head on the table. Franco arrived with the bill and beer coaster, bent down low to tap her and talk to her. She raised one elbow as if trying to fend him off.

"Franco!" Bertram shouted, standing up and pulling his wallet from his hip pocket.

At that same moment Marianne Schubert appeared. It had been a long time since I'd seen her.

"All over," Franco cried, "closed!"

Bertram sat back down. She walked past our table, greeted Bertram with a "Hello, Peter," and gave me a nod.

"I'll pay," she said to Franco, and had him give her the bill and the coaster.

"Now I get it," Bertram whispered. "The Amazon and Beyer's Hanni. Who would've thought it!"

"You mean *our* Beyer?" I asked.

"Precisely, his mistress and Marianne. Don't you see now why everything at Furniture Paradise ends up in Beyer's lap? I knew Marianne's husband and figured that between the two of them I could get a foot in the door at Paradise. There's some real money there. But if they're as close as this, you could stand on your head all day."

"Did you get it or not?" Hanni asked loudly. I couldn't understand Marianne's reply.

"You said you'd get one!" Hanni suddenly seemed very upset. "'In the legs,' that's what you should've said. Why didn't you tell her 'in the legs'? Just like you!" she shouted. "In the heart or the head! Just like you!"

Marianne came past us.

"Grappa, amaretto, cognac?" Franco asked. She handed him the bill and a fifty, and clasping her wallet between folded hands, she leaned against the bar.

I don't know why we stayed on. We didn't say a thing, and the bottle was empty besides. We just went on sitting there. I wondered if I should collect the change from the telephone and take it to her table.

Hanni's head lurched forward. This startled her, and she tipped a glass over. It struck the ashtray, rolled away in a long arc, fell to the floor, and lay there on the carpet. She crossed her arms and bedded her head on them, her elbows sticking way out.

"Can I help?" Bertram called out. Marianne shrugged. Franco was faster. It first looked as if he were bending down to pick up the glass. Instead, Franco took hold of Hanni behind the knees, slipped in under her left arm, and—as the chair tumbled backward—lifted her up. Marianne tried to prop up Hanni's dangling head. Meanwhile I had stood up and, after checking under her table to see if she'd left anything else, picked up her purse. Bertram was carrying her coat. We all left together.

Franco obviously had had some practice at this and had no trouble putting Hanni into the front seat after it was adjusted to recline. Bertram carefully spread Hanni's coat over her.

"Should I help get her out once you're there?" I asked, handing Marianne the purse.

"Do you live in Altenburg North?"

"Yes," I said, and wondered if Bertram might possibly know I was lying.

"Then you two don't need me anymore," he promptly said, and shook my hand firmly. "Toodle-insky, Marianne," he called out.

"Can we give you a ride?" she asked.

"No need," Bertram shouted, and waved one last time as he left.

"Ciao, Franco," I said.

Marianne drove carefully, taking curves very slowly. It had been a while since I'd squeezed into a backseat. Hanni's forehead kept slipping closer to my right knee. I watched Marianne in the rearview mirror. Our eyes met at one point, but we didn't say anything.

I stood at the entrance with Hanni in my arms while Marianne found a parking spot. I imagined how it would look to someone stepping to his window at night and seeing a guy carrying a woman around with him. I wished Hanni would come to, smile, and then go back to sleep.

Marianne, who arrived with key in hand and Hanni's coat over her shoulder, was fighting a frog in her throat. "Can you manage it, it's the fourth floor?"

I was gradually going numb in the arms.

Marianne's apartment smelled good, a little like Intershop stores used to smell. She collected a *Burda* fashion magazine, a *TV & Film,* and a green library book from the sofa. Summoning my last ounce of energy, I crouched down and carefully laid Hanni on it. Marianne told me to take off those shoes. "Her shoes, not yours!" she hissed when I loosened my shoelaces. I held Hanni's ankles firmly and easily slipped the first shoe from her heel. But with the second one I accidentally crooked her leg up and saw her panties again.

Marianne brought a blanket, tucked it in behind Hanni's shoulders and along the sides, and even wrapped her feet in it. I tied my shoes again. Hanni was breathing heavily, as if she were about to start snoring. A little bubble burst between her lips.

Marianne set a blue plastic bucket with a little water in it at the head of the couch, cleared her throat, and said, "That's that."

We sat in the kitchen, where the wall on my left was plastered with postcards. "All from my daughter," Marianne said. "Yesterday Connie called from Caracas. Would you've known offhand that Caracas is in Venezuela?"

"No," I said.

"I think Connie sometimes doesn't know herself where she is anymore," she said.

We drank tea and then coffee. I couldn't tell her how long Hanni had been sitting in the restaurant. "But long enough to get very drunk and make two phone calls," I said.

"Two?" Marianne asked. "I was lying awake and had got up to get a beer when I saw the answering machine blinking. And I took off right away."

"Alcohol's the only thing that helps when there's a full moon," I said.

"If anyone had ever told me that you'd be sitting here in my kitchen . . . I know your father, too . . . Comrade Meurer," she said. "A school principal by trade."

"He's at Dösen now," I said.

"At Dösen? I saw him myself at most two or three times, back then," Marianne said. "But did you know that there was no one who was a greater subject of conversation here around this table than your father? You do believe me, don't you?"

I nodded. I wanted to tell her that Ernst wasn't my real father at all. But she would've probably taken that wrong.

We ate pretzel sticks with our coffee and talked about how scary things were and how a lot of people were afraid even to go out after dark anymore, which was little short of hysteria.

"You just have to look at the doors to people's apartments," I said, "and all the locks they have now."

"Recently, when I'm alone in the furniture store at night," she began, "I've started being afraid, too. That hasn't happened for a long time. People who are afraid have something to lose. So I can't be as bad off as I think, otherwise I wouldn't really care. And I didn't for a while there. But now I often think it'll happen any second, they'll burst in and clean the place out. But that doesn't mean they'll let me have a gun permit." She stifled a yawn. "The psychologist, there's always a psychologist on the panel, she asked what I'd do if someone came at me. I said, shoot. But at what, she wanted to know. Then I said there's only two spots you can be sure about, the heart and the head. You'd really shoot, she said. Of course, I said, what else? She said I couldn't have a gun permit, that she couldn't recommend it, that her guidelines prohibited her from recommending it. I said thanks. At least that made things nice and clear."

Marianne picked up the last two pretzel sticks and offered me one. The other disappeared into her mouth, slow and steady. She chewed it thoroughly and then ran her tongue across her teeth.

"Well look who's here!" she cried. Hanni was standing in the door, rubbing her right heel across the instep of her other foot. One half of her face was all red. "Did we wake you up?" Marianne asked.

Hanni seemed to want to say something, but was holding her forearm across her mouth. Finally she raised her head and said, "Hello."

"Hello," I said, and stood up. Marianne introduced us.

That's how Hanni and I became acquainted. Three months later she asked me what I thought about marriage. That was the best thing that's happened in my life so far.

My mother really went bananas. But Ernst and Martin and Danny, even Sarah, Hanni's daughter, they all thought it was okay.

At the wedding Ernst suddenly came over to Marianne's table. He and Marianne danced, but didn't say a word. But when he brought her back to her seat, he thanked her with a bow. She left right after that. She'd already suggested that we be on a first-name basis. We've got the full-page for Furniture Paradise now. I let Bertram take credit for that coup. Which made Marianne absolutely furious. She said that Bertram had often tried to get his foot in the door, and that it was stupid of me, inexcusably stupid, to miss out on a monthly commission of a good eight hundred marks. She could've spared herself the trouble. "I didn't do it for Bertram!" she said.

I know Marianne's right, even if I won't admit it, and of course I don't want Hanni to know anything about it. Mainly because turning down that much money was really uncalled for, completely pointless. I should've known a payoff wouldn't work, that I couldn't buy my way out, that it's not about Bertram at all. I should have known that much when I saw Hanni in her pink panties the second time, at the latest.

CHAPTER 25

my god, is she beautiful!

How Edgar Körner tells some stories and invites Jenny and
Maik to a motel. He suddenly wants to move on. He doesn't
succeed. The waitress attends to a youthful hero.

"I was taking pictures that morning, at the Iglesia de San Cristóbal.
There was a grungy old man sitting outside, who stood up and ran
off when he saw my camera. That noon, the same old man waved
me into a parking place on the Calle de Sebastian. I gave him three
hundred pesos for it. When I drove off two hours later, he was still
standing there, with a thin cane in his hand. I gave him what
change I had. Late that afternoon he was sitting at the bar in the
Bar de Colonial drinking beer—or what they call beer. Just as I
came in he spat on the floor, grabbed for a napkin, blew his nose in
it, and threw it on the floor." Edgar flung his napkin down beside
the table. "Like that. Then he blew his nose again in a new napkin
and—tossed it away. We were sitting facing each other, at one of
those horseshoe-shaped bars." Edgar drew two right angles in the
air. "The old man acknowledged me and called over something.
There was spit clinging to the corners of his mouth, and at the
front, on his lips, too. It looked like he was trying to estimate the
distance between us. He slipped off his barstool, but thank God sat
back up on it again, and went on drinking." Edgar first gazed at
Jenny, till she avoided his eyes, then at Maik, who had left half his

schnitzel on his plate and was smoking. Edgar turned his coffee cup around by the handle, the way you move the hand of a clock.

"Okay," he said. "So at the head of the bar, sort of halfway between us, were two guys with their heads close together. Suddenly"—Edgar stretched his upper body—"one of them grabbed hold of the waiter. He just reached behind without moving anything else, and grabbed him by the hip pocket. The waiter was completely baffled and didn't even defend himself. But then they started screaming at each other, cursing each other nose to nose. The man emptied his espresso into the saucer, soaking the sugar packet, came over to me brandishing his arm in the air, ordered another espresso, then waved it away again in disgust, and banged his fist on the bar. At that same moment I got a whiff of the old man. He raised his glass to toast me and shouted 'Good morning!'" Edgar held his cup in both hands as if trying to warm them. "Two waiters moved in on him, one on each side. The old man stared into his beer, looked up as if reconsidering, and shouted 'Good afternoon!' The waiters hissed at him, got a fix on me out of the corners of their eyes, and banged the old man on the back of the head, real quick, once, twice, three times— I don't know if it was the flat of their hands or their fists. And even though the old man's head shot forward at each blow, he didn't defend himself. He just held on tight to his glass." Edgar put down the empty cup and bent over for his napkin. "You guys want anything else?"

"And then?" Jenny asked. Maik lit another cigarette.

"He really stank something awful," Edgar said. "I finished my beer and left."

"And the old man?" she asked.

"They threw him out, I'm sure." Edgar looked at them both. Maik was staring outside. You couldn't see the autobahn from here.

Edgar broke off some French bread and sopped up tomato sauce from the edge of his plate.

"Why are you telling us this?" Maik asked without looking at Edgar.

"So I won't fall asleep. Since you two never open your mouths."

"Wrong," Maik said. "Because I told you I work behind a bar, and waiters don't count with you, that's why."

"Kid," Edgar cried, "I thought you were a bartender!" He kneaded his napkin into a ball and stuffed it in his cup. The waitress was standing there with the empty plates stacked up her arm.

"Everything's fine, Britti," Edgar said.

"Thanks," Jenny said, "it was delicious."

When Maik didn't look up, the waitress moved on.

"I like old people," Jenny said.

Edgar chewed and nodded for a good long time.

"With them you can really see how it works. You ask them, and first they tell you one thing. You ask again, and then they'll tell you something else. And then you ask them a third time. And then you've finally got your answer."

"Don't you want the right answer from the start?" Edgar asked.

"No. Let's say I ask about number seven. Old people will tell you about number four, and if you ask again, about number six, and then about number three. And when I give up, they just say: four plus six minus three equals seven. But that's not a good comparison."

"Sure it is," Edgar said. "I get it, it's a good comparison."

"You know what I'm talking about?"

"I don't know if this fits in," Edgar said, "but there was something that happened to me at the movies once. We got there too late, the only seats left were in the first row. We headed down into the dark. It was all from a bird's-eye view, a flight above the jungle. I closed my eyes to keep from getting dizzy. Then right next to me I heard a deep clucking sound, a marvelous laugh."

"Maiki, what's wrong?" Jenny asked. Maik let the lighter drop into his breast pocket and leaned back.

"I'm tired too," Edgar said, and slid his chair back as if he was going to get up.

"No," Jenny said, "I want to hear this, please."

Edgar glanced at Maik. "Okay," he said, "movies, first row, a laugh next to me . . ."

"A marvelous laugh," Jenny said.

"Exactly. And always at places that were somehow unusual, where nobody else laughed. She had her legs crossed, and was jiggling her right foot. Sometimes I could see her calf and ankle. I'd stare at her and then the clucking would stop. And that jiggling foot, like an invitation. I touched my elbow to hers, she didn't even notice. I thought, I just have to put my arm around her, and she'll lean against me, like it's the most natural thing in the world, as if it just has to be. And at the same time I wanted to stroke her calf. I had to control myself, really control myself, we were sitting that close to each other. I kept thinking, My God, is she beautiful! I wanted to kiss her every time she clucked."

"And—did you?"

"I couldn't figure out who was sitting next to her. A man—yes, but it wasn't clear if he was there with her. I was sure of only one thing, that I was going to speak to her, even if I had to desert my friends to do it."

"She wasn't alone, then?" Jenny asked. The waitress set a fresh ashtray on the table. Maik stubbed out his cigarette.

"No," Edgar said. "She wasn't alone. She was there with a whole group." He paused.

"So what happened?"

Edgar shook his head. "It'd been too dark to see. She was retarded, the whole bunch of them were retarded."

"Oh shit," Jenny said.

"I'd fallen in love with an idiot."

"Incredible."

"Yes," he said. "And the worst part was that I still wanted her all the same."

"You what?"

"I'd fallen in love, it was a done deed." Edgar leaned back, his fingers resting on the edge of the table. Jenny smiled. Maik had fished his lighter from his pocket again and was playing with it.

All around them were solo drivers or couples who ate in silence. Farther to the front, between the cash register and the entrance, were tables where things were getting louder.

"We really should be going," Edgar said, and laid the room key between Jenny and Maik. "Go on ahead. I'll take care of this."

"Everything okay, Maiki?" Jenny took the key and stood up. "Thanks," she said.

Maik stared at the heavy metal key chain with its embossed number 7 in her hand. Without looking at Edgar, he shoved his chair back and followed her.

"Where'd those kids come from? Can I take this?"

Edgar nodded. "They're really not kids anymore," he said. "But in some ways they are, aren't they?"

"You stole his girl out from under him," the waitress said, "with your horror stories."

"Oh come on, Britti," he said.

"You saw for yourself. He left pretty pissed."

"I don't want anything from that little girl, you know that. Bring two coffees and let those idiots up front fend for themselves."

"It's none of my business, Eddie. You can do what you want. You will anyway." She cleared the table, bunching the napkins into a wad.

"Those two are total opposites. She's from East Berlin and he's from Stuttgart. I have no idea what the tiff is all about. You feel sorry for the boy?"

"You gonna tell me," she said, turning half around, "all boys go through this phase?"

"I like them both, honest. I'm just glad I don't have to stand by the road with a backpack. There are times when I'm really glad about that."

"All on one check?"

"Go for it." He watched her pass the cash register and slow down just before the automatic door and turn into the kitchen on the right. He took a toothpick, broke it, and broke the two halves in half again. His fingernails were clean. He watched the tables near the counter. A woman had turned her chair around and was talking in a loud voice to some men at the next table. Brit came back with one large coffee.

"You mad at me?" Edgar tossed the toothpick splinters into the ashtray. Brit set the coffee down in front of him, crumbed the tablecloth—the little brush vanished into her apron pocket.

"They'd wanted to tour France. Somebody stole their money, and now they're broke, or at least that's what they say."

"You're sleeping in your rig and paying for a room for them?"

"Is that so awful?"

"Unusual at least."

"What else?"

"You're just a generous guy, at least if the young ladies let you stare halfway down to their belly buttons, right?"

"Britti," Edgar said, and laid a hundred-mark bill on the table. "Tell them tomorrow morning that it's all taken care of, okay? I'm paying for their breakfast, too."

"So what now?"

"I'm driving as far as Herlehausen, just in case it's bumper-to-bumper tomorrow."

"Legally?"

"I've got a good hour left."

"They won't come in for breakfast, not if they don't have any money."

"I want to drive on, Britti. It's better this way, I think."

"Oh good grief," she said.

"What do you mean, 'good grief'?"

"You don't have to lay it on so thick. Besides, I'm not on the breakfast shift, as you can see."

"I'll pay for it now, though. If they don't come, credit me for it. That okay, Britti?"

"What if they steal stuff?"

"Listen to yourself."

"I'm just saying . . ."

"Little lambs . . ."

"They're no lambs, Eddie, neither one of them."

"That enough?" He tapped the money.

"Computer's down." She sat down facing him, totaled the bill, and tore it off the pad.

"What sort of crowd is that up front?" Edgar asked.

"Pretty rotten today," she said.

"Bunch of pigs."

"Yeah," she said, and fumbled in her money pouch. "Pigs of the world, unite. . . ."

"It's okay. If they don't show up again, just credit my account, okay?"

"You're so easy," she said, and waved her order pad under his nose.

"Ought to throw that riffraff out."

"Who, me? As long as the coffee's flowing . . ."

"What do you mean, coffee? They're drunk."

Brit set the vinegar back in the condiment rack. "You could use a shave, Eddie."

"Just for you," he called after her. Then he opened both little plastic tubs of cream, emptied them, and stuffed his wallet into his vest.

He took a long time washing his face in the rest room. In the mirror he watched water dribble down his chin. He turned his head back and forth to dry his face.

He sipped his coffee and watched the two men standing chest to chest like soccer players, shouting at each other. It was German, but he couldn't make it out. An older couple turned on their heels at the entrance. Edgar felt for his keys and his wallet. By working your way along the window tables, you could slip out unnoticed. More and more people were getting up now.

Edgar recognized the kid by his thick strawberry blond hair and by the way he rolled his shoulders. He forced his way between the two men as if trying to take the shortest route to get to Edgar, but that was as far as he got. He was stuck between them. His backpack and the room key fell to the floor.

Then the men pulled back. The restaurant got much quieter. Slowly, very slowly, Maik raised his left hand. He held it up like a book in front of his eyes and squinted, as if it were too dark to read. He didn't move, just looked at the palm of his hand. Blood was running down his arm to the elbow and dripping on the floor. The men had vanished.

Brit stepped forward, took Maik by the shoulder, bent down, and looked up into his face. The other waitress picked up the room key. The two of them led Maik to the nearest table and pulled out a chair for him. A woman came over from the counter. The older couple who had been waiting outside took up position in front of him. A first-aid kit was retrieved from the kitchen. More and more people gathered in a circle around Maik, talking to him as if he needed calming. Gazing over their heads, Edgar could see the boy's pale face.

"You idiot," Edgar shouted once he had pushed his way inside the circle. "You stupid idiot!" Maik slid down farther in his chair, stretched out his legs, and smiled at him. Someone bandaged his hand. Brit kept running her hand through his hair. The backpack with its tied-up bedroll lay beside his chair.

"What a stupid idiot you are," Edgar said, and tapped his forehead.

Without taking his eyes off Edgar, Maik reached across the table with his unbandaged hand, groping for the room key, and threw it at Edgar's feet. He burst into laughter, loud and surprisingly shrill; Edgar pulled back, leaving the key and metal ring with the number 7 on it lying exactly halfway between them.

CHAPTER 26

blinking baby

Berlin, a Sunday evening in August. Lydia tells about Jenny,
Maik, Jan, and Alex, and eats rice pudding. An old man is
sitting out on his balcony. There's a signal light on the
windowsill. Who and what belongs where.

The rice pudding is still lukewarm as I dish myself a plateful. I
make a dent in the middle and fill it with pieces of canned mandarin orange. The juice gathers in a thin circle around the edge of
the plate. I sprinkle it evenly all over with sugar and cinnamon and
hold the spoon almost vertical so that the whole thing doesn't
spill over.

The signal light on the windowsill has stopped blinking. It
reacts immediately to light and dark. The glass is yellowish, almost
orange, with a metal triangle at the top to hang it by. The black let-
tering on the yellow case reads SIGNALITE.

My kitchen window looks out onto the courtyard. The old man
is still sitting out on his balcony in the ell to my left. He suns himself in the afternoon. Usually he listens to Mozart and Wagner, and
other things that sound familiar, although I don't really know what
they are. When the old man opens the balcony door, what you see
first are the trembling fingers of his left hand, which he uses to
steady himself on the frame. He supports himself with a cane in
his right hand. His feet and calves are swollen and purplish. He
walks as if he were wearing incredibly heavy boots and checking at
every step to see if the floor will hold. It's a long time before the old

man sits down, his hands clutching the handle of the cane, one atop the other, or each pressed to a thigh. About every half hour he slides his chair a little to stay even with the sun. By four o'clock he's turned around directly toward me. He wears white underpants, a bathrobe, and sunglasses. Strands of hair reach down over his bald spot to his collar. He evidently fell asleep during the oboe concerto. It's almost six in the evening now.

This heat leaves me exhausted all day. I lie awake at night. It doesn't even help if there's a draft.

This morning two guys were kicking a tin can back and forth right outside our building. That was about five o'clock. Then crows started carrying on a conversation. I swear they were talking about something. And finally, a telephone rang somewhere close by, all the windows are wide open. Just when I finally fell asleep, Jan rang the doorbell. He'd come directly from Tresor Disco. The toilet attendants and bouncers wanted to go home. There was no second shift because of vacations. So they had to close down early. Jan wanted to show me a signal light he and Alex had stolen from a construction site on Bötzow Strasse. They'd been hopping around in their disco bunker all night, waving this signal light. What happened then I'm not sure. Jan just said that it was all over between him and Alex, the end, over and done with, and finally asked if he could move in with me for just a few days. But I'm not going to let him even get to square one with that.

Then, around eleven, up popped Jenny and Maik. France didn't last even a week. Maik's left hand was bandaged up and in a sling. I keep their keys. They share a two-and-a-half-room apartment with Alex and Jan one floor down.

Jenny came back alone this afternoon. She took off again a half hour ago, and I don't know if I should be angry or hurt or just take it all as a sign of helplessness, maybe even of trust. There was a time when I would've laughed it off.

Of course I'm glad they come to see me. I could be her mother, theoretically speaking. At times we're a kind of family. They don't even notice when they're starting to get on my nerves. They think they have to look after me because I'm lonely. That's why they placed a personal ad for me in *zitty*. And ever since they saw some of Patrick's photographs lying around here, they want me to write him. I've told them several times that Patrick was the reason why I had to get out of Altenburg. That night with the Holitzschek woman was the last straw. Her and her not-so-secret secret. Besides, as I always say, getting out of there was just the first step toward putting some order back in my life. And I'm not about to let that order fly out the window, even if Jenny and the three guys do carry on as if being alone were the worst thing ever. I always thought it was completely different for really young kids. Plus the fact—which they don't even take into account—that Patrick has found a new girlfriend and a new job.

Jenny was hungry at any rate. She opened the fridge and shouted, "When are you ever going to eat all this?" Her hand was resting on the shelf she was checking out.

"I can warm up the lasagna," I said. "There's veggie lasagna left over from lunch."

She took a package of nasi-goreng from the freezer and turned it over a few times until she found the cooking instructions. That pastel blue sleeveless blouse I got rid of is too big for her. "You can do it in a pan, too," Jenny said. "Want some?"

"Why not the veggie lasagna?" I asked.

Then Jenny held up a can. "Mandarin oranges! Can I open it? There's still one left." She shoved the nasi-goreng back in the freezer. "My mother never puts cans in the fridge, uses too much electricity," she said, bending down and pulling out a jelly jar to see what was behind it.

"Mmmm, rice pudding!" She held up a package of Ravensberg Rice Pudding with both hands. "Lyyyydia—please, please, please, please!" The vegetable bin was sticking out. That's why the fridge door wouldn't close.

"You got cinnamon, sugar and cinnamon?" she asked.

"Jenny," I said, "the fridge." She just forced the door shut, grabbed a paring knife from the drawer, sawed along the dotted line of the rice-pudding package, and tore off the tip. "Where's the garbage can?" she asked. I showed her the bag for recycled paper under the sink.

The next thing she shouted was: "Yuck, look at this apple!" It had a big brown spot. Jenny turned over the other apples and grapefruit in the straw basket. "This's the only one," she said, halving it with the bread knife. "This got its own place, too?" I showed her the green tub for biodegradables and told her about Jan and Alex and the signal light.

"When you're still flying and they close down, it's like having your heart give out," Jenny explained to me. She meant dancing and the stuff they swallow to get high. "That light really bugs me," she said. "What a stupid gizmo. Even when I can't see it, I can feel it. Why'd they bring something like that home? It really gets to me."

"Jan says it's his baby now," I said. "For at least as long as he's alone."

"Great! His baby, not mine," she said. "First of all, he's already in the sack with Alex again, and second, they wouldn't let me keep the cat, either. Baby!" she shouted. "Another baby! That gizmo starts blinking whenever it gets a little darker. It really bugs me." She diced the apple. You could see a white stripe on her tanned right shoulder where her blouse had slipped down.

I asked about Maik's hand. Jenny sniffed. "He's packing his stuff right now. *I* told him to pack. Can I turn this on?" She fidgeted at the radio dials. "First he says I shouldn't worry about money. And five days later he's broke. I was furious, nothing but restaurants and bars. What station is this? I wanted to see Paris! Instead we spent two days hanging around cemeteries in Reims. Now he's acting as if *I* ran through all his money." She turned the radio off again. "Maik got caught in the middle somewhere, two guys were arguing, and airhead that he is, Mr. Bigshot stuck his hand in between." Jenny had opened the oven and pulled out the skillets. "There was this really nice guy who'd given us a ride," she said. "Maik wanted to go to Stuttgart, to see his parents. I said, no problem, go ahead, but count me out. I said not in a truck, but Maik asked the driver anyway. It had Berlin written on it, but the driver was headed for Meerane, wherever that is. A Volvo rig full of Spanish oranges he'd picked up in France. Eddie talked the whole time. If he stopped talking, he said, he'd fall asleep. We were supposed to entertain him, fifty jokes before we got to the Hermsdorf interchange. That pissed Maik off, and he told him to turn on the radio instead. Well, you know," Jenny said, and set the medium-sized skillet on the stove. "At the Kirchheim interchange Eddie said he wanted to pay for our dinner and a night in a motel. That was okay by me, paying the way for two people who're broke. I'd already told him the story about the lifeguard. We understood each other."

I didn't know what she was talking about.

"Come on," she said, "I know you know the swimming-pool story."

"No, I don't," I said.

"Easy to see how well you listen," Jenny said, and held the spark lighter to the burner. "That's the day before I got my first ID card. In April of '89. I was at an indoor pool with a girlfriend. We wanted to jump in, but this woman lifeguard demanded we put our clothes back on and leave, because some training session was about to start. I got out my watch—there was at least another twenty minutes to go." Jenny put butter in the skillet, bent down, and turned up the heat.

"You'd just been messing around till then?"

"We'd paid. Besides, there was still time left. We already had our bathing caps on. Suddenly a whole pack of competition swimmers—that's what they called them—storms in. They started playing dodge ball with us, pushing us around in a circle. I just kept thinking, Don't cry, don't cry. Nobody gave a shit about us. But we jumped into the water anyway, with our knees all scraped up. When we turned in our locker keys at the entrance, that same lifeguard was sitting at the desk and even said 'Thank you.'" Jenny swirled the melted butter around in the skillet. "And for the first time in my life I'd seen what grown-ups are really like and how you're treated when higher-ups can get back at you without ever getting their hands dirty. I was going to tell my mother about it that night. But once she was standing there beside my bed, I knew I couldn't say anything about it. It would've been worse, a whole lot worse, for her than it'd been for me. I couldn't do that to her."

Jenny tossed the diced apple into the skillet. She'd shaken off her run-down sandals as she moved about, and now used her toes to pull the scale out from under the shelving, stood on it, stepped off, and tried a second time.

"Look at that," she cried. "That can't be. A hundred and eleven. I don't even weigh a hundred!" Her shoulder blades stood out like two wings. "A hundred and eleven! Have a look for yourself!" She got out of the way to let me try and watched the pointer.

"A hundred fifty," I said, "works fine."

"What? You weigh a hundred and fifty?" Jenny looked me up and down.

I shoved the scale back under the shelving and asked again about Maik's hand.

"I couldn't really tell the story, because Maik was constantly interrupting," Jenny said, stepping over her sandals to put a bowl and a package of cinnamon on the table, and then shoved the sugar bowl toward me.

"He kept horning in," she said, "until Eddie asked him to please leave me alone and let me talk. And when that didn't help he yelled at him to shut his trap. He was right, Lydie, he really was." Jenny glanced over at me. I told her to use a wooden spoon instead of a fork and to turn down the heat.

"So when Maik and I were alone in the motel room—Eddie

was still sitting in the restaurant—Maik starts in on me. Why had I told Eddie that story when I'd never told it to him before. Imagine anybody coming at you with something like that—but it's typical Maik. Besides, he pisses in the shower."

"All men do," I said.

"Maik started talking bullshit. He wouldn't stand in my way if I wanted to earn a little extra tonight. That's the kind of crap he was giving me. Well, that did it for *me*," Jenny cried. "I'd told him one time," she said, "about a guy I'd got together with occasionally, before Maik and I were an item. He was a lot older, but okay, very polite and generous and absolutely nuts about me. Everything I did drove him wild. He was always slipping me a little money, instead of presents. But for some reason he couldn't get it on, and I figured maybe it was paternal, an instinct to protect me or what-ever. But then out of the blue he read me this filthy story, a kind of S and M thing that would've been totally absurd if it hadn't been him. And so everything just fell apart for me, the whole image I had of him. And I told Maik about it, which was way unnecessary. And since then he thinks I'm hiding things from him, some S and M rough stuff or whatever's going on inside that wacko brain of his. Just because the guy gave me some money. But that's Maik all over. It wasn't till they brought him back that I realized he'd locked me in the room. One of the waitresses drove us to the hospital and back. Meanwhile the other one had found a guy who'd take us to Berlin. He didn't say a single word the whole way here and dropped us off at Wannsee station."

I told her she should wear something under that blouse, because otherwise just one little gesture and you could see every-thing.

"Not there," I said when Jenny pressed her chin to her chest. "Here, at the sleeves."

"A little unappetizing?" she asked. "They kind of stick out side-ways—repulsive, huh?" Suddenly she threw her arms around my neck. I just had time to get to my feet. I held Jenny tight and stroked her hair. My left shoulder felt wet. That's how I noticed she was crying. But then, as abruptly as Jenny had thrown herself at me, she pulled away.

I mixed the sugar and cinnamon, set the table for two, and asked if she'd like anything to drink.

"Same as you," Jenny said, stirring the rice pudding into the diced apples. She tore the package all the way open. "Serve chilled, with muesli," she read, and turned the heat up again. The can of mandarin oranges in hand, she started looking for an opener. The rice pudding began bubbling at the edges. "Could you?" she asked, handing me the can and the opener, and stirred the mixture.

Suddenly Jenny said, "You're probably right, maybe being alone is best."

Just as I got the can open, the doorbell rang. "It's for you," I said, and didn't stand up until it rang a second time.

Jenny went out. I heard her open the door. But she didn't say anything. Then the door closed again. I waited. I called Jenny's name and finally went looking for her. I was alone.

I took the rice pudding off the stove, then stood awhile at the apartment door and waited. There was no one in the stairwell, either. I turned the burner off and ran myself a bath. That always helps. Sitting in the tub, I played with an empty shampoo bottle. I picked it up with my feet and set it on the bathtub rim, concentrated, and just nudged it with my toes so that it fell back into the water. It's a kind of billiards I play, and it's good for the stomach muscles, too.

When the doorbell rang again, I ran to the door in my bathrobe. There on my doormat was the signal light, blinking away. I bent down over the banister—nothing. I took the signal light back to the kitchen and set it on the windowsill, where it immediately stopped blinking.

I eat the whole plateful, but still don't know what to think about this stunt. I dish up the rest of the rice pudding. First I wash the skillet, which only fits at an angle partway in the sink. Then I fill the empty pudding package with water so it'll be easier to rinse later. Then I eat some more.

There's not a sound coming from either the courtyard or the apartment below. If those four were my kids, I'd blame myself and feel guilty that they're so rude, so chaotic. Or I'd convince myself that it was the bad neighborhood or hard times somehow or the heat.

The old man is still sleeping. When he wakes up, he'll wonder where the day has got to. A perfect excuse. But he probably doesn't need excuses anymore. Last spring, he always left green bananas on his balcony. He used the crook of his cane to pull them over, feel them, and then shove them away again. One corner of his bathrobe would dangle back and forth. His joints are going to hurt. I can't sleep even in a bed, and he can take his catnap right there on a chair just like that. He'll probably feel it worst in his neck and shoulders, and tonight he'll lie awake just like me, listening to music, wondering about the blinking light, and asking himself what it means. Maybe it could have a soothing effect, too. If you close your eyes it might have a soothing effect, sort of like the ticking of the alarm clock used to. I was eleven and twelve and thirteen and never told my mother, not just because I was afraid, but because I thought it would be worse for her than for me and that I couldn't do that to her. But then she divorced the man who fathered me, divorced him for completely different reasons.

Once I've finished it all, I'll rinse the plate and the rice-pudding package. Maybe it'd be better if I put SIGNALITE in the wardrobe, under my winter things, or in the bathroom and leave the light on. Tomorrow morning I have to take the recyclable paper down— they empty the yellow cans on Mondays. I'll lay Jenny's sandals on her doormat and put SIGNALITE beside them. And if Jan doesn't want his baby anymore, now that Alex is back, then he'll just have to return it to that construction site on Bötzow Strasse. That would be the perfect solution and everything would be in its place again.

CHAPTER 27

the wrong man

How Patrick leaves Danny. A scene in the living room. Lydia's letter and her extra pounds. Tino, Terry, and the monster.

Patrick is sitting in a large gray armchair across from the broken television. To his left is a window, to his right a dining room table where Danny is sitting with the back of her chair to Patrick. A light supper for three has not been cleared away yet. Two of the four yellow globes above the table are on, shedding dull light. Below them a candle burns. From neighboring apartments come sounds of televisions.

Danny holds a cigarette to the candle. She turns to one side, her left forearm over the back of the chair, and pulls her legs up, propping her heels on the edge of the chair seat.

Patrick slips into his black shoes, loosens the laces of the right one, tugs until they're of equal length, and ties a bow. He does the same with the left. Patrick asks, "He asleep?"

Danny shrugs. She clasps the toes of first one foot, then the other, with her right hand, as if she's cold. "You know what Billi said to me? 'He lost his job and looked for a new one. His wife ran off and he's found a new one. What else does he want?' That's what Billi said." Danny blows smoke toward the closed living room door in front of her. "It was nice in Kohren-Sahlis, wasn't it?"

"Very nice," Patrick says.

"Sometimes you have to force Tino to be happy. Kids need definite boundaries to move around in."

"We had good luck with the weather."

"To think he let you put him on your shoulders, Pat—that was really more than just a crack in the ice, don't you think? And when you two went rowing, and he listened to you and tried so hard. . . . A miracle, really." She scratches her shin and touches her chin to her knee for a moment. "It's gonna be awfully hard on him."

Patrick folds his hands over his stomach, but then immediately puts them back on the arms of the chair.

"You still have to call your friend Enrico," Danny said. "Wouldn't you know, just when I'm finally getting used to him. Two bags of dirty laundry as a calling card—talk about unique! I still don't know what that green stuff was. As if he'd stuffed his pockets full of birch leaves or brussels-sprout crumbs. And him standing there in that stained T-shirt, his mouth wide open, as if he was about ready to barf again. I thought I wasn't hearing right when he started in again about his stomach cancer. For a writer he's a little short on imagination—no, awfully short. Have you ever told him that? And does he really know all that much about China and Schopenhauer . . . but then I don't know enough to tell, come to that. At least he spared me the Brazil story." Danny put her feet on top of the big brown-checked slippers in front of her chair. "You can't even ask him to set the table. He always messes it up somehow, with silverware strewn around like pickup sticks. I'm surprised at your patience. Really surprised. Just because he says he had nothing to do with that crazy woman? And what if he's lying to you, what if he was involved with her? Maybe she wanted to sleep with him?"

"No," Patrick says, and sucks his lips in. "Most definitely not."

"What do you know about it. . . ." Danny rubs her right foot on her left ankle and slides into the slippers. "Terry has fleas again." She crosses her legs. The right slipper is perched just on her toe tips. "I've always asked myself what would bring a woman to leave you—let me finish—and then take up with a guy like that. It amazes me. Every time he shows up here, I ask myself why in the world—"

"Lydia . . ."

"No! Please don't, Pat. Don't mention her name here."

"I just wanted to say that she had her reasons." He shoots Danny a glance.

"Pat." She puts her cigarette out in a saucer. "He's the kind who finishes every other sentence by saying he's going to end it all. That's Herr Enrico Friedrich, wannabe writer. So somebody sits down next to him, holds his hand, and explains why he shouldn't do it. That'd be you. Week after week you cheer him up, tell him about all the wonderful things in life, try to ease his fears. He can apply for rent support, he's got health insurance, he can even get a new washing machine from social services." Danny holds three widespread fingers up. "But the real fun for him is in messing up everything you suggest. That's his job and his hobby. Nobody, no job, no joy, no nothing, nothing, nothing. I take it as a downright insult, at least to everyone around him. And then for an encore he barfs other people's beds full and sobs himself silly because he's lonely. And if somebody finally says that maybe it would be best if he did what he's been talking about all this time—good God, is it any wonder? Besides, you didn't say it to him. You said it to her in confidence. So what? You never claimed you'd be happy if he did. It's so absurd! And people who are always babbling about it never do it anyway. There's that, besides. The ones who really do it never talk about it. Or am I way off track? Isn't that so, Pat?"

"Usually," he says without looking up.

"Do you think that's a good reason? Is that any reason to just pick up and leave somebody you've lived with for years, just because he says about a mutual acquaintance: 'He won't make it'? Because of four perfectly justified words? And doesn't even have the guts to look you in the face. Just scribbles her adios on a scrap of paper, and that's that? You were right! More right today than ever. He won't make it!" She gives her hair several tugs and pulls a few strands back down behind her ears. "I'm just asking questions, Pat, that's all. And I know what I know about you. You told me all this yourself. I'm not making anything up. Or that whole circus on account of that Czech woman, the cleaning lady who was the reason why Fräulein Schumacher couldn't sleep a wink for a whole weekend—rings around her eyes as if you'd beaten her black-and-blue. Is it a crime to hire somebody to clean for you? I'm not making this up, Pat, and people don't change." Danny runs her fingers through her hair. "What would you've done that night if you'd caught her with Enrico, if she'd still been there? I never asked you that. And how could you think a kid would solve all your problems? You want every woman to bear you a kid? Like the baboons in that temple in Bangkok? All that matters to them, too, is their own genes."

Patrick slides forward in his armchair.

"Sorry," she says. "Sorry. Don't you really want anything more to eat? I made all this salad for nothing."

Patrick remains at the edge of his seat. He says, "I'll call a repairman tomorrow."

"Why?"

"Because the TV's busted."

"Why do *you* want to call the repairman?"

"Danny . . ."

"Why do *you* want to call the repairman, I asked? Why can't *I* do that?"

"Because I said I'd do it. I promised Tino."

"And what are you going to tell the repairman? That he should call me? Just what are you going to tell him? I don't understand you. You never think things through. Maybe that's it. You just don't think things through. I'm not even asking you to think about us. Just to think things through. That's all."

Danny holds another cigarette to the candle. "You don't have anything to say? Evidently tolerance has broken out on all sides."

"What am I supposed to say?"

"Well, maybe your little thing about lighting cigarettes on a candle, how it sends a sailor to his watery grave. . . ."

"I thought that drives you up the wall."

"There're worse things," she says. As she speaks, smoke rolls out of her mouth. "Do you know why I liked you from the start? Because that first day in the office you said, 'That's your favorite way to stand, isn't it?'"

Danny puts the toes of her right foot behind her left heel. Cigarette still in her mouth, she stands up, bracing herself on the table and chair. "Or like this." She switches feet. "Right? Almost every picture is like that."

Patrick nods. She plops back down on her chair.

"I thought, finally a man who really observes things, who knows that a woman wants to be treated like a woman. Somebody I don't have to hang my diploma above the sink for, for him to realize that I can do something else besides." Her long thumbnail flicks at the cigarette filter. "Do you know the first time you disappointed me, really disappointed me? When Beyer said our names couldn't appear that time things got so bad with the Fascis and Punks."

"They're still bad."

"But I mean back then, when you didn't even protest. I felt you'd betrayed me. And not just you. I almost lost it, because of those crocodile eyes, remember? And you were just scared shitless."

"Not for myself."

"I know, she'd just moved in with you. If it'd been me, I would've demanded your name appear. Wasn't she even a little surprised it didn't?"

"No."

"I thought we were a good fit, because we knew each other. That makes a person more realistic, there's not that one hundred percent expectation—maybe it's not the love of your life, but it's not bad. You can let it grow. And the way you handle Tino. And that we're not like most people, who think that if they can make it big, come New Year's Eve '99 they won't be all alone."

"Danny, I'd still like to help you two out. I'll send money, for Tino."

"Another great idea you can forget."

"Things'll be tight, with just you and the boy. You don't get anything from Martin, or at least not much."

"You're incredible, Pat, really incredible. Am I supposed to hand Tino a hundred marks when he asks about you, or two hundred maybe? I should've told you to please tear up that letter and throw it away, or said let's burn it in the ashtray, in that one, that one up there." She nods toward the TV. "What would you've done if I'd demanded you tear up the letter unread and burn it?" After a pause she says, "Well?"

"Danny."

"I mean, I could've thrown it away, not even shown it to you. Or it might've got lost, lost in limbo somewhere at the post office? I saw the return address. The woman has no inhibitions. Have you even thought about what might've happened then? Want me to tell you? But I don't have to, or do I? When I said you don't think things through, I meant this part of it, too. You've said yourself the woman is sick—but you just had to prove you could live with her, wake her up again, as you so nicely put it, have kids with her and a great life just in general. That was your grand ambition. And you said you knew she wouldn't be easy. You compared your relationship to trees in Siberia, that take longer to grow but break normal saws in half—or am I confusing things here? And all the while, I kept asking myself, why's he telling me this? Maybe it's just how men think. But why do I have to listen to it? I don't want to know any of this!" Danny gives her head a couple of raps with her knuckles. "I'm so damned good at noticing things. It's all in here, every bit of it. Did you know, by the way, that you're a provincial love object? Do you know what that is? I've been thinking about it. And put simply it means: you were the best she could find in Altenburg. You were her stopgap, her quick fix. Better to move in with somebody than to have nobody at all. It's that simple. But in great big Berlin, where Lydia Schumacher had such a wide choice, you wouldn't even enter into the equation. That's what she was trying to tell you. I notice things. And the way she beat every bit of ambition out of you, by showing you just who you are. Step by step she demolished your self-image, and she was always in the right, and called you a 'bullshit artist,' not in a nasty way, just sort of offhand, as if she no longer expected anything different from you, that's what you said. Until it finally dawned on you that she's sick. A woman who's had a constant headache for the last five years. . . . But why go on. None of these Westie chicks can take it. . . ."

"But she's not a . . ."

"So what? She acts like it. She's sick. Even Enrico figured out that much. After that political bigwig's wife, Holitzschek, or whatever her name is, after she slipped him the hint that Lydia Schumacher is more than a little screwy, even he caught on. Why do you suppose she left town? The only explanation is because she was afraid of Holitzschek, because she knew there was no fooling her. Ask your friend Enrico. He figured it out. She saw right through her, Holitzschek did, she's a psychiatrist. Have you forgotten all that?" Danny pours herself some more tea. "Want some?"

Patrick shakes his head. Danny takes a sip and sets the cup back down.

"All the same, I was jealous of her. All that stuff you told me—declarations of love, pure and simple. And because she's 'all legs.'"

"Danny!"

"Don't say you don't like it. It's nothing more than a thigh that's two or three inches longer and one or two inches less big around. That's all it is! And what tact you showed, telling me she's all legs! Well, at least I know where that leaves me."

"I'm sorry, Danny."

"What're you apologizing for?"

"I'm sorry."

"What do you mean by that?"

"That I'm sorry."

"I don't get your point! I'm asking you, what's that supposed to mean?" Danny pulls the saucer to the edge of the table and stubs her cigarette out. "Would you please explain it to me? Does that mean you loved me until yesterday afternoon? But that since yesterday afternoon you can't stand living here, with Tino and me? Is that what it means?"

"It means that I'm sorry," Patrick says. "And besides, she's gotten fat."

"What?"

"She wrote that she's gained some weight. Has put on almost twenty-five—"

"Twenty-five?"

"—pounds."

"I'll be damned, twenty-five pounds? Since when do *you* like your women fat? Guess I should've sat around here stuffing myself, instead of bothering with exercise and saunas? Wrong, no matter what you do—but that's nothing new, either."

"You didn't do anything wrong. It has nothing at all to do with you. . . ."

"That's enough, Pat, you can stop right there, please. . . ."

"Maybe it's fate. Maybe it's simply my fate," he says.

He sits there, not moving, until Danny whispers, "Damn, I'm stupid." She presses clenched fists to her eyes. "Loving a guy like this."

Patrick looks at the TV screen mirroring the living room back at him. "He'll be asleep by now," Patrick says. Tilting both shoes back on their heels, he taps the toes together a few times. "I'll give

you a call, okay?" he says, and stands up, walks around the armchair, reaches for his suitcase and his black travel bag.

"Good luck, Danny." He looks at her big slippers and the flea
bite on her ankle, at the backs of her hands, at her fingers without
any rings, at her polished fingernails. As he leaves, the zipper on his
travel bag scrapes against the rippled glass of the door pane. Then
comes the sound of a lock falling into place.

Danny sits there. Suddenly a child's voice calls out, punching
each word hard, "Moms! Moms! Moms!" Now a door is shoved
open. Danny moistens the tips of her forefinger and thumb with
spit and puts out the candle. "Moms!" Tino cries as he comes in
and looks around. He's wearing white pajamas with little blue
squiggles.

"What's wrong?" Danny asks, wiping her fingertips on her
sleeve and standing up. Tino spreads his arms. She lifts him up,
carries him out, and slams the door behind her. There is silence
except for the sound of the television next door. Suddenly out of
nowhere a dog, a fox terrier, appears, jumps up on Danny's chair
and from there to the table. He hungrily sets to work on the supper
leftovers. You can hear a series of smacking sounds, except when
he thrusts his head forward to gulp something down. Before going
for more, he licks his chops and checks the door. Now and then he
scratches his neck with his hind leg. After a few minutes he leaves
the table and jumps up on the gray monster of an armchair, and
seems to vanish into it.

CHAPTER 28

snow and trash

Raffael the taxi driver talks about trouble with a writer and a stove. Enrico Friedrich has changed his first name and wants to break a leg. Unpleasant neighbors. How you can be happy anywhere.

It was well after midnight by the time Petra and I got home from her brother's birthday in Leipzig. I drove around Sperlingsberg—where we've been living now for just under a year—looking for a parking place. I thought I saw a figure in a long coat standing among the bushes beside the door to our building—and it was the middle of August. We found a parking spot, and as we walked toward our building, I spotted the same silhouette again— a man, judging from the height.

"Don't be afraid," I said, pressing Petra's arm to me, "it's a flasher." She didn't understand. "A flasher," I repeated, and pulled out my keys. By this hour there was no light at our entrance. None in the entrances nearby, either.

"Good evening," a male voice called. "She just won't do it. Nothing's good enough for her." The figure took a step toward us and raised its head. It had one arm extended, as if pointing to something at its feet.

"Herr Friedrich?" Petra asked.

"Sometimes it's over, one, two, three," he said, "and she's done her business. But not tonight. Going to start raining any minute."

"Ah," Petra said, "look at that. I've never seen that before, a cat on a leash." The animal crouched down in the grass in front of us. You could make out its collar clearly.

"Practical solution," Friedrich said. "She never wants to go out. She gets frightened so easy. But I need a little fresh air."

Even from six feet away, you could smell his breath, vodka presumably. His bathrobe, a rusty brown with a pattern of gray petals, gave off a medicinal odor as well.

Petra bent down, wiggling her fingers. The cat presented a flank. "What's her name?"

"Kitty," he said. "Actually it's a tom—or rather was one."

"Oh really?" Petra looked up and stared at Friedrich's leg sticking out of the bathrobe. "What happened to you?"

"Multiple fracture," he said, gathering his bathrobe tight and rapping the cast. "My bones are too light, break easy as hell." From his mouth came a clattering noise. His long underwear had been cut away for the cast.

"Good God," Petra said.

"The stove," he explained. "I was trying to get rid of the antique, on a dolly, but I slipped and . . ." Friedrich waved his arms vaguely, then struck the cast with the edge of one hand and clicked his tongue. "So the antique's still in the hallway, right where it fell."

"We kept ours," Petra said.

Friedrich grinned. "Just in case . . ."

"Just in case," I said. "Only thing that'd still work in a real emergency." Friedrich screwed his mouth to one side and chewed at his lower lip.

"Fine idea," he said, "damn fine idea."

"The name beside your doorbell?" Petra asked, as if talking to the cat. "I thought . . ."

"Heinrich is just the Germanized version. I wanted to take care of it now. Better to do it before things take off."

"Take off?" I asked.

He looked me over. "My career," he said hesitantly.

"But Enrico sounded so good," Petra said, looking up again. "I thought maybe some relative of yours had moved in."

The cat was no longer interested in Petra's outstretched arm and wiggling fingers.

"Just Germanized," Friedrich repeated, and chewed some more on his lower lip. He ran his cast over the sidewalk concrete, like a man trying to scrape something off the sole of his shoe.

"You in any pain?" I asked.

"With these fad names nobody ever knows what language they really come from," Friedrich said. "And language is all I care about, nothing else."

"Oh, I see," Petra said.

"No," he said, "nothing chauvinistic, definitely not."

"What are you working on at the moment? Something on the order of *Buddenbrooks* or *Hamlet*?"

"Better if you leave Kitty be. Going to rain any minute now."

Petra stood up instantly.

"I'm working on several things at once," Friedrich explained. "Each helps move the other along. They don't like it for you to be logical and systematic. Publishers don't."

Petra nodded. "I did some writing myself at one time."

We watched the cat prowl through the grass for a while.

"Good night," Petra said, offering Friedrich her hand.

"Good night," I said.

"Ditto," he replied.

By the time we got into bed it was in fact raining. I wondered if Friedrich and his cat were still outside, because I hadn't heard a sound in the stairwell.

Petra now said we should get rid of our little stove, too, and clean out the old coal bin. I had renovated the whole apartment before we moved in, and she'd wanted to keep the old stove then, since the coal had come with the apartment.

"Friedrich was pretty well loaded," I said.

"Always is," Petra said. "These days, though, he's bathing in cheap brandy."

"That's it! Cheap brandy," I said, and tried to imitate the way he clicked his tongue.

The trouble with Friedrich, who no longer went by Enrico, began at the end of September, on a Wednesday. Petra called me at the taxi switchboard a little before four that afternoon. She wanted me to come home right away. I was alone and asked how she figured that would work—my leaving the phones unattended. She said she didn't care, that she wasn't going to set another foot out of the house, and slammed the receiver. Now that my taxi business was doing better, especially since our move from Altenburg North to Sperlingsberg, exchanges like that had become rare between us. The subject of divorce never came up, either.

When I got home at six, Petra was lying stretched across our bed. All I could understand was that someone had accosted her on the stairs and asked if she could break his leg for him. I didn't know who she was talking about.

"Friedrich!" Petra shouted. "It was Friedrich, who else?"

In situations like this, her cheekbones seem to stand out more strongly, and the veins in her neck are visible. For a moment she looked like the picture of a Bosnian woman that was in the local section of the paper, the one who'd thrown herself from the window of the shelter for political refugees.

I tried to give Petra a hug or at least clasp her hands in mine. David, who'd just turned sixteen, appeared in the hall, heading for the kitchen. I heard the refrigerator door shut. Without so much as a glance our way, he went back to his room. He elbowed the door closed behind him. At least he'd turned the music down.

"Friedrich was sloshed," Petra said. "We're face-to-face outside our door, and that's what he asks me to do! Since I'm a biology teacher, he says, I'd know how to . . ." She sobbed, and I kissed her trembling hands. "I'd know how to do it right. He wanted me to show him the spot where it breaks easiest. But he didn't say 'break,' he just did that sound with his tongue. It was so sickening!"

"Like this?" I asked, and clicked my tongue.

"Ugh!" Petra cried, squirming in disgust. I guided her to an armchair in the living room and held her hands between mine.

"He actually believes I'd spend my time thinking about . . ."

"Why does he want to know?" I asked, and tried to keep my voice calm and deep.

"I asked him that, too," she said, her hands still clasped around my neck, her mouth at my ear. "But he just started in again about how hard it was to do it yourself and how he didn't know enough anatomy. Can you believe it!"

I caressed Petra's back. "Maybe he just wants to stay on disability," I said. "He can draw a check and write novels."

I tried to loosen myself from Petra's embrace. She held me tight. Her shoulder was pressed against my chin. "And I'm not supposed to tell anyone, not even you," she said. After a pause she whispered, "He's coming tomorrow. . . ." She put her nose in the air and held her breath. "Jesus!" she gasped. It sounded as if she had the sniffles.

Petra said that Friedrich was now sporting a beard and was more bloated than ever, that the cast was gone, but he was still wearing that bathrobe. "And the stench!"

"Cheap brandy?"

She nodded. "And schnapps."

"Don't you worry," I said once I was able to move my head again. We both had a cognac. Then I went up to the fourth floor.

HEINRICH FRIEDRICH was the name printed under the doorbell. Nothing happened after the first dingdong. After the second, a vacuum cleaner started up in the next apartment and bumped against the front door a few times. A half hour later I climbed the two stories again and knocked. I wasn't sure whether the doormat had been missing the first time or not. Frau Bodin opened her door behind me to wipe off the threshold. We exchanged nods.

Around ten that same evening, I positioned myself in a chair next to our apartment door, just in case Friedrich came downstairs with his cat.

David asked if I needed any help. "Wants to be certified disabled—that's what he's up to, of course," he said. "The things they come up with!"

I asked who he meant by "they." He pointed upstairs with his thumb. "All the crazies, like Friedrich and his crew."

Petra was lying in bed reading. I could hear her turn pages. All of a sudden there she was standing in front of me like a little kid. "I'm afraid," she said. I put my arms around her waist and pulled her onto my lap. I held Petra tight, until my feet fell asleep.

The next afternoon I picked her up at her school and drove her home. Friedrich's bathroom window was tilted open, but he didn't answer his door. All the next week, too, he remained invisible. I learned from Frau Hartung, who lives above us, that every Tuesday and Friday Friedrich goes to the supermarket, pulling a handcart behind him. He has trouble schlepping his hamster pouch full of bottles up the stairs.

On a Sunday in the middle of November, I disassembled the old stove—piling the tiles, firebrick, stovepipe, feet, housing, door, and grate in our cellar and emptying the rest into the big garbage bin. I was just finishing my shower when the doorbell rang.

Friedrich's face was bloated. His hair was shiny and plastered to his head as if he'd just come in out of the rain. His pale chin shimmered under a black beard. He wore a red scarf around his neck and was holding a large padded envelope with both hands.

"Your wife wanted to read this," he said. I thanked him. His chest and stomach bulged under his sweats. This time Friedrich didn't stink, or at least I couldn't smell anything. He nodded and turned around. His bare feet were thrust into a pair of flip-flops. Like warning stripes on the rear of a truck, the blue-and-orange stripes on the soles slapped at his heels—now one, now the other—and squeaked as he climbed the stairs.

"Friedrich," Petra said without even looking up. She was sitting in an armchair, holding a minivac between her knees.

I pulled the manuscript out of its envelope. The title page read: *Silence*. And under that, somewhat smaller: A Novel. And then, larger again: Heinrich Friedrich.

What junk. I didn't understand any of it. I opened the typed manuscript to several pages at random. I didn't understand a sentence. That is, I found hardly any sentences, only strings of words with inserted handwritten corrections. In some places Friedrich had scribbled a whole new paragraph in the margin. I gave it to Petra. His name on the envelope was crossed out. And he had scratched off a label in the lower left-hand corner.

"So that's how he spends his time," Petra said.

I took another look inside the envelope. I hadn't missed anything.

"I don't know," Petra replied when I asked her what she had just read. "I couldn't say for the life of me."

It was the same with me.

"Puts you into a really foul mood," she said. "Somebody ought to tell him it's a no-go."

"You don't think he has any talent? Maybe he can write something good, too."

"Doubt it," she said. "I shouldn't've thrown my stuff out. It wasn't all that bad, at least showed some talent, or so people told me. You would've liked it."

I asked what she meant by that.

"It kept you in suspense. You always wanted to know what happened next."

Over the next few days, we constantly heard Friedrich on the stairs. Evidently he was clearing the trash out of his apartment. By Tuesday evening you couldn't close the paper bin that always gets emptied on Wednesday. An empty binder lying on top read: Enrico Friedrich—The Poems. Another one read: Enrico Friedrich—The Correspondence. Plus scraps of newspapers, brochures, Xeroxes, and handwritten pages. I was able to make out the title of one: "The Cat Never Leaves the Light." He was taking his stove apart, too. Petra watched at the peephole each evening, when between nine and ten he'd huff and puff past our door carrying buckets full of debris. She said he was clearing the way for a fresh start and that for the time being his manuscript was better off with us than in the chaos upstairs. "If he needs it he'll come get it."

The first Sunday in Advent, around noon, Frau Hartung was mopping the stairs when it happened. She claimed later that Friedrich stared her right in the eye as he fell. I was sitting in the kitchen, reading the paper. Frau Hartung's scream and the echo of the banister startled me. The banister rumbled, boom—boom—boom. You'd have to bang it with your fists to get a notion of what it was like.

Friedrich lay one flight up, just below the window, his face turned upward, his right leg bent at an unnatural angle. It was a while before I even noticed the blood running from his nose and mouth. His left eye was open, but you couldn't see his right one. Nobody wanted to touch him.

I called an ambulance. They'd already been informed and soon arrived with siren howling and blue lights flashing. Twenty minutes later they drove off without Friedrich. How he managed to fall one and a half floors was and still is a riddle to me. There's almost no open shaft in that narrow stairwell. Plus Friedrich must have taken a very unlucky blow to the head.

The police sealed his apartment. Everyone in the building was interrogated. We used the occasion to get rid of both manuscript and padded envelope.

At first I thought Friedrich must have come to his own realization that nobody wanted to read his stuff, and that's why he'd thrown himself head over heels down the stairs. But Petra said that's hardly a reason to commit suicide. After all, she had given up writing too, and looked for some other line of work. "I'm sure he just wanted to break a leg," she said, "and have the taxpayers pick up the tab. But anybody who's that clumsy . . ."

The next time the trash was collected, the container of debris that included the remains of Friedrich's stove didn't get emptied, nor the week after that. Frau Hartung said that it was too heavy, they couldn't lift it, their hydraulic system wasn't up to it.

A couple of days later, a letter without any stamp appeared in our mailbox. It was signed by all the residents.

"I don't get it!" Petra cried. "I simply don't get it." We were supposed to take care of the container, because the residents of the building did not see why they should pay to have our old stove removed. That had never been customary practice here. This last sentence clearly alluded to the fact that we'd moved in only a year before.

"Show them the tiles in the cellar. Show them the stuff!" Petra shouted. "Things here just get worse and worse and worse." She sat down and began composing a letter on the spot. I preferred to go from door to door and explain to everyone that those were not our tiles, that while it was true that I'd thrown one or two in the container, all the rest were still piled in the cellar. I wondered how it was that their letter came to be written, whether they'd all sat down together or if someone had gone door to door, and who the initiator might be. And what people were saying about us. Now that they'd signed it without even giving it a second thought, the only way they could justify what they'd done would be to invent arguments against us. I heard Petra tear up one sheet of paper after the other. It was pointless.

The following day, there were chains and padlocks on all the trash containers—except the one with Friedrich's tiles. We, apparently, were the only residents without keys.

The next Wednesday, Petra woke me shortly before six. I put on my sneakers and the overalls I wear when I'm remodeling. It was snowing—the first snow of the year. Herr Bodin was just coming back in from outside, chains and padlocks in hand. Evidently he was in charge of the whole complex. We exchanged glances, but no greetings.

I waited under the overhang at the door and watched the two garbagemen shove one container after the other onto the forklift and then pull a lever. Each container was first raised a little and then heaved upward with a half turn until its little wheels were pointed skyward and the lid opened on its own above the hopper.

In my mind's eye I could already see Friedrich's trash container floating in the air, but in fact the hydraulic system balked. They couldn't budge it an inch off the ground. They tried a second time. Finally they rolled it back and loaded the last container on the forklift.

I had to scream to be heard above the racket the truck was making. I pulled out fifty marks, but they shook their heads. I kept holding the bill out to them and told them to take the money anyway. We had to figure out something. They were wearing wool caps and yellow hooded jumpsuits. They said they had to move on. I gave them another fifty.

They helped me up and then passed me a pickax and shovel. The tiles were frozen fast. I flailed away at them with the pickax. I gathered up whatever came loose and tossed it into an empty container they had rolled up beside me. I tried using the shovel. Most of the debris was either so bulky it slipped off again or so light that the wind picked it up and carried it off. I shouted for them to put their hoods over their caps because of the dust. But they didn't respond, just went on smoking with their backs to me, while snow fell into their dangling hoods.

I hacked and grubbed and shoveled and wondered if I'd find the cadaver of the cat here under all this trash, which might well support the suicide theory. Or what if Friedrich had given it away beforehand. Maybe the police had simply overlooked it and locked it in the apartment. A tile fell off my shovel and shattered on the pavement. The men looked around. They each picked up a few pieces and threw them into the empty container. Then they turned around and went on smoking, and I was looking into those hoods again. The truck was still making one helluva racket. That couldn't just be the engine. Some sort of machine was probably compacting the trash. I decided to ask about it once I was done.

It was slow progress, but at least I was getting somewhere. I had matters in hand so to speak, and that put my mind at ease. In fact I really felt good up there. Maybe because I was putting one problem behind me. It was just a matter of time. Suddenly every problem seemed easily solvable. I was feeling almost cocky, as if my taxi business and my debts didn't even exist. I wasn't thinking about Petra, who was standing behind the living room curtains, or about David, who was asleep, or about Friedrich and his bad luck or our lousy neighbors. It was another one of those happy moments when you believe that everything will work out and then you'll be able to just pack your bags and take off, alone or with Orlando, or with a wife who looks like that Bosnian woman. I clicked my tongue, and it was the loudest click I'd ever managed. One of the men even turned around. I laughed and roared for him to put his hood up, damn it. He turned away, and I shoveled some more. And then I started hacking away again. But every time I raised my head, I was looking directly into those two garbagemen's hoods. I could see snow sticking to them, collecting inside them, more and more and more snow.

CHAPTER 29

fish

Jenny tells about a new job and Martin Meurer. The boss shows them the ropes. Where is the North Sea? At first, everything goes well. Then Jenny has to do a bit of interpreting. What happened to the fish during Noah's Flood? Topped off with a brass band.

He's standing between two chairs, is wearing green gym shorts and trying to climb into a diving suit, the one with red stripes that I tried on yesterday. The one with blue stripes is lying on the table. We shake hands. He says, "Martin Meurer," and I say, "Jenny."

"The other one is even smaller," he says, "but the flippers are good." I turn my back to him and undress. And pop a button off on my jacket. I get into the blue-striped diving suit and tug the hood up. You can't see my hair or my ears or my neck. It makes my face look almost chubby. I pack up my things and wait until he finally gets his flippers on.

He's holding a plastic bag in his right hand, diving goggles and snorkel in his left, and walks as carefully as a stork down the hall toward Kerndel's office. He knocks twice. I tell him to open the door. We sit down in the two chairs along the wall to our left and wait.

"I look like a nun," I say.

"No," he says. "Like some reporter playing astronaut. You ever done it before?"

f i s h

"What?" I ask.

"This. You got into your gear so fast."

"I was here yesterday," I say, "but they won't let you do it alone."

"It's pretty warm in these," he says.

"My feet are cold," I say.

"My feet are cold too," he says. "But the rest of me—"

"Hello, Jenny!" Kerndel exclaims. "Well, how's it going?"

We stand up. "Meurer," he says, introducing himself and clamping the plastic bag between his knees. "Martin Meurer."

Kerndel puts out his hand. We sit back down. Kerndel leans against the desk, picks up a piece of paper, and turns it over. He goes through the same routine as yesterday.

"And then you ask your questions. 'Where is the North Sea?' Or, 'Can you tell us where we can find the North Sea around here?' Or, 'How do I get to the North Sea?' However you want to put it, but North Sea has to be in there, got it?"

"Yes," I say, "no problem."

Kerndel looks at him. "Got it?"

"Got it," Martin replies, lifting his right flipper and slapping it on the carpet.

"And always be cheerful and spread good cheer," I say.

"You bet!" Kerndel says. "Otherwise you two can stay at home." He slides a little farther along the edge of the desk and stares at his own pale hand rubbing the piece of paper up and down his thigh like a washrag. It's made to look like a large ticket, one part of which can be torn off along a perforated line ("Tear Here—Keep in Your Wallet"), the other is a map of the city. Stylized red fish mark the spots where the local branches of the North Sea restaurant chain are located. The largest part of the map, however, shows a photograph of the tan, wind-rippled dunes of a desert, above which white letters against a bluish purple sky read: "Where is the North Sea?"

"And what if they say no?"

"But we do!" I say. "Schul Strasse 10a and Schul Strasse 15! You're invited to a fish dinner. It's our May special. And then we hand them the piece of paper."

"The flyer," Kerndel says, correcting me. "And what if they say yes?" Kerndel looks at Martin.

"How do we get there?" he says, and slaps his flipper again.

"Jenny?" Kerndel says. "What if they say yes?"

"Great! Take us there?" I say.

"You got all that now?" Kerndel stares at Martin until he says "Yes." Then he has him repeat the May special: "Baked plaice with tartar sauce, parsley potatoes, mixed salad, and a point-three liter Coca-Cola. Regular 15.40, now only 12.95."

"It's all here on the flyer," Kerndel says. "But don't read it. That's tacky. There'll be no reading. Now, once more."

"Baked plaice with tartar sauce, parsley potatoes, green salad, plus a large Coke, only 12.95," I say.

"Regular 15.40," Kerndel adds. "Mixed salad and Coca-Cola, point-three liters. Put your goggles on. And now talk. Let's hear it, come on. . . ."

"How do I get to the North Sea?" I ask. "Do you know where the North Sea is?" Kerndel points to Martin.

"Which way to the North Sea? I want to get to the North Sea! The Sea's the place for me to be! Can you help me out?"

"Too nasal, both too nasal, better without goggles," he says. "No, don't take them off. Put them on your forehead. Push the goggles up." The telephone rings, but then stops after the second ring. "And put this like this." Kerndel has stood up and is tugging Martin's snorkel lower. "A little more. That's it! And never too many flyers in your hand at once, four or five at most, no doubling up, okay? All right?"

We nod.

"So what happened to the fish during Noah's Flood?" Kerndel asks, and claps his hands. He lays an arm around my shoulder and pulls me to him. "Now go get 'em." He walks around his desk and picks up the receiver. "It'll be a snap!"

We leave our own bags in the secretary's closet and are given blue shoulder bags filled with flyers.

"Can you manage these?" she asks. "A thousand in each." She holds the door open for us. "Just follow this hallway."

Martin halts outside the back door, looks at me, and says, "We've got to go for 'em all, every man, every woman, right from the start. Otherwise we get nowhere. If we cop out even once . . ."

I wonder if maybe he was a teacher at one time. I haven't even got the door closed, and he's off and running. Two boys, fourteen or fifteen at most, stare at him. "Well, can't you figure it out?" he asks. They give our flippers and shoulder bags the once-over. "We want to get to the North Sea," I say. They shake their heads. "Please. The Sea's the place for you and me," he says. "Well, go see for yourselves," he says. Finally they take the flyers.

We head for the pedestrian zone. I say let's leave out kids like them. "Puberty," he says, and nods.

And it really goes well. We get into it quick. Usually I start, then he chimes in, "Right, we want to get to the North Sea." "That's it, the North Sea," I say then, or, "You really don't know where it is?" And then he goes, "We'll let you in on a little secret." After a short pause we finish off by reciting the address together. People laugh and take the flyers without the least hesitation.

"I'm sorry," Martin says suddenly. "That was stupid of me." I don't know what he's talking about. "Wishing that last bunch 'Bon appétit.'"

I tell him I don't think it's such a bad idea, and so when it's my turn for the flyer I add "Bon appétit" too. Some people respond with "Thanks" or "Same to you."

"They're really curious, actually want us to speak to them," he says. "Not shy at all."

If there are a couple of people standing around us, others come over on their own. There's even a little jostling, and we pass out flyers only to people who put out a hand.

"Wonder if he's having us watched?" I ask softly.

"Sure," he says.

"I tried to sound as natural as you," Martin says. "But he wasn't convinced."

"You kept playing with your flipper," I say.

"What?"

"You wouldn't stop slapping your flipper, like this——" And I do it for him. "Didn't you notice?"

He shook his head. "Maybe that's why he was like that."

"He's like that, period," I say. "Nothing you can do about it."

Where the pedestrian zone crosses Schloss Platz, a brass band is playing out in front of a white tent that comes to a high point. It looks Oriental. Next to it is a man being interviewed for television. He has a round yellow sticker on his blue jacket. It reads: "Our Beef—As Safe As It Is Tasty!" The musicians are wearing the same sticker, as are the women busy grilling steaks and sausages. I now notice people all around me wearing this beef sticker. They're distributing flyers that are larger than ours.

"Would you work for them?" he asks.

"Sure," I say. "Do you think what we're offering is so great?"

"I don't know," he says. "The fish in the picture looks like it's been breaded to death, probably hard as a rock, and it's only 2.45 cheaper. Think it'll sell?"

When I ask him where he's from, Martin just says, "From the East, from Thuringia." He's visiting his mother here in Stuttgart.

"Kerndel," he says, "didn't mention a word about the pay, the hundred twenty a day."

"They've got to make good on that," I say. "It's what the ad said."

He nods. Suddenly he says, "One flyer would work for a whole family."

f i s h

My first thought is that he's trying to be witty. "And for friends and acquaintances," I respond.

"That's true too. If we keep going at this rate, we'll be done by early afternoon."

We still have the shops in the pedestrian zone to go, but even when we don't speak to people, they stop and stick out a hand. The band keeps playing without a break.

"You mentioned that thing with the flipper," he says.

"And?"

"Do you know that you never stop smiling?"

"You don't either," I say.

About an hour later it starts to drizzle. Most people stay close to the store windows, moving along under the awnings and from overhang to overhang.

While he goes on working outside, I step into the shops. A woman waves to me and calls out, "Hi there, Froggy."

I don't interrupt conversations. But when they see me or turn around to look at me, I pretend I'm lost and softly ask, "Excuse me, but do you know where the North Sea might be?" They're shocked for a moment. But once they start laughing I hand them the flyer.

When I don't spot Martin outside the window, I go back out. I retrace our steps a little, but can't find him. But there are North Sea flyers lying everywhere. He's sitting with his back to a flagpole and doesn't answer me. His left eye is swollen. He glances up briefly and asks if I've seen his snorkel lying around anywhere. I try to collect a few of Kerndel's flyers, but they're stuck to the wet pavement, and every time I try to bend down to pick one up, I step on it with my flippers.

"They give you a bad time, too?" Martin asks when I'm standing in front of him again.

"No," I say, "why?"

"The way you're looking at me."

"That's quite a shiner," I say.

"Have you seen my snorkel?"

I go on looking for a while. All I find is a few more flyers, and I go back to him.

"Sorry," he says, lifting up his snorkel and tapping the mouth-piece against his left flipper. "Was under my flipper, didn't even notice."

"Should I get you some ice?"

"You know what kept running through my mind? That thing about the fish and Noah. I was paralyzed, totally paralyzed," he says. "First the guy looked down and then he glared at me and asked his wife if she knew me. I was standing on his shoes, with the tips of my flippers, just a little. I didn't even feel it, and he can't 've felt it, either. His wife said she did *not* know me. I think it might've even lifted me off the ground a little."

"Are you sick to your stomach?"

"That thing about Noah is so goddamn stupid," he says. "I didn't say anything different than usual. Just the same as always."

"We've got to go see Kerndel," I say. "For the insurance. This is an accident."

"I'm not going back there." He slapped the pavement with his flipper.

"I know why it happened," I say, and wait for him to look at me.

"He didn't like the sound of my accent."

"He asked his wife if she knew you, right? And when you said no, he punched you, right?"

"How could I possibly know her? This is the first time I've even been in Stuttgart."

"He was trying to find out if this was a setup," I say. "That's why."

Martin doesn't get it.

"He figured it might be a big-time setup job, with a hidden camera, or that you might be somebody who'd lost a bar bet," I explain. "Nobody else'd be doing it, nobody your age. The guy thought you were trying to jerk him around. That's all."

f i s h

He looks at me as if I'd slapped him in the face.

"Not that it's true, of course," I say. "I just mean, that's what that idiot must've been thinking. You're really good, you've got a way of making people happy. You really do spread good cheer, and not just these scraps of paper. I'd like to see anybody do it better. Besides, you're in great shape."

He spits between his flippers.

"You made everybody feel good," I say. "We ought to get a lot more money, and not just from Kerndel but from the mayor, even from insurance companies, for making people feel better."

Martin looks at me. His left eye is swollen shut now.

"The guy's an asshole. The kind that doesn't believe it's possible for someone just to be nice," I say.

"No one bothered to help," he says, and spits again. "Nobody budged."

"That's asking too much of them," I say. "People didn't know what they were supposed to make of it, they had no idea what was going on. They'd never seen anything like it. In the middle of the pedestrian zone they see a frogman get punched out. Maybe they thought it doesn't hurt when you're wrapped up in rubber, or that it was part of the act. They didn't want to make asses of themselves if it turned out to be performance art or street theater."

I tell Martin about the old man who died on his balcony in our back courtyard, the guy with the bananas and the loud music. We all thought he was sleeping. And he sat out there in the rain, all night.

"All night?"

"Yes," I say. "It was too dark to see. It wasn't till morning, when we noticed him still sitting there. . . . Come on, we're gonna go see Kerndel."

Martin closes his eyes, just like I saw a woman do in the subway once. She just calmly closed her eyes, and never moved a muscle till the doors opened. Martin shakes his head.

"Yes we are," I say, "we've got to."

I hold his goggles and snorkel while he stands up. His shoulder bag is filthy. He gingerly pulls his hood up over his head.

"I'm not going back to Kerndel," Martin says. It takes him a long time to put his goggles on.

"So where to now?" I ask.

"Anywhere," he says, "as far from here as possible." He spits again, puts the snorkel in his mouth, and secures it in place under the band of his goggles. Finally he slings his bag over his shoulder.

I do the same thing. Then we set off. People are standing under awnings and building overhangs, waiting for the rain to stop. Except for a guy on a bike, we have the pedestrian zone to ourselves. We splash through the puddles. At one point I notice someone waving to us and shouting, something about the North Sea, of course. You can even imagine that these people are lining the street for us. We hold hands, because the goggles restrict our peripheral vision and neither of us can tell if the other is still walking alongside or not. The band is inside the tent again, playing something louder and faster, a polka I think. Actually, I don't even know how a polka sounds. Maybe it's just a march or something. Whatever it is, Martin and I fall in step with it. And that doesn't change even when we leave the pedestrian zone.

Printed in the United States
by Baker & Taylor Publisher Services